series, and has also written romance novels as Sarah
Temple and Young Adult novels as Cheryl Lanham.
She lives in Southern California.

Visit Emily Brightwell's website at
www.emilybrightwell.com

Also by Emily Brightwell

The Inspector and Mrs Jeffries
The Ghost and Mrs Jeffries
Mrs Jeffries Dusts for Clues
Mrs Jeffries on the Trail
Mrs Jeffries on the Ball
Mrs Jeffries Plays the Cook
Mrs Jeffries and the Missing Alibi
Mrs Jeffries Stands Corrected
Mrs Jeffries Takes the Stage
Mrs Jeffries Questions the Answer
Mrs Jeffries Reveals Her Art
Mrs Jeffries Takes the Cake
Mrs Jeffries Rocks the Boat
Mrs Jeffries Weeds the Plot
Mrs Jeffries Pinches the Post
Mrs Jeffries Pleads Her Case
Mrs Jeffries Sweeps the Chimney
Mrs Jeffries Stalks the Hunter
Mrs Jeffries and the Silent Knight
Mrs Jeffries Appeals the Verdict
Mrs Jeffries and the Best Laid Plans
Mrs Jeffries and the Feast of St Stephen
Mrs Jeffries Holds the Trump
Mrs Jeffries in the Nick of Time
Mrs Jeffries and the Yuletide Weddings
Mrs Jeffries Speaks Her Mind
Mrs Jeffries Forges Ahead
Mrs Jeffries and the Mistletoe Mix-Up
Mrs Jeffries Defends Her Own

Mrs Jeffries Takes Stock

Emily Brightwell

Constable • London

CONSTABLE

First published in the US in 1994 by The Berkley Publishing Group,
an imprint of Penguin Group (USA) Inc.

This edition published in Great Britain in 2014 by Constable

A CIP catalogue record for this book
is available from the British Library.

ISBN 978-1-47210-890-6 (paperback)
ISBN 978-1-47210-900-2 (ebook)

Typeset in Bembo by TW Typesetting, Plymouth, Devon
Printed and bound by CPI Group (UK) Ltd, Croydon, CR0 4YY

Constable
is an imprint of
Constable & Robinson Ltd
100 Victoria Embankment
London EC4Y 0DY

An Hachette UK Company
www.hachette.co.uk

www.constablerobinson.com

To Marjory Robinson,
one of the rare people
whose love of books and reading
touched many lives

CHAPTER ONE

INSPECTOR GERALD WITHERSPOON clasped his hand-kerchief to his nose and sneezed. He flinched as the undignified noise echoed off the silent walls of St Thomas Hospital.

'Bless you, sir,' Constable Barnes said kindly. He smiled sympathetically at the inspector and edged closer to the sheet-shrouded body lying on the table. 'Now I expect you'll be wanting to examine the victim.'

'Ah . . . ah . . . choo.' Witherspoon sneezed again. 'Oh drat. This cold is dreadful,' he complained. 'I really should be home in bed, not standing about a chilly hospital mortuary. It'll be a wonder if I don't catch my death in here.'

'Yes, sir, I'm sure you're right. But unfortunately you've not got much choice in the matter. If you'd have a look at the deceased, sir.' Barnes reached for the edge of the sheet.

'Spring colds are the worst,' the inspector continued, ignoring the constable's attempts to get him to look at the body one second before he had to. 'They hang on for ages. I seem to have spent the last two weeks coughing my head off and fighting off the chills.'

'Makes you miserable, colds do,' Barnes agreed with a cheerful smile. 'Guess I'm one of the lucky ones. I never get them. Now, sir, if you'd just have a quick look at the deceased, we could get you out of here, back to the station and fix you up with a nice cuppa tea.'

Witherspoon wiped his watery eyes and noticed Barnes was watching him expectantly. He sighed. 'I suppose you're right. I best get this over with. One must do one's duty.' He broke off as another sneeze racked him. 'Oh drat. Duty or not, I don't see why I had to be called from my sickbed on this one. Why isn't Inspector Nivens here? He was up for the next murder.'

'Well, sir, there's a bit of a problem with that.' Barnes gave up trying to lift the sheet.

'Problem?' Witherspoon looked puzzled. 'I don't see why there's a problem. There's a murdered man lying here and Inspector Nivens was promised the next murder. I heard the chief tell him so myself. It was right after Nivens recovered Lady Spangler's jewels. The Home Office was so grateful that Nivens managed to avert a scandal. I mean, after all, we all knew the jewels hadn't really been stolen.' He shook his head. 'Women are such strange creatures, Constable. I don't think I'll ever understand them. Imagine giving all those valuables to that young bounder.'

'Yes, sir,' Barnes replied dryly, his craggy face set in lines of patience. 'Lady Spangler was foolish, but she's not the first to have her head turned by someone half her age. There's plenty of men about who've done the same thing. But grateful as everyone was for Inspector Nivens's discretion, there's still a bit of a wrinkle in giving him this case.' The constable gave up waiting for the inspector to make a move towards the corpse. Barnes's feet were cold and he wanted a cup of tea, too. He decided to take matters into his own hands. He lunged at the sheet, tossed it back, and revealed the body before the inspector could witter on about his cold.

Witherspoon moaned and quickly closed his eyes. He really didn't want to look. Bodies weren't very nice. Even the tidy ones that weren't drenched in blood were awful, and this one was a drowning. Or a shooting, or something equally wretched. He couldn't quite remember exactly what Barnes had told him earlier. Gracious, it's a wonder he could even remember his own name, considering how miserable he was.

'This one isn't too bad,' Barnes murmured as he stared at the bloated corpse. 'Not like that last one we had. Pity Nivens won't get a crack at this case, but it can't be helped. Nivens might be a suspect himself.'

'What?' The inspector's eyes flew open.

The constable chuckled. 'Only foolin', sir. Of course Inspector Nivens isn't really a suspect. But the reason he isn't getting this one is because he knew the victim. Actually did business with the man, so to speak. The dead man's name is Jake Randall. He's American. He were found this morning floating in the Thames, and he weren't going for a swim, either. He's got a bullet in his chest.'

'And you say Inspector Nivens did business with the deceased?' Witherspoon asked curiously. He forced himself to look at the dead man and then wished he hadn't.

The body was puffed, the skin a pale grey and the bullet hole in the man's chest a dark gaping pit. Witherspoon quickly averted his eyes and silently thanked his lucky stars that at least with this cold his nose was so clogged up he couldn't smell anything.

'Not directly. Inspector Nivens owns stock in Randall's mining company. He's not a major shareholder, mind you. But he owns enough to make it a bit awkward for him to take the case. Name of the company is Randall and Watson.'

'That's not exactly doing business with the man,' Witherspoon exclaimed. 'I own shares in government bonds. That hardly means I'm doing business with Her Majesty.'

'True.' The constable took his helmet off, shook off the remaining drops of rainwater and then flicked a last few drops off his curly grey hair. 'But then, Her Majesty is hardly bein' accused of defrauding her investors.'

'Oh dear.' Witherspoon sighed. Behind the lenses of his spectacles, his clear blue-grey eyes narrowed in concern. 'I take it that means that Mr Randall was suspected of defrauding his investors.'

Barnes shook his head slowly, his craggy face sombre. 'That's about the size of it, sir.' He popped his helmet back on and adjusted the strap. 'I got a bit of background information out of Inspector Nivens. He was called to the scene when they fished this bloke out of the river this morning. 'Course, soon as the inspector saw who he was, he took himself off the case. That's when the chief sent me round to get you.'

Witherspoon blew his nose so hard his bowler hat slipped forward onto his forehead. He pushed the hat firmly back into place over his thinning brown hair and cleared his throat. 'What else did Inspector Nivens tell you?'

'Not all that much, sir,' Barnes admitted. 'But he did say the victim was supposed to have met with the other stockholders in his company a couple of days ago. They had a meeting scheduled for Monday, March seventh. Randall never showed.'

'Where did Mr Randall live?'

'He had a set of rooms near Hyde Park. I've already sent someone round to speak to the landlady,' Barnes said. 'She said that Jake Randall moved out on the first of this month. Supposedly, he's been living at a hotel since then. The landlady didn't know which one it was, and Inspector Nivens didn't know either.'

'Hmmm . . .' Witherspoon muttered. He closed his eyes briefly and tried to think of something to ask. 'Er, perhaps we'd better send a few lads round the hotels and try and find which one the deceased was staying at.'

'Yes, sir.' Barnes coughed slightly. 'I've already done that. I thought it might help us establish the last time the man was seen alive.'

'Good work, Constable,' Witherspoon replied. 'I don't suppose Dr Potter's made any estimate as to how long the victim's been dead?'

Barnes raised one shaggy grey eyebrow. 'Hardly, sir. You know Dr Potter; the man won't even tell you it's daytime unless he looks outside first.' He paused and glanced over his shoulder toward the door. Except for the body on the table, the small room was empty. 'I hope you don't mind, sir,' Barnes said, dropping his voice to a whisper, 'but I saw that young chap Dr Bosworth when they brought the body in, and I took the liberty of havin' a quick word with him.'

Witherspoon wondered why Constable Barnes was whispering . . . or maybe his cold was so bad he was starting to lose his hearing. 'Really. About what?'

'About havin' a look at the body, sir.' Barnes raked the door with another furtive glance. 'Remember on that case we had last year, sir. It were Dr Bosworth that found out the victim was pregnant, and that information helped us find out who killed her.'

Witherspoon stared at him in admiration. 'Very good, Constable.' Barnes was referring to a case where Dr Bosworth's medical knowledge had shed a whole new light on the investigation. 'And what did the doctor say?'

'He didn't have much time to look this morning,' Barnes acknowledged. 'The best he could come up with was an estimate on the time of death. Bosworth thinks Randall was probably shot on the evening of March the seventh. That'd make it two days ago.'

'Oh dear.' The inspector's long nose wrinkled as he fought to hold back another sneeze. He struggled mightily for a few seconds and actually smiled as he realized he'd won. 'Too bad he didn't have time to give the victim a thorough examination.'

'He's going to have another go at it tomorrow afternoon,' Barnes said quickly. 'Dr Potter won't be here then. He'll have to be testifying at the inquest. He's doing the autopsy in the morning. Dr Bosworth wanted to wait until after the bloke were sliced open before he started snoopin' about. Claimed it would be easier that way. He'll be able to have a right good look at the innards; said he'd be able to tell us quite a bit then.'

Witherspoon hoped he didn't look as green as he felt. But really, Constable Barnes obviously had a strong stomach. 'Er, excellent.'

The household at Upper Edmonton Gardens, home of Inspector Gerald Witherspoon, was in an uproar. Mrs Jeffries, the housekeeper, stared at the mutinous faces surrounding the kitchen table and sighed inwardly. 'Really,' she said calmly, 'I don't know what all the fuss is about.'

'That's easy for you to say,' Mrs Goodge, the cook, said. 'You're not the one that's going to have to try to feed this household on a pittance.' She jabbed one plump red finger at the piece of notepaper lying in front of Mrs Jeffries. 'You've got to talk to the inspector. This is daft. I don't mind bein' a bit frugal. But what he wants is ridiculous. And prices are going up all the time. What's he expect me to do? Feed everyone fried bread instead of decent cuts of meat?' Her chin bobbed up and down as she spoke, dislodging a tendril of white hair from under her cook's hat.

'And what about the coal supplies?' Wiggins, the footman, interjected. He stared earnestly at the housekeeper, his round, placid face creased in worry. 'This house don't stay warm by itself, you know. We've got to keep the fires going or we'll all freeze. It gets bloomin' cold up in that attic. Even Fred notices it.' He glanced down at the shaggy black-and-brown mongrel resting next to his chair. Fred, when he heard his name called, lifted his head and then settled back down to sleep.

'Does this mean we're goin' to get our wages cut?' Betsy, the maid, asked. Young, pretty, and with plenty of natural intelligence, she got right to the heart of what was really worrying all of them.

'Of course it doesn't mean you're going to get your wages reduced,' Mrs Jeffries assured them quickly. 'The inspector merely wants us to trim the household expenses a bit, that's all.'

'I'm not cuttin' back on the 'orses' feed,' Smythe, the coachman, added. He crossed his arms over his broad chest and leaned back in his seat. He was a big man, with dark brown hair and harsh, almost brutal features, save for a pair of twinkling brown eyes. His eyes weren't twinkling now, though. 'Just because the inspector don't use Bow and Arrow all that much don't mean they ain't deservin' the best.'

'Please, calm down,' Mrs Jeffries commanded. 'You're all jumping to conclusions much too quickly. All the inspector is saying is that we've got to cut back a bit on the household expenses. He's not going to starve his horses, freeze his servants, or force us to eat bread and water.' Her normally placid face creased in a frown, and her brown eyes narrowed in irritation. 'Furthermore, I should think you'd all be a bit ashamed. Have you ever known the inspector to be unfair? Has he ever treated any of us with less than the utmost kindness?'

Smythe cleared his throat. 'Uh, we didn't mean no disrespect to the inspector,' he said uneasily, 'but you've got to admit it's a bit of a worry. I mean, 'im all of a sudden comin' up with this grand scheme to save a few pounds each month. We all knows how much we owes the inspector.'

Wiggins shoved a lock of dark brown hair off his forehead. 'What's this all about, then? What's wrong? The inspector ain't losin' his position, is he?'

'No,' Mrs Jeffries replied firmly. She didn't like making them feel guilty, but really, she had to do something. This discussion was getting completely out of hand. Besides, complaining about the inspector's newest household management scheme wouldn't do them a bit of good. It was far better to go along with his plan and let the inspector see the results of 'cutting back' himself. Mrs Jeffries was confident that within a very few weeks the household would be back to its normal routine. 'The inspector isn't losing his position, Wiggins,' she said. 'But – and I suppose it's only fair you should know this – some of his investments aren't doing all that well.'

'Cor blimey.' Wiggins shook his head. 'That doesn't sound good.'

'Here now. I'm sorry about the inspector's investments, but how on earth am I expected to entertain on this amount of money?' Mrs Goodge asked. She jabbed her finger again at the dreaded piece of paper.

Mrs Jeffries stared at the cook in amazement. 'Entertain? I'm afraid I don't understand what you mean. The inspector never entertains.'

'I weren't talkin' about him,' Mrs Goodge replied earnestly. She waved her arm around the table. 'I was talkin' about us. We've got Luty Belle and Hatchet comin' by for tea tomorrow—' She broke off and snatched a plate of cherry tarts out from under Wiggins's fingers. 'We'd best save these,' she continued, ignoring the footman's yelp of outrage. 'These'll do

9

for tomorrow, and I can save the last of them currants for a batch of buns. Though goodness knows what I'll do if we have to start helpin' the inspector on one of his cases. I won't be able to get anyone to tell me a bloomin' thing if I don't have some decent food to put on their stomachs.'

Mrs Jeffries sighed. She knew Mrs Goodge was referring to the fact that all of the servants at Upper Edmonton Gardens helped Inspector Witherspoon solve his most difficult murder cases. Naturally, the inspector had no idea whatsoever that he was getting any help. She smiled at the others. Despite their complaints, they were a devoted lot. They dashed all over London questioning servants, following suspects, and chasing after clues. And they did it all because they loved and admired their dear Inspector Witherspoon. And, of course, because they were all natural-born snoops. As Betsy once said, following suspects and ferreting out clues was a lot more interesting than changing bed sheets or polishing floors. Even Mrs Goodge, who rarely left the kitchen, did her fair share.

The cook had a virtual army of delivery boys, chimney sweeps, gas men, and fruit peddlers that she fed and watered. When they were on a case, Mrs Goodge could ferret out the most minute bits and pieces of gossip and information. No wonder she was in a mood, Mrs Jeffries thought. Without adequate supplies, she wouldn't be able to contribute anything. And the housekeeper knew how important it was for the elderly woman to contribute as much as the rest of them.

Mrs Jeffries gave her a reassuring smile. 'Don't worry, Mrs Goodge,' she said confidently, 'we're not investigating anything at the moment, and perhaps by the time we are, the household will be back to normal.'

Mrs Goodge snorted. 'Well, I certainly hope so.'

'So do I,' Betsy said. She jerked her chin towards the piece of paper. 'Maybe if we had a decent murder to investigate, we wouldn't mind puttin' up with this . . .' She stopped speaking and tried to remember the words the housekeeper had used.

'Household management scheme,' Smythe said, giving the girl a cheeky grin.

'Cor blimey, Betsy,' Wiggins protested. 'Haven't we had enough murders? A body could do with a bit of peace and quiet every now and again. Besides, it's not right, wantin' someone dead just so we can 'ave a bit of sport.'

'I wasn't sayin' that,' Betsy said defensively, her lovely cheeks flaming red. She appealed to Mrs Jeffries. 'You know that's not what I meant at all.'

'Of course you didn't,' Mrs Jeffries said soothingly. Actually, she rather agreed with Betsy. Life was so much more interesting when they were digging about in one of the inspector's cases. 'Wiggins is merely teasing you. After all, you do go after him rather mercilessly at times.'

'Only because the lad asks for it,' Smythe put in. He reached over and cuffed the grinning footman on the head. 'Always hangin' about moonin' over some girl . . .'

Wiggins's various infatuations with the young females of London were legion.

'Nonetheless,' Mrs Jeffries said briskly, 'you can't blame him for wanting to get a bit of his own back.'

'Hmmph,' Mrs Goodge snorted again. 'We only tease the ones we like,' she muttered. 'If we didn't care for the boy, we wouldn't say a word about all that silly poetry he writes for them girls.'

'Me poems ain't silly,' Wiggins yelped. 'Elsie Tanner told me that one I wrote her was the prettiest thing she'd ever heard.'

'Heard?' Smythe said. 'Don't you mean "read".'

Wiggins shrugged. 'Well, I had to read it to 'er meself.'

'That's "myself",' Mrs Jeffries corrected him quickly. She didn't correct the other servants because their speech offended her; she corrected them so they could improve their lot in life. They were all highly intelligent, hardworking people, and the housekeeper was secretly determined that one day they'd have an opportunity to advance themselves. Inspector Witherspoon was the kindest of masters. He treated his servants as human beings rather than objects put on this earth to answer his every whim. Yet kind as he was, Mrs Jeffries harboured the hope that one day the younger servants would have to call no man master. One day they'd be master of their own fates.

'Right,' Wiggins said. 'I had to read it to her myself. Elsie can't read. But she said it were wonderful.'

'She may have thought it were wonderful,' Mrs Goodge said, 'but that didn't stop her from gettin' engaged to Lady Cannonberry's gardener.'

Smythe glanced at Wiggins. The footman dropped his gaze and stared at the tabletop as a blush crept up his cheeks. The lad was good-natured about their teasing but he was still raw over the subject of Elsie Tanner.

Wiggins hadn't been in love with the lass or anything like that, but he'd been smitten enough to get his feelings hurt bad when she up and got herself engaged to another bloke.

Smythe decided to change the subject. 'Do you think we'll be gettin' somethin' interestin' to do soon?' he asked the housekeeper.

Mrs Jeffries smiled sadly. 'Not for a while, I'm afraid. You see, the inspector told me that the next murder that comes along goes to Inspector Nivens.'

'Inspector Nivens?' they all chorused at once.

'But that's daft!' Mrs Goodge exclaimed.

'Nivens couldn't find a singer at a music hall, let alone catch a killer,' Smythe charged.

'He's always lookin' down his nose at people,' Betsy said earnestly. 'How can someone like that ever learn anything?'

'Well, I think it's about time that someone other than our inspector had to do it,' Wiggins said. 'It isn't fair that he always gets stuck with the bad ones.'

'Oh dear, sir,' Mrs Jeffries said to Inspector Witherspoon as she ushered him into the drawing room, 'you really shouldn't have gone out. Not with that terrible cold.'

'I didn't have much choice, Mrs Jeffries,' he replied as he settled himself in his favourite wing chair by the fireplace. He glanced around the normally cozy drawing room. 'When one is summoned, one must go. I say, it's a bit chilly in here. Why isn't the fire going?'

'I didn't think you wanted one, sir,' she replied calmly. 'After you left this afternoon, I assumed that

13

you wouldn't be in here very long. Wiggins has laid a fire in your room, sir. Naturally, as you've instructed us to be more careful about our expenditures, I didn't think you'd want to waste a bucket of coal to heat a room you'd only be sitting in for a few minutes.'

Witherspoon frowned slightly, but said nothing.

Mrs Jeffries firmly clamped down on the surge of hope welling up inside her as she poured the inspector a glass of sherry. She'd known when the inspector was summoned by the chief inspector earlier that afternoon that something important was happening, but she hadn't dared let herself believe it might be another murder investigation. That's why she hadn't said anything to the others. She didn't want to get their hopes up.

'Here, sir.' She handed him a glass of pale amber liquid. 'This ought to take the chill off.'

'Thank you, Mrs Jeffries,' he replied absently as he took the glass from her fingers and raised it to his lips. As the liquid hit his tongue his eyes bulged. 'I say, this doesn't taste like our usual sherry?'

'It's not, sir,' she said, giving him a placid smile. 'You finished the last of your usual kind yesterday. Naturally, in accordance with your instructions to trim our spending, I ordered this brand. It's Spanish, you know. Far less costly than Harvey's. The wine merchant assured me it would do nicely. Now, sir, why don't you tell me why you were summoned out of your sickbed today?'

Witherspoon tentatively took another sip. He grimaced. The wine merchant might say it would do nicely, he thought, but he wasn't the one having to drink the ruddy stuff. Still, he couldn't complain to Mrs Jeffries. She was only following his instructions.

'Inspector?' Mrs Jeffries prompted gently.

'Ah, oh yes. Why was I summoned to the Yard.' He laid his glass to one side. 'Because of a murder, of course.'

Mrs Jeffries sat up straighter. 'A murder?'

He nodded weakly and plucked his handkerchief out of his pocket. 'I'm afraid so. Fellow by the name of Jake Randall was found floating in the Thames.'

'Floating in the Thames,' she repeated slowly, her mind working furiously. She knew that murder by drowning was difficult to prove, impossible really, unless there was an eyewitness or unless the body was marked in such a way as to rule out any other conclusion. She'd learned quite a bit living with her late husband, a police constable in Yorkshire for over twenty years. 'How extraordinary. What makes the police think it's murder and not an accidental drowning?'

The inspector sneezed so hard he didn't hear the question. He pulled out his handkerchief and blew his nose. 'Uh, I say, Mrs Jeffries, what is Mrs Goodge cooking up for dinner tonight?'

'Spring stew of veal and brown bread pudding,' she answered quickly, knowing the inspector would be far more receptive to her questions once he knew he was going to be fed properly.

Witherspoon brightened considerably. 'That's one of my favourite dishes. One of my favourites.' He tucked his hankie back in his pocket. 'Now, what was that you asked?'

Betsy stuck her head in the drawing room. 'Dinner's

15

served,' she announced just as there was a knock on the front door.

'Answer the door, Betsy,' Mrs Jeffries said as she rose to her feet.

'Odd time for someone to come calling,' the inspector murmured. He was really quite hungry. He hoped he wasn't being called out again. Surely they wouldn't have found another corpse floating in the river. Even his luck wasn't that bad.

Betsy returned a moment later. Inspector Nigel Nivens was right behind her. Mrs Jeffries stiffened. She didn't like Inspector Nivens, and she was fairly certain he didn't like her either.

He was a man of medium height, with dark-blond hair slicked straight back from his high forehead. His chin was weak, his grey eyes cold and shifty, and he was forever trying to figure out precisely how Inspector Witherspoon solved all those complicated murder cases.

Nivens flicked the housekeeper a brief, suspicious glance before turning to Inspector Witherspoon. 'Good evening, Witherspoon,' he said politely. 'Mrs Jeffries.' He acknowledged her presence with a slight nod. 'I'm terribly sorry to barge in like this, but it's imperative that I speak with you. It's about that man they fished out of the Thames today. Jake Randall.'

'You're not barging in, dear fellow,' Witherspoon said with a welcoming smile. 'It's nice to see you again.'

'Should I ask Betsy to hold dinner?' Mrs Jeffries asked softly. Really, sometimes she felt like shaking her employer. He was so very innocent. He didn't have the slightest notion that Inspector Nivens thought he was a fool. Nivens's sarcasm and innuendo rolled right off Inspector Witherspoon's back.

Witherspoon's brows rose. 'I don't think that will be necessary,' he replied. 'I'm sure that Inspector Nivens will dine with me.' He looked hopefully at the other man. 'Won't you?'

Nivens smiled. 'As long as it's no trouble, I'd be delighted.'

'It's not a bit of trouble,' the inspector assured him. 'Come along, the dining room is through here,' He led the way out of the room with Nivens trailing at his heels. Mrs Jeffries, sure that something was up because she knew good and well that Inspector Nivens hadn't called around to inquire about her employer's health, followed at a more cautious pace. But she was determined to find out why the odious man had come. If he was going to browbeat the inspector into giving up this case . . . well, she'd just have to take matters into her own hands.

She didn't have to wait long. Just as the two men were entering the dining room, Witherspoon said, 'I'm jolly sorry you're not getting this case. I know how much you wanted a chance at a murder.'

'I'm sorry, too. But circumstances being as they are, we've no choice in the matter.' Nivens turned his head and saw her loitering in the hall. She gave him an innocent smile.

'I knew the victim, you see,' Nivens said when it was clear that Mrs Jeffries wasn't going to be cowed. 'And I've got some information I think will help with your investigation. Details, that sort of thing.'

'Yes, I'm sure you'll be most helpful,' Witherspoon

murmured. He really didn't want to talk about murder while he ate his dinner. But obviously, Inspector Nivens felt it was important enough to come round personally. He was duty bound to listen attentively, even if his stomach was growling and his head was so stuffed he could barely think. He gestured toward the chair on his right and sat down. 'Do sit down, Inspector.'

Mrs Jeffries heard Betsy coming up the backstairs with the main course. She turned and fairly flew down the hall.

'Here,' she hissed to the surprised maid, 'I'll serve. You nip back into the drawing room.'

'What for?' Betsy's blue eyes mirrored her confusion. Serving dinner was one of her duties.

'Because I want to know everything that Inspector Nivens says tonight, and I'm fairly certain he'll take care not to say anything important while I'm in the room.'

'What are you on about, Mrs J?'

'Murder,' she hissed. 'If Nivens doesn't see me hovering about the dining room, he'll assume I'm eavesdropping by the door and he might close up tighter than a bank vault. Even worse, the odious little man might deliberately give the inspector the wrong information just so he can try to trap me. We can't take that risk.'

Mrs Jeffries knew she wasn't being her normal articulate self, but she was in a hurry. She was certain that Nigel Nivens suspected that Inspector Witherspoon's 'phenomenal success' at solving murders was due to the fact that he had help. She was equally certain that he'd guessed precisely where that help had come from. But she didn't have time to explain all this to Betsy right now.

'You mean Nivens is onto us?'

'Perhaps,' she whispered. 'And I want him to see me serving dinner. It might allay his suspicions. So I want you to go into the drawing room. If you huddle down behind that wing chair opposite the fireplace and put your ear to the wall, you can hear every word that's being said in the dining room.'

'You mean you want me to eavesdrop?'

'Of course I want you to.' The housekeeper took the platter out of the girl's hand. 'Murder's been done and our inspector is on the case.'

She didn't have to explain further. Betsy nodded and slipped down the hallway into the drawing room. Mrs Jeffries continued into the dining room.

Secure in the knowledge that Betsy was listening to every word, Mrs Jeffries calmly served dinner. She was aware that every time she entered the room, Nivens broke off and waited until she'd left before speaking again. She deliberately made as much noise as possible as she went back and forth between the kitchen and dining room. She clicked her heels loudly against the hallway floor, stomped up and down the steps hard enough to cause the banister to vibrate, and banged the plates together every time she served a course. She was sure her plan was working.

She placed a plate of brown bread pudding in front of the two inspectors and turned for the door. She left it open as she tromped down the hall, her footsteps loud enough to wake the dead. She smiled to herself as she reached the staircase leading to the kitchen. From behind her, she could hear the murmur of voices.

Nivens, secure in the knowledge that she couldn't

possibly be eavesdropping, was talking his head off. He was annoying, but she wasn't in the least worried. Even if Betsy suddenly went stone-deaf, she'd still find out what was going on.

Inspector Witherspoon told her everything.

CHAPTER TWO

Betsy kept one eye on the door and pressed her ear to the wall. The voices of the two men were low, but very clear. From outside the front window, she heard the rattle and clop of a carriage. She frowned and shot a quick glare toward the road as the noise of the horses' hooves and rumble of the wheels drowned out Inspector Nivens's first words. Blast, she thought, pressing her head closer to the wall; if this keeps up, I won't hear a bloomin' thing.

From behind the panelling, she heard Inspector Witherspoon say, 'Now precisely what was it you wanted to tell me, Inspector Nivens? Oh, do help yourself to more veal; it's one of cook's best recipes.'

There was the scrape of silverware against china. Betsy guessed that Nivens was loading his plate up. He looked like the kind that'd make a pig of himself, she thought. She hoped he wouldn't keep his mouth so full that he couldn't talk. Then relief filled her as she heard Nivens start speaking. Betsy held her breath, hoping he wouldn't take too long to say something interesting.

'As I'm sure you know, Jake Randall was pulled from

the Thames this morning,' Nivens said. 'We know it was murder because he had a bullet in his chest.'

'I saw the body this afternoon,' Witherspoon replied. Betsy had to strain to catch his words. His voice seemed to have gone a bit faint.

'I assume Constable Barnes told you why I had to give up the case,' Nivens continued.

She heard a muffled grunt in reply.

'My business with Mr Randall wasn't extensive,' Nivens said, 'nor was it directly with Mr Randall himself. It's true I own shares in Randall and Watson Mining Company, but I purchased that stock through a Mr Lester Hinkle. He represents several small investors like myself. That's really all there is to it. I'd never even met the victim, but you know what a stickler for propriety the chief is, and I thought it best to take myself off the case.'

'Er, excuse my asking, but if you'd never met Mr Randall,' the inspector said hesitantly, 'then how did you know it was him when you saw the body?'

There was a long pause before Nivens answered. 'We may not have been acquainted, but I had seen him before. When Mr Hinkle recommended I purchase the shares, I took it upon myself to inquire into Mr Randall's background. During the course of that inquiry, I happened to see him coming out of Hinkle's office on Throgmorton Street.'

'Hmmm, I see. What kind of mine is it?' Witherspoon asked.

'Silver,' Nivens answered. 'It's in the United States, in Colorado to be exact.'

'Hmmm,' the inspector said.

Betsy rolled her eyes. If Inspector Witherspoon didn't get on with it, she'd be here all night.

Inspector Nivens, perhaps coming to the same conclusion that Betsy had, suddenly got to the heart of his story.

'A few days ago,' he said, 'Mr Hinkle contacted me. He said he had it on good authority that Jake Randall wasn't using our investment money to buy equipment, hire miners, or dig for silver. It seems that one of Mr Hinkle's relations happened to be visiting Colorado. He visited the mine site and found it was nothing more than a hole in the side of a mountain.' Nivens stopped and Betsy took the chance to rub the crick out of her neck.

She quickly put her ear back against the wall when she heard Nivens start up again.

'Furthermore, Mr Hinkle's relation had taken the trouble to meet the other owner of the mine, a man called Tib Watson. These Americans have such strange names.' He paused. 'Watson was nothing more than an old drunk. The only mining equipment he had was a pickaxe and a half-blind old mule.' Nivens snorted in anger.

'Oh dear, that doesn't sound at all right,' Witherspoon murmured sympathetically.

'It wasn't right. Naturally, Mr Hinkle was concerned. Not only had he invested my money and the money of several other people, but he'd also invested a huge amount of his own,' Nivens complained bitterly. 'He came to me because I'm with the police. He wanted to know if we should have Mr Randall arrested. I told him that he didn't have enough evidence. I offered to contact the American authorities, but Mr Hinkle was afraid the press would get wind of it, so he asked me not to do anything yet. He decided to talk with other shareholders about the situation. He did that and they decided their best course of action would be to confront Mr Randall and ask him for an explanation.'

Betsy's foot began to cramp. She eased it out from beneath her, cringing as the sole of her shoe scraped noisily against the floorboards. But she needn't have worried about being overheard. Both men were too intent upon their subject to take any notice of unusual noises.

She shifted slightly into a more comfortable position. Through the wall, she heard the inspector ask the obvious question.

'But surely, if you knew there was no mining going on and you'd all given him money, you could have picked Mr Randall up for fraud.'

'Hardly, Inspector Witherspoon.'

Betsy's eyes narrowed at the cool contempt she heard in Nivens's voice. How dare he speak to their inspector in that tone?

'Why ever not?' Witherspoon asked innocently.

'To prove fraud, you must prove intent,' Nivens replied. 'But that's neither here nor there. We couldn't prove intent, nor did we have enough evidence to arrest Randall. The unsubstantiated word of someone's cousin isn't reason enough to arrest a man with the kind of important connections that Randall had. The other shareholders decided to have a meeting and confront Jake Randall. He was either going to have to give them back their money or come up with a reasonable

24

explanation. The meeting was scheduled for March seventh. Randall agreed to be there. But he wasn't. On March ninth his body was found.'

'Er, uh, who else was due at this meeting?'

'All the other shareholders. One of whom is Rushton Benfield; he's the son of Sir Thaddeus Benfield. Mr Benfield is the main reason Lester Hinkle bought into the company. As you know, the Benfields are one of the most prominent families in England.'

Betsy heard the sound of a chair scraping across the floor and decided that Nivens had stuffed himself so full he needed more room.

Nivens continued, 'The other stockholders are John Cubberly, a businessman. He lives on Davies Street just off Chester Square. The meeting was going to take place at his home. The other major shareholder is a gentleman named Edward Dillingham. Hinkle, Benfield, Cubberly and Dillingham essentially represented all the stockholders in Randall and Watson. Between them, they'd put in over fifty thousand pounds.'

'Oh dear, dear.' Witherspoon clucked his tongue. 'That's a frightful amount of money.'

'Yes, it is. I'm sure you can appreciate how all the stockholders felt when they were confronted with the rumour that Jake Randall wasn't to be trusted.'

'Hmm . . . uh, if Mr Randall had only recently sold stock in his company,' Witherspoon said, 'perhaps he hadn't had time to buy any equipment or hire any workers.'

That's a good point, Betsy thought. She thought it was most clever of the inspector to ask. She heard Nivens laugh harshly.

'He'd had plenty of time,' Nivens cried. 'Six months, in fact. You see, this was the second time he'd issued stock. Six months ago, these same investors put up the initial development money for the mine. This second issue was merely to raise more capital.'

Betsy jumped as she heard a loud crack. It sounded like someone had smacked the top of the table with their fist. Betsy grinned. Ol' Nivens had worked himself up to a real fit! Served him right, too, she thought.

The air in the kitchen crackled with excitement. Mrs Jeffries had taken a few minutes between serving the dinner courses to tip Mrs Goodge off to the fact that they now had a murder to investigate. The cook hadn't wasted a moment. By the time Inspector Witherspoon had said good-bye to his guest and retired for the night, she'd managed to get the rest of the servants into the kitchen and around the table.

Mrs Jeffries sat down and waited until Mrs Goodge had filled five mugs with hot, steaming tea.

'Is the inspector abed yet?' Betsy asked, glancing uneasily to the door that led to steps.

'He retired half an hour ago,' Mrs Jeffries replied. 'And don't worry, he didn't have any idea that you were listening to his discussion with Inspector Nivens.'

'Betsy were listenin'?' Wiggins exclaimed. 'Whatever for?' He turned and frowned at the maid. ''Ere, that's not very nice, listenin' in on the inspector.'

'It's all right, Wiggins,' Mrs Jeffries interjected. 'I told her to do it. We've no time to waste on this case. If I'd had to wait until breakfast tomorrow to pry the details out of the inspector, we'd have lost a whole morning. None of us can investigate anything without knowing the facts of the case.'

'All right.' Mrs Goodge planted her elbows on the table. 'Let's have it, then. Who got done in?'

'The victim was an American named Jake Randall,' Mrs Jeffries began. She didn't stop until she'd told them everything she'd learned. 'So you see, we're not precisely sure even where the man lived.'

'I think I can help a bit there,' Betsy said.

'Did Nivens know, then?' Smythe asked.

'Not exactly, but I did hear Nivens tell the inspector they think they may have found the hotel Randall was stayin' at.'

'Why don't you start at the beginning and tell us everything,' Mrs Jeffries suggested. She was quite relieved that Smythe wasn't in a state over Betsy having gotten a start on the investigation. The two of them had been quite competitive on their last couple of cases, and Mrs Jeffries was glad to see that this particular nonsense had run its course.

'All right, then,' Betsy said. Blessed with both good hearing and a remarkable memory for details, she repeated the information Inspector Nivens had given Inspector Witherspoon.

Everyone listened carefully.

When Betsy had finished, Mrs Goodge shook her head. 'Let's see now, I want to make sure I've got it right. This Jake Randall had sold off shares in a mining company that weren't no good. All the people that had bought those stocks and given him their money got wind of what he was up to and demanded a meeting.'

'That's right,' Betsy said.

'And then, instead of Randall showin' up for that meetin', he's found a couple of days later floating in the river with a bullet through his heart.' Mrs Goodge pursed her lips. 'Sounds to me like one of them that lost their money done him in.'

'But we don't know that for sure,' Smythe said cautiously. He looked at Mrs Jeffries, his expression puzzled. 'There's somethin' I don't understand 'ere.'

'What is it?'

'Where's the money? Did he 'ave it on 'im, or was it in the bank? I mean, why would one of the stockholders shoot Randall unless it meant they was goin' to get their money back?'

Mrs Jeffries looked thoughtful. 'You know, you're absolutely right. And I think that's one of the first things we've got to find out. What happened to the money?'

'I wish Inspector Witherspoon had thought to ask that,' Betsy said. 'It'd save us a bit of time. If that money is sitting in a bank somewhere, then it's a sure bet that none of the shareholders did the man in.'

Wiggins frowned. ''Ow do you figure that? Could be one of 'em was angry about what he'd tried to do and decided to teach him a lesson.'

'They wouldn't teach him a lesson until after they got their money back, now, would they?' Betsy persisted. 'That class of people don't do murder over somethin' like that.'

'Meanin' that it's only the lower classes that murder 'cause they're angry,' Smythe put in. He raised one eyebrow and stared at the maid. 'Come on, girl, you know better than that. You've snooped about in enough of the inspector's cases to know that the rich ain't any different from the poor when it comes to hatin' and madness. But they are better at hidin' it than the rest of us.'

'I'm not sayin' they're different. I'm just sayin' that unless one of those investors could have gotten his money back by killin' Randall, they wouldn't have bothered.' Betsy shrugged. 'Why take the risk of murderin' someone when it'd be a lot easier just to hire a solicitor and take the man to court? That's the way the rich take care of their problems. They go to the law.'

'I don't understand if he was drowned or if he was shot,' Wiggins interrupted.

'What difference does it make?' Mrs Goodge asked impatiently. 'Drowned or shot, he's still dead.'

Mrs Jeffries did think the cause of death was important, but she didn't wish to embarrass the cook by arguing the point. 'We don't know the exact cause of death,' she replied. 'But that matter should be cleared up by tomorrow. That's when they're having the inquest. Dr Potter's doing the autopsy.'

There was a collective groan.

'I know,' Mrs Jeffries said soothingly, 'But it can't be helped. Let's just hope that Dr Potter surprises us and actually knows something useful.'

Betsy, her blue eyes sparkling, eagerly leaned forward. 'What do we do first?'

Mrs Jeffries considered the question. 'We've learned enough to get started with our inquiries,' she mused, 'yet we don't have much in the way of facts.'

'We know where the body come up, don't we?' Smythe asked.

'Yes, just under Waterloo Bridge,' Mrs Jeffries

replied thoughtfully. She frowned. 'But I'm not sure that will do us much good. The body may have been spotted there, but considering the currents and tides in the river, we've no reason to think that Randall was shot anywhere near the bridge.'

Wiggins gasped. 'You mean he was shot somewhere else and the body just floated down the Thames until someone happened to see it?'

'No, no, Wiggins,' Mrs Jeffries explained hastily. 'Dead bodies don't float, they generally sink to the bottom for a few days, bloat up a bit and then pop to the surface. But the point is, we've no idea if the victim died of drowning or the bullet wound. In either case, the body could have gone into the river several miles from where it was actually found.' She knew this because her late husband had investigated several deaths by drowning.

'Why don't I take a run down to Waterloo Bridge anyway?' Smythe suggested. 'You never know, Mrs J. We might get lucky.'

She looked at the coachman. 'All right. But afterwards, I think you'd better take on the task of learning everything you can about Rushton Benfield.'

'Do you know where he lives?'

'No,' she replied. 'But he shouldn't be hard to find. His father is Sir Thaddeus Benfield.'

'I can help there,' Mrs Goodge said. 'Well, I can tell you where Sir Thaddeus lives. He's got a fancy house near Regent's Park. I expect if Smythe hits the locals round there, he can find out where young Mr Benfield calls home these days.'

Mrs Jeffries nodded. She was no longer amazed by

the cook's enormous amount of information on the gentry of London.

'Excellent. Now, Wiggins,' she said, ignoring the boy's less-than-enthusiastic expression, 'I want you to find out everything you can about Lester Hinkle.'

Betsy suddenly interrupted. 'Lester Hinkle lives near the Cubberlys' – he lives right on Chester Square. I heard Inspector Nivens tellin' our inspector that before he left. He give Inspector Witherspoon all their addresses exceptin' for Mr Benfield's.'

'Very good, Betsy.' Mrs Jeffries beamed proudly at the girl.

'What do you want me to learn about this 'ere Mr 'inkle?' the footman asked grudgingly.

'Everything you can, but most especially, I want to find out as much as possible about his movements between March seventh and ninth.'

Mrs Goodge leaned her ample bulk forward. 'Why just them dates?'

'Because the meeting was called for March seventh and the body was found on March ninth. As Mr Randall didn't show up for the meeting, there's a possibility he was already dead.'

'Cor blimey,' Wiggins groaned. 'That's gonna be right 'ard. What if I can't learn nuthin'?'

Mrs Jeffries sighed. Wiggins was obviously assailed by self-doubt again. She wondered if it had anything to do with Elsie Tanner's defection. Amazing really, how one totally unrelated event in a life could affect everything else. She peered closely at the boy. His mouth was turned down, there were faint circles under his eyes, and his usually round cheeks were pale and sunken.

Oh dear, she thought, he really was in a bad way. Perhaps she'd better put her foot down if there were any more teasing. Wiggins had always been good-natured about it in the past, but he didn't look at all his normal, jolly self. 'Of course you'll learn something,' Mrs Jeffries assured him. 'You always do. Why, you were instrumental in solving our last two cases.'

Wiggins raised his eyes and stared at her hopefully. 'Really?'

'You and Fred both,' the housekeeper said enthusiastically. 'That's why I don't think you'll have any trouble getting all sorts of information about Mr Hinkle. Just do what you normally do: make contact with a footman or a gardener or perhaps a pretty housemaid and use your charm.'

'My charm?' Wiggins grinned. 'Well, if you say so, Mrs Jeffries. By the way, where is Fred?' He ducked his head and looked for the stray dog he'd brought in a few months back. 'Fred,' he called softly, 'here, boy . . .'

'He's not here,' Mrs Jeffries said hastily. 'He's in the inspector's room.'

'Again!' Wiggins's good mood began to vanish. 'What's he doin' in there? 'E's my dog, you know. 'E's supposed to sleep up with us.'

'Well . . .' Mrs Jeffries tried to think of a diplomatic response. 'Of course he's your dog and we all know how devoted he is to you. But the inspector's become very fond of him, too.'

'But Fred's my dog,' the footman complained. ''E ought to be with me, not the inspector. I thought dogs was supposed to be loyal.'

'Fred is loyal,' Mrs Jeffries argued. 'But like all

creatures, he likes his comfort. And I think it is warmer in the inspector's bedroom.' She didn't add that Witherspoon was always slipping Fred little treats and that she suspected he let the dog sleep at the foot of the bed and not the floor.

If she'd known how difficult bringing the dog into the house was going to be, she'd have thought differently about allowing it to happen. It wasn't that Fred was any trouble. Except for being overly fond of sausages and occasionally stealing one off the table when no one was looking, he was a fine animal. The problem was that both Wiggins and the inspector felt the dog belonged to them. And they were just a tad jealous of one another.

But Mrs Jeffries really felt that Inspector Witherspoon should have the animal. Wiggins was one of them. They formed an unusual, but very real family circle, even though none of them were related by blood. The inspector, on the other hand, though he had the respect and devotion of his servants, was very much alone.

They had each other. Inspector Witherspoon had no one. Mrs Jeffries refused to give up on her ambition of acquiring a wife for him, but the man was so ridiculously shy around women, she knew it might be ages before she could complete that task. In the meantime, Fred would just have to do. Witherspoon needed the dog far more than Wiggins did. But she wasn't about to tell Wiggins that. 'You don't want Fred to catch cold, do you?'

'Course not,' Wiggins said. 'But it in't that cold up in our room, is it, Smythe?'

'I wouldn't call it toasty,' the coachman said dryly. 'And you do insist on keepin' that ruddy window cracked a few inches. Poor mutt probably feels the chill.'

'There, you see, we're all agreed. Fred should just go right on sleeping in the inspector's room.' Mrs Jeffries smiled confidently.

'You've got the dog all day to yourself,' Betsy put in. 'The inspector only gets to see him of an evening, and he's got right fond of the animal.'

Wiggins nodded, but grumbled under his breath.

Thinking the matter settled, Betsy eagerly turned to the housekeeper. 'What do you want me to do tomorrow?'

'If you'll pop round and see what you can find out about the Cubberly's,' Mrs Jeffries said slowly, 'I'll see what I can learn about Edward Dillingham.'

'So we'll have all four of 'em that were due at that meeting covered, right?' Smythe said.

'Correct.'

'I reckon you want me to suss out what gossip there is about all of them,' Mrs Goodge said. Her broad face was creased in a worried frown. 'That's not goin' to be easy, seein' as we're supposed to be cuttin' back and all.'

'Come on, Mrs Goodge,' Betsy said cheerfully, 'surely you can make do.'

'That's easy for you to say, you won't have half a dozen people droppin' round and expectin' a decent bite to eat. The more buns and cakes I stuff down their throats, the longer they stay. The longer they stay, the more they talk.' The cook cast a quick glance toward the pantries off the hallway. 'I expect you're right, though. If I trim back a bit on meals, I ought to be able to make do.'

'I still don't understand what learnin' about these four people is goin' to do,' Wiggins complained. 'We don't know for sure if they 'ad anything to do with Randall's murder. No one even seems to know the last time the bloke was seen alive. He could have been murdered days before he were even due at the meeting at the Cubberly house.'

Mrs Jeffries gave the footman a surprised look. He was right. Suddenly it became imperative to find out when Jake Randall was killed, or failing that, to find out when he was last seen alive.

'Good morning, sir,' Mrs Jeffries said cheerfully as she carried the inspector's breakfast into the dining room. 'I hope you slept well.'

Witherspoon yawned. 'Very well, thank you.' He smiled as she put a plate of hot food in front of him. Then he saw what was on it. 'Er, no bacon and eggs this morning?'

'Oh no, sir.' Mrs Jeffries turned her head so he wouldn't see the impish twinkle in her eyes. She'd known that Mrs Goodge was up to something this morning. The cook had been chuckling to herself as she'd cooked the inspector's breakfast. 'Mrs Goodge has found several breakfast dishes that are far less costly than bacon and eggs. She hopes you like this one.'

Witherspoon picked up his fork and prodded the square brownish-grey object. 'Yes,' he murmured, 'I'm sure I will. What is it exactly?'

'Marrow toast.' She poured herself a cup of tea and

took the chair next to the inspector. When she looked up, he'd blanched. 'Oh dear, sir, are you feeling ill this morning?'

Witherspoon pushed his plate away. 'Just a touch off-colour,' he replied. 'I expect it's just this wretched cold. Er, I think I'll just have tea this morning.'

'Are you sure, sir?' she asked. 'I could ask Mrs Goodge to fix some porridge for you.'

'No, no, it's quite all right.' Witherspoon held up a hand and gave her a weak smile. 'Tea will do nicely. I mustn't complain because everyone's following my instructions so very enthusiastically. I appreciate all Mrs Goodge's efforts to trim back the food budget. I'm sure her marrow toast is wonderful, but I do have a poor stomach this morning.'

'All right, sir.' Mrs Jeffries took a sip of tea. She stifled a pang of conscience. They were laying it on a bit thick. Mrs Goodge had spent half the morning poring over cookery books. She'd come up with the most appallingly cheap and nasty recipe she could for breakfast. It would be interesting to see what she came up with for dinner. But the inspector had to under-stand that if one cut back, one had far less comfort and pleasure in life. She knew perfectly well that Inspec-tor Witherspoon wasn't in any real financial difficulty. He'd merely panicked when the price of some of his shares had dropped. 'Do you have a full day planned?'

'Indeed I do, Mrs Jeffries,' Witherspoon replied. 'Today I've got Jake Randall's inquest. Then I thought I'd pop round to Davies Street and begin questioning some of the victim's business associates.'

'Do you think your men will have any luck in

finding out where Mr Randall has been staying?' she asked casually. 'You did mention that he'd left his lodgings on the first of the month.'

'Oh, I'm sure we'll find out soon. Nivens said he was seen going into a hotel near the Strand last week.' Witherspoon gave her his worldly smile. 'From what I know of the victim, he enjoyed the finer things of life. He was probably staying at one of the larger hotels. You know my methods, Mrs Jeffries. It's vitally important that we trace the man's movements prior to his death.'

Mrs Jeffries desperately wanted to ask him about the fifty thousand pounds, but she wasn't certain this was the right time. 'Do you think Dr Potter will be able to give you an estimate on the time of death?'

Witherspoon shrugged. 'I suppose he'll try, but you know Potter; he's very cautious. Actually, though, we've had a spot of luck there.'

'How so, sir?'

'Dr Bosworth is also going to have a look at the victim,' the inspector explained. 'He's quite a bright chap, and I'm hoping to get a bit more information out of him.'

'Isn't that a bit unusual, sir?' Mrs Jeffries asked. She was delighted that the inspector had realized that young Bosworth had more brains in his little finger than Dr Potter had in his entire head.

'A tad,' he replied cautiously. 'Actually, it's quite unofficial and there's no disrespect intended towards Dr Potter. He's a fine physician. But Dr Bosworth is so much more up-to-date on . . . well . . . medicine. Did you know he spent several years studying in the United States? The chap really likes looking at corpses, and, from what I gather, the Americans have plenty of them.'

'As usual, sir, you've got everything well in hand.'

Mrs Jeffries stood on the Lambeth Palace Road and stared at one of the several doors of St Thomas's Hospital. The huge building had far too many entrances for her liking. It was only by a tedious process of elimination that she had determined this one was the most likely choice for her to catch her prey.

A blast of sharp March wind gusted off the river. She pulled her cloak tighter and hoped she wasn't on a fool's errand. Perhaps Dr Bosworth wouldn't be able to tell her anything at all useful. But she felt she must try.

The door opened and several men dressed in heavy overcoats stepped outside. Right behind them, another single figure emerged. Mrs Jeffries darted across the busy road. She caught up with Dr Bosworth and fell into step with him. 'Hello, Dr Bosworth,' she said cheerfully.

Surprised, he stared at her. 'Hello,' he replied cautiously.

She laughed gaily. 'We have met before, sir. A few months ago, I accompanied a friend to the mortuary. You very kindly assisted us.'

He smiled suddenly, his blue eyes lighting up in recognition. 'Yes, of course. You were with that American lady. How very nice to see you again, Mrs . . .'

'Jeffries.'

'I'm so sorry,' he mumbled, a blush creeping up his cheeks, 'but I've an appalling memory for names.'

'That's quite all right. Do you mind if I walk with

you? One feels so much safer these days in the company of a strong, young man.'

Bosworth straightened. 'I'd be delighted to accompany you, Mrs Jeffries. I'm just on my way over the bridge to the station.'

'I'm on my way to Great George Street,' she replied, 'This is most kind of you, Doctor. Sometimes one just doesn't feel safe upon the streets anymore. Not like when I was a girl,' she continued chattily, though actually, when she was younger, there was just as much crime and violence as there was now. 'But of course, you know all about how unsafe the streets are, what with helping the police and all.'

Bosworth's chest swelled. 'Really, Mrs Jeffries, I don't do all that much.'

'Why, sir, I know that's not true. Inspector Witherspoon has mentioned several times how very brilliant you are.'

'Inspector Witherspoon,' he said, clearly puzzled.

'Yes, I'm his housekeeper. Had you forgotten?'

'Yes, yes, of course,' He beamed with pleasure. 'That's right, you work for the gentleman. I must say, it's very kind of him to mention me. But in all honesty, I haven't done all that much.'

'You're much too modest, Doctor,' she said, taking his arm as they started across Westminster Bridge. 'The inspector tells me you're going to examine his latest victim. He's every confidence you'll be able to tell him far more than Dr Potter. No disrespect meant for Dr Potter, of course. But I understand you're rather an expert on bodies. You studied in the United States, I believe.'

'Yes,' he said enthusiastically. 'I was in San Francisco, and I made the acquaintance of the most remarkable doctor. Chap named Spurgeon Smith. Quite a peculiar fellow, really. Spent more time with cadavers than he did with patients. But gracious, he was a fountainhead of knowledge.'

Mrs Jeffries slowed her pace. They were halfway across the bridge and she didn't want the doctor to arrive at the Westminster Bridge Station before he'd told her what he'd learned from examining Jake Randall's body. She listened patiently while he went on about his stay in the American west. Then she steered the conversation toward Randall.

Dr Bosworth took the bait. His own footsteps slowed as he told her about his findings. 'Of course, I realize it isn't admissible evidence in court,' he continued, 'but according to Dr Smith, they used to dredge up bodies out of the San Francisco Bay all of the time. One can determine how long the body had been in the water by testing for various gases. Now, Dr Potter wouldn't even hear of doing such a thing, but as he wasn't there and the test is relatively simple I took a chance and tested the victim anyway.'

'How very commendable of you, sir.' She smiled encouragingly. 'And what were your conclusions?'

'I'd say the body was in the water for at least thirty-six hours. But of course, that's only an estimate. The tests aren't infallible. Dr Smith says there are so many other factors that can affect decomposition.'

Mrs Jeffries glanced over the side of the bridge at the river. 'But wouldn't the body have gone out on the tide?'

Bosworth chuckled. 'Generally, yes. But the victim had a long flat bruise on his leg, like he'd been pinned beneath a piling or something. My conclusion is that he was killed very close to where he came up. It's a fairly well-populated stretch of river. The body was spotted literally as it floated to the surface.'

'Did Mr Randall drown, then?'

'Oh no. He was dead before he hit the water,' Dr Bosworth said cheerfully. He looked enormously pleased with himself. 'The bullet killed him. A shot directly to the heart from a Colt .45 will generally finish you straight off.'

Stunned, Mrs Jeffries stopped. She looked at him in amazement. 'You mean you know what kind of gun was used?'

Bosworth shrugged modestly. 'Oh yes. It's not admissible in one of our courts, of course. But I'd stake my life that Jake Randall was shot by a Colt .45. They call it the "peacemaker" over in America. You know, Mrs Jeffries, we don't see all that many bullet wounds here, but they do in America,' he said wistfully. 'There certainly isn't any shortage of murders over there. I'm sure Dr Potter would tell me it's impossible to know. But believe me, after a year of working with Dr Smith on the Barbary Coast, I've seen enough entrance wounds to be able to identify half a dozen different kinds of guns.'

'Gracious, Dr Bosworth.' Mrs Jeffries was truly impressed. 'Why on earth don't the police use your remarkable abilities?'

Bosworth sighed. 'To be perfectly honest, it's my own fault that I haven't advanced further. You see, the only way to advance is to have important people as your patients.'

'But surely you're a very good physician,' she protested.

'Oh, I'm competent,' he admitted, 'but I don't much care for live patients. I'm afraid I'm a bit like my friend Dr Smith. I much prefer the dead ones. They don't complain if you make a mistake and, of course, if you make a really dreadful mistake, you can't hurt them. They're already dead.'

CHAPTER THREE

INSPECTOR WITHERSPOON AND Constable Barnes waited patiently in the drawing room of the Cubberly home. The large, well-appointed room wasn't quite as nice as one's first impression suggested. The inspector squinted through his spectacles as he gazed at his surroundings. The crimson velvet curtains were badly frayed along the railing, the gold-leaf carpet was thin and worn in spots, and in the corners there was a layer of dust on the dark hardwood floors. 'Bit odd, this place,' he muttered softly.

'Yes, sir,' Barnes agreed, He, too, was taking in the details of the room. 'Beneath all the elegance, it's a bit tatty, isn't it? Not what you'd think the place would be like judgin' from the neighbourhood. Did you notice the banister, sir? When the maid went up the stairs, it rattled every time she touched it.'

Witherspoon hadn't noticed. He'd been too busy staring at the elderly, slovenly dressed woman who'd answered the door to take any notice of the staircase. Naturally, one didn't want to be judgemental, but in a home like this, one would have expected a neatly uniformed housemaid or butler to answer the door.

From behind them, they heard footsteps approaching. Witherspoon and Barnes both turned as a dark-haired man with mutton-chop whiskers entered the room. He stopped by the door and stared at them coldly out of the smallest blue eyes the inspector had ever seen.

'I take it you're the police,' he said.

'I'm Inspector Gerald Witherspoon and this is Constable Barnes.' He held out his hand. 'We're sorry to disturb you, but we're here to ask you a few questions.'

'Yes, expected you would be. I'm John Cubberly.' He hesitated for a moment before shaking the inspector's hand. He dropped it quickly. 'You're here about Jake Randall?'

Witherspoon nodded. 'When was the last time you saw Mr Randall?'

Cubberly shrugged. 'I'm not precisely sure of the date. I think it was a fortnight ago.'

'We understand that you were one of the major investors in Mr Randall's mining company, is that correct?' Witherspoon asked. He had a feeling this interview was going to be tedious. Mr Cubberly had not asked them to sit down. In all fairness, he's not obliged to, the inspector thought. But really, it would be ever so much more comfortable if they could all have a seat.

'That's correct.' Cubberly smiled slightly.

Drat, the inspector thought, this is going to be tedious. The man obviously wasn't going to volunteer anything. 'You were expecting Mr Randall here for a meeting on March the seventh, weren't you?'

'Yes. But he didn't come.'

'I see.' Witherspoon's stomach growled. Embarrassed,

he began talking quickly. 'What was the purpose of this meeting, Mr Cubberly?'

'The purpose?' Cubberly repeated hesitantly. 'Well, I suppose you could say we – by that I mean myself and the other stockholders – called the meeting because we'd heard some very alarming rumours concerning Mr Randall.'

'What kind of rumours?' Witherspoon desperately wanted a cup of tea. His throat was absolutely parched.

'We'd heard that Randall hadn't invested any of the money he'd raised in the mine.' Cubberly turned and began to pace slowly back and forth between the two policemen and the marble fireplace. 'Naturally, considering the amount of money we'd all put in, we became concerned. We asked Mr Randall here to explain his actions, but as I've said, he didn't show up.'

'And who are the other gentlemen who were scheduled to come that day?' Witherspoon already knew that information, but he'd just remembered something his housekeeper had once said. 'Oh yes, sir,' she'd said, 'my late husband always made it a point never to tell people anything. He waited for them to tell him what he already knew. He claimed that was one of the ways he could tell if someone was lying.'

'There were four of us. Myself, Rushton Benfield, Edward Dillingham, and Lester Hinkle. Together, we constitute the major investors in the company.'

Witherspoon nodded. 'I see. Could you tell me, sir, what did you and the others decide to do when Mr Randall failed to keep his appointment?'

'Do?' Cubberly stopped pacing. 'We didn't do anything. When he didn't show up, the others left as well.

There wasn't much point in having a meeting unless Randall was here.'

'I'm sorry, sir,' the inspector said, 'but I really don't understand that. By your own admission, you were concerned that Mr Randall had stolen your money—'

'Stolen?' Cubberly interrupted. 'We never accused him of stealing. We merely wanted him to explain the situation.'

'Are you saying, sir, that you don't think he was stealing from you?' Constable Barnes asked quietly.

'We didn't know for sure,' Cubberly snapped. 'All we wanted was an explanation. You're making it sound like we'd already tried and convicted the man. That's not the case at all.'

Witherspoon persisted; he wasn't sure what he was getting at, but he had the feeling it was important. 'But surely, when Mr Randall didn't show up as scheduled, you and the others reached some sort of decision.'

'Well, we did think it might be prudent to contact the bank where the funds were being held,' Cubberly admitted slowly.

'And what bank would that be, sir?' Witherspoon asked.

Cubberly stared at them for a moment before answering. 'It's the London and San Francisco Bank on Old Broad Street. Randall chose it.'

Witherspoon nodded. 'Which one of you contacted the bank?'

'Rushton Benfield. He'd opened the account with Randall. That was one of our terms and conditions.'

'Was the money there?' For once, Witherspoon was certain this was a pertinent question.

'I don't know.' Cubberly shrugged as though the matter was of no importance. 'Benfield hasn't called round to tell me.'

'And you didn't think it important enough to contact him to find out?' Barnes asked incredulously.

'As a matter of fact, no.' Cubberly resumed his pacing. 'The mining venture isn't my only investment. I'm a very busy man. Naturally, I assumed that if Mr Benfield found something amiss, he'd inform the rest of us. As he has not done so, then I think it's safe to assume that all the money is accounted for.'

Witherspoon was confused, but determined not to let it show. He didn't wish to accuse Mr Cubberly of lying, but really, the man must think the police were absolute fools if he expected them to believe he had so little interest in whether or not his money was safe!

'Now, sir' – Cubberly rubbed his hands together – 'if you've no further questions—' He broke off as the door opened and a short, slender red-haired woman stepped inside. She paused in the doorway and stared at the two policemen.

Her eyes were a pale, clear brown and they slanted at the corners over a long, sharp nose and pointy chin. She reminded the inspector of an intelligent fox. She wore an elegant day dress of dark green and her thin hair was pulled back in a tight bun beneath a grey hair net.

Cubberly frowned at her. 'What is it, Hilda?'

'I'm sorry, John,' she replied. 'I didn't realize you had anyone with you.'

'Just the police,' he said brusquely, 'and they'll be gone in a few moments.'

47

'I'm Hilda Cubberly,' she announced. 'Are you here about Jake Randall's murder?'

'Of course they're here about Randall,' Cubberly said impatiently. 'Why else would they be here? Now, what was it you wanted?'

Hilda Cubberly didn't seem offended by her husband's manner. 'The new girl is here for the house-maid's position. You said you wanted to interview her.'

'Tell her to wait,' he ordered. 'As I said, the police are almost ready to leave.'

'I'm afraid we've a few more questions, sir,' the inspector said.

'Well then, get on with them, man,' Cubberly snapped. 'I've already explained I'm very busy. Besides, I don't know what else I could possibly tell you. I haven't seen Jake Randall in two weeks.'

'Really, John,' Mrs Cubberly interrupted irritably. 'Have you forgotten? You saw him going into St George's Baths on Buckingham Palace Road just last week. You told me about it when you got home.' She turned to the inspector. 'Honestly,' she complained, 'he's getting so absent-minded.'

Cubberly hesitated and then smiled weakly. 'Why yes, now that you mention it, I did see Randall. I'd forgotten.'

Gracious, Witherspoon thought, Mrs Cubberly has a rather sharp tongue.

Mrs Cubberly gave a delicate, ladylike snort, as though she expected no better from a male. 'If you gentlemen will excuse me, I must get back to the housekeeper's rooms. I'll bring the girl down in ten

48

minutes,' she called over her shoulder to her husband as she left the room.

'Did you speak with Mr Randall when you saw him last week?' the inspector asked.

'No. I was in a hurry.'

Witherspoon wondered what else he might have forgotten. But he couldn't see that Cubberly's forgetting to mention a small detail could have any bearing on the murder. 'How did you and the others contact Mr Randall? To get him to the meeting, I mean. Did someone go round personally and tell him he must be here?'

'We sent a note to his rooms.'

'When?'

Cubberly stared at him suspiciously. 'The day before the meeting.'

'That would be on March the sixth?'

'Yes,' he replied slowly. 'I suppose that's right. Wait a moment; I've made a mistake. Benfield didn't take the note to his rooms; he took it to Randall's club. Yes, that's right. Randall had moved into a hotel by then. But we know he got the note. The porter at the club assured us he'd given it to him.'

Witherspoon paused on the bottom step, took out his handkerchief and blew his nose.

Barnes clucked his tongue sympathetically. 'Still got me cold, I see, sir.'

'Yes, I'm afraid I'm going to have it forever. I say, Constable, what did you think of Mr Cubberly?'

Barnes, who had the highest respect for Inspector Witherspoon, even if he was occasionally confused by his methods, answered honestly. 'I think he was hidin' something, sir.'

'I had that impression, too, Constable,' the inspector replied as they started up Davies Street towards Chester Square. 'And I must say, I didn't like the way he side-stepped that question about the note.'

'You mean the way he suddenly remembered that the note couldn't have gone to Randall's rooms?' Barnes chuckled. 'He's a sly one. Almost stepped right into your trap.'

Witherspoon wasn't aware he'd been setting a trap, but he didn't want his constable to know that. 'Er, yes, well, clever is as clever does.'

'Still, I suppose he couldn't have done it; not if he were home like he said he was.' Barnes stopped and glanced back at the house. 'Do you think I ought to nip back and have a word with the servants? It's no good asking Mrs Cubberly to confirm he were home the rest of the day. A wife'll say anything her husband wants.'

'I think we ought to do that tomorrow,' Witherspoon said. 'We'll interview the other shareholders before we begin verifying alibis. Have the uniformed lads come up with the name of Randall's hotel yet?'

'Not yet, sir. He wasn't stayin' at the one on the Strand. But we're still workin' on it. What did you think of Dr Potter's evidence this morning?'

'I'm sure Dr Potter did his best,' Witherspoon replied, forcing himself to be fair. 'But frankly, I do wish the man would be more precise in his opinions. The only thing he was certain about was that the man was dead. According to him, Randall could have been shot on the seventh, eighth or even the ninth of March. That's hardly helpful. I do hope young Dr Bosworth will have more useful information for us.'

'He will, sir. I told him we'd pop round to St Thomas's late this afternoon. Is that all right with you, sir?'

'That'll be fine.'

'Are we going to the bank now, sir?'

Witherspoon sighed. He had a long day ahead of him. Between spending the morning at the inquest and then dashing all the way over here to begin the interviews, he was exhausted. But he knew his duty. It was imperative that they confirm that the investment money was still in the bank. Then he had to interview the other three investors in the company. After that, there was Dr Bosworth to see. His stomach growled again, reminding him of how hungry he was. A vision of roast beef and new potatoes popped into his head. Witherspoon licked his lips.

Then he remembered Mrs Goodge's marrow toast and he shuddered. Surely the cook didn't mean to turn every meal into a pauper's feast. They came out onto Eccleston Street. The inspector spotted a tea shop on the corner next to the bank. His mouth watered and he quickened his steps. Perhaps they could pop into that tea shop for some sticky buns. The inspector dearly loved sticky buns. 'We'll go to the bank after we finish the interviews this afternoon. I say, I could do with some tea, Constable,' he announced. 'I don't know about you, but I'm famished.'

'He's a nice little dog,' the housemaid said as she patted Fred gently. 'Mr Hinkle's got a dog, too, but he's so old and cranky he growls if you try and touch him. Not like your Fred 'ere.'

Wiggins smiled at the lovely brown-eyed girl who was fussing over his dog. He was right proud of himself. He'd only been on the job, so to speak, for half an hour and already he'd met someone from the Hinkle household. And she was so pretty, too. 'Uh, what kind of dog is it?'

'An old bulldog. His name's Albert.' She straightened and shifted the basket she was carrying back onto her arms. 'Well, I expect I'd better get crackin'. I've got to take this 'ere basket over to the church.'

'Can I carry it for ya?' he asked. 'I'm goin' that way myself.'

'That's very nice of you,' she replied shyly, 'All right, if it's no trouble. It'd be nice to have some company. It's a long walk to St Bartholomew's.' She gave him her burden. 'It's a poor basket. Mr Hinkle sends food over to 'em every Friday.'

'Is that who you work for?' Wiggins started slowly up the street.

'Yes, Mr and Mrs Lester Hinkle. I've been there three years, ever since I was fourteen.' She fell into step next to Wiggins. Fred gave up trying to sniff the contents of the basket and trotted after them.

'Your Mr Hinkle sounds like he's a good one to work for, then. I mean, 'is 'eart must be in the right place if he gives food to the poor.'

'Oh, he's a nice man, he is. By the way, my name's Jane. Jane Malone.'

'Pleased to meet you, Miss Malone,' Wiggins said politely. He'd much rather spend his time finding out about Miss Malone than Lester Hinkle, but he knew he'd better have something to report when he got back to Upper Edmonton Gardens. Besides, he'd already come up with a right clever way of finding out what he needed to know.

'Hinkle, Hinkle,' he mumbled. 'I say, isn't he the bloke that got coshed over the 'ead by that robber?'

'What you talkin' about?' Jane stopped and stared at him. Fred stopped, too, and had another sniff at the basket.

'I read about it in the papers,' Wiggins continued. 'The story were right on the front page. It said a feller got 'it on the 'ead by some robbers outside Victoria Station this past Monday. That'd be March the seventh. Was it your Mr Hinkle?'

Jane laughed. 'Nah, must be someone else.' She looked at him curiously. 'You read the papers, do you?'

'Every day,' he said proudly. 'But are you sure it weren't your Mr Hinkle?'

Jane absently patted Fred on the head and started walking again. 'I'm sure. Last Monday, my Mr Hinkle was at a meeting over near Chester Square. I 'eard he and the missus talkin' about it when he come home that night.'

'Oh.' Wiggins tried to think what to ask next. 'Well, maybe he got coshed after the meetin'.'

Jane cast him a curious glance. 'No. He weren't nowhere near Victoria Station. I 'eard Mr Hinkle tellin' Mrs Hinkle that he'd spent the entire day chasin' about lookin' for some feller who never showed up. He didn't get home that night till past ten. I know, 'cause I let him in and he were right as rain. I'da noticed if he'd had his 'ead bashed in.' She stopped abruptly and faced Wiggins. 'Look 'ere, why are you askin' all these questions?'

Luty Belle Crookshank cocked her snow-white head to one side and regarded Mrs Jeffries thoughtfully out of her bright black eyes. 'You know, Hepzibah, you've been watchin' that door like you're expectin' the Queen herself to come sashayin' through it any minute.'

'Have I really?' Mrs Jeffries said innocently. She forced herself to smile calmly. She'd only made it back to the house herself moments before Luty Belle and Hatchet arrived for tea. Betsy had only just come in, Mrs Goodge was in a foul mood because she'd found out nothing from any of her sources, and Wiggins and Smythe were nowhere to be seen. She wasn't worried about the footman's safety, but she was concerned he'd come flying in with Fred at his heels and give the game away. Luty Belle and Hatchet were trusted friends. Indeed, they'd helped out on two of the inspector's other cases. But Mrs Jeffries didn't want to take advantage of the elderly American. And of course, there was her age.

'Yes,' Luty said bluntly. 'You have. What's wrong?'

'Nothing's really wrong,' Mrs Jeffries said. She helped herself to another tart. 'I suppose I'm a bit concerned about Wiggins. He's so very fond of you. I'm surprised he isn't back yet.'

'Not like the lad to be late for tea,' Mrs Goodge said darkly.

'He'll be here any minute,' Betsy said cheerfully.

'Where is he?' Luty asked.

Unfortunately, they all spoke at once.

'He's gone to the butcher's,' Mrs Jeffries replied.

'He's walkin' the dog,' Mrs Goodge said.

'He's helpin' Smythe to wash down the carriage,' Betsy said.

'I knew it.' Luty banged her teacup down and glared at the three women. 'You're up to something.' She turned to her butler. 'They's up to something, ain't they, Hatchet?'

Hatchet, a tall, dignified white-haired man, tilted his chin and studied each of them carefully. 'Yes, madam, I believe you're correct. Mrs Jeffries has indeed given the backdoor an unwarranted amount of attention. Mrs Goodge has been most distracted, and even Miss Betsy has fidgeted about in her chair like a schoolgirl waiting for the teacher to leave the room. My guess, madam,' he continued as he turned and stared at his employer, 'is that they've embarked upon another murder investigation.'

Mrs Goodge gasped, Betsy flushed guiltily, and even Mrs Jeffries was embarrassed.

'Now, Luty,' the housekeeper began.

The backdoor burst open and Wiggins and Fred flew inside. 'You'll never guess what I've found out. On the day of the murder, Lester Hinkle told his missus he's spent the whole day chasin' after—' He broke off and blushed crimson as he caught sight of Luty Belle and Hatchet.

'Aha.' Luty jumped to her feet and placed her hands on her hips. 'I told ya,' she shouted.

'True, madam,' Hatchet said. 'You did. And I think it's most unsporting of them to not to let us in on it.'

'Now, Luty,' Mrs Jeffries began again.

'Don't you "now, Luty", me,' the elderly American snapped. 'You know good and well that Hatchet and I like to help you investigate. I thought we was friends. I thought I could count on you.'

'But of course we're friends,' Mrs Jeffries said quickly, 'and we were going to tell you about the case. I was merely waiting until everyone was present.'

Luty regarded her suspiciously. Then she glanced at Hatchet. One of his white patrician eyebrows was raised in disbelief. 'What do ya think, Hatchet? Was they gonna tell us?'

The butler considered the matter. 'Madam, I would never deign to consider that Mrs Jeffries was capable of lying to us.'

Luty snorted but sat back down. 'I wouldn't like to think you was keepin' this from me 'cause of my age, Hepzibah.'

'That was the furthest thing from my mind,' Mrs Jeffries replied. She hated lying, but obviously, she'd severely miscalculated how much being included meant to Luty. She wouldn't make that mistake again. 'While we're waiting for Smythe to arrive, why don't I fill you in on all the details.'

Smythe arrived fifteen minutes later. He cuffed Wiggins on the back, winked at Betsy, and smiled broadly at Luty. 'I see you've let her in on it.'

'But of course,' Mrs Jeffries said. 'And now that you're here, we can all share what we've learned. Then Luty and Hatchet will be fully informed.'

'Git off my foot, Fred.' Luty shoved the hound off her feet, patted his head, and slipped him a bite of her cake. Fred gulped down the treat and butted her knees with his head.

'It's your own fault, madam,' Hatchet pointed out. 'You do keep slipping the animal bites.'

'I only give the critter a little seedcake,' Luty protested. 'Can't stand to see a creature hungry. Afore any of you start, I've got a couple of questions. Exactly where was this silver mine?'

'Didn't I mention that?' Mrs Jeffries said. 'It's in Colorado.'

'You told me that,' Luty replied. 'But does anyone know exactly where in Colorado?'

They all looked at one another. None of them knew.

'Is it important?' Mrs Goodge asked.

'Well' – Luty drummed her fingers on the top of the table – 'it could be. Why don't you see if you can find out exactly where this place is, and when you do, be sure and let me know.'

'All right.' Mrs Jeffries didn't see that it mattered all that much. But she'd do as Luty requested. She had great respect for her intelligence. 'Now, who would like to go first?'

'I've not got all that much,' Betsy said glumly. 'I tell ya, that Cubberly household must be the worst place in the world to work. I spent half the day hangin' about waitin' for a servant to come out and the only thing I saw was the inspector and Constable Barnes. They must lock their servants up.'

'Don't be discouraged, Betsy,' Mrs Jeffries said kindly. 'You tried your best and tomorrow is another day.'

'Oh, I didn't let that stop me,' the maid said. 'When

it were clear that I wasn't going to find someone from the household, I made the rounds of the local shops.'

Mrs Jeffries beamed in approval. Betsy was very good at prying information out of tight-lipped merchants and chatty shopgirls. 'Excellent.'

'Still didn't find out much. But I did learn that Mr Cubberly is a right old miser, and he and Mrs Cubberly have only been married two years.'

'Hmmm,' Mrs Jeffries said thoughtfully. 'I wonder if his miserliness is recent. If so, it could mean he was desperate for money.'

Betsy shook her head. 'I don't think so. From what I heard, he's always been tightfisted. He makes his servants pay for their tea and sugar every month. I heard that from a shop assistant that used to be sweet on one of the Cubberly maids. He even made the scullery maid repay him when she borrowed his wife's glycerine for her chapped hands. He wouldn't buy soft soap for his floors, he was always haggling with the butcher and the grocer over their bills, and Mrs Cubberly complained to anyone that would listen that she hadn't had a new dress since she married him.'

Luty snorted in disgust. 'Sounds just like Jake Turtle.'

'Who's he?' Wiggins asked.

'The biggest skinflint that ever lived,' Luty said. 'He kept the first dollar he ever made. His wife finally got so tired of livin' on beans and wild greens that she locked him out in the snow during a blizzard. Froze to death. He was clutchin' his purse right next to his heart when they found him the next day.'

'Was his wife tried for murder?' Betsy asked.

Luty cackled. 'Murder? Nah. Martha Tuttle claimed

that Jake went outside on his own. Said he'd dropped a penny in the snow and wanted to find it. Her story was she went on to bed and didn't hear him bangin' on the door to git back inside. 'Course ol' Jake was such a miser, we half believed her.'

They laughed, and even Hatchet cracked a smile.

'I reckon I'll go next,' Mrs Goodge announced. 'Not that I've all that much to tell, and if you don't mind my saying so, it's the inspector's fault.'

'Really, Mrs Goodge—' Mrs Jeffries began, but the cook cut her off.

'But it is his fault,' she said stubbornly. 'If he didn't have us cuttin' back every which way so he can save a few pennies, I'da had a much better day. One cup of tea is barely enough to wet someone's whistle. They won't talk if you don't feed them.'

'What's she talkin' about?' Luty asked curiously.

'The inspector has asked all of us to decrease our household expenditure a bit, that's all,' Mrs Jeffries said soothingly. 'Mrs Goodge has merely had a less than successful day.'

'I didn't find out anything,' the cook wailed. She looked like she was going to burst into tears.

Mrs Jeffries knew that Mrs Goodge was more upset over her failure to learn anything useful than she was with the inspector's newest household management scheme.

'Don't distress yourself, Mrs Goodge,' she said sympathetically. 'You know perfectly well you're absolutely brilliant at prying information out of your network of sources. But even the most brilliant of people occasionally have a bad day.' She reached over and patted her friend's work-worn hands. 'Tomorrow will be better. I'm sure that by this time tomorrow evening, you'll have learned more than the rest of us put together.'

'Sure you will, Mrs G,' the coachman put in.

'Don't feel bad. I didn't learn much today either,' Betsy added.

'You're better at findin' out things than you are at cookin',' Wiggins said. 'And we all know what a great cook you are. Just give it another day or two. That's all you need do.'

Mrs Goodge sighed and hastily brushed at her eyes. 'Got a piece of grit in my eye,' she muttered. 'All right, I'll try again tomorrow.'

Mrs Jeffries was deeply touched by the others. All of them had realized what was bothering Mrs Goodge, and all of them had done their best to make her feel included, important and, most of all, needed. 'I haven't had all that much success with my inquiries today either,' she said. 'However, I did have a chat with that nice Dr Bosworth. You remember him, don't you, Luty? He works at St Thomas's.'

Luty nodded.

Mrs Jeffries went on to tell them about Dr Bosworth's contention that the victim had been killed on the evening of the seventh. 'But the most interesting thing I learned was that Dr Bosworth is almost certain that Jake Randall was shot with a Colt .45.'

'How could he possibly be sure of such a thing?' Hatchet asked.

'That's what I asked him,' Mrs Jeffries said, 'but as it turns out, Dr Bosworth spent a lot of time in San Francisco working with a doctor there named Spurgeon

Smith. As he put it, they have an awful lot more bodies with bullets in them than the English do. He's seen dozens of bullet wounds. Bosworth claims he can now identify half a dozen weapons just by the kind of wound they make entering the body. I don't know if what he's saying is correct or not, but it sounded quite possible to me.'

'I reckon it's true,' Luty muttered. 'Stands to reason, don't it? Nell's bells, even I can tell the difference between a shotgun hole in someone's gut and one of them fancy little derringers.'

'So that means that Jake Randall was shot with an American gun,' Hatchet said.

Betsy, who didn't know all that much about fire-arms, asked, 'Can you only get that gun in America?'

'I expect you kin git it in England,' Luty replied. 'But it's far more common over there than it is over here.'

'Hmmph,' Mrs Goodge muttered. 'Sounds to me like you found out a lot of useful information.'

'Yes, but not about Edward Dillingham.' Mrs Jeffries sighed. 'I drew a complete blank there. The only person who came out of the Dillingham house was an elderly gentleman. Quite well dressed. He was carrying a Bible. The butcher's boy told me he was Phineas Dillingham, Edward's father. As he hasn't anything to do with Jake Randall, I didn't bother following him.' She glanced at Wiggins. 'As you seem to have actually learned something useful, why don't you go next?'

Wiggins shrugged. 'All I heard was that Lester Hinkle didn't come home from the meetin' on the seventh until around ten o'clock that evening. And when he come in, he told his missus that he's spent the day on a wild-goose chase. Said he'd been lookin' for someone.'

'Jake Randall probably.' Mrs Jeffries straightened. 'I wonder if he found him.'

'Jane didn't know that. All she overheard was him complainin' to Mrs Hinkle that he'd been all over London and he was bloomin' tired.'

'If he used the expression "wild-goose chase", then we can surmise that he was unsuccessful,' Mrs Jeffries mused.

'If he was lookin' for Randall,' Luty pointed out.

'Really, madam,' Hatchet interrupted. 'Who else would Hinkle be looking for?'

'Rushton Benfield,' Smythe said softly.

They all stared at him.

'Wait a minute,' Wiggins protested. 'I'm not through yet.'

'Sorry,' the coachman said. He sat back in his chair. 'I'll wait my turn.'

'Now, what else did you learn, Wiggins?' Mrs Jeffries asked patiently.

The footman squirmed in his seat. 'Well, not much, really. But Jane did tell me that Mr Hinkle's been worried lately. And she thinks it's because he's got some money problems. She 'eard Mr Hinkle tellin' Mrs Hinkle that if they didn't get their 'ands on some money soon, they'd be ruined.'

'Mr Hinkle must have been frantic when Jake Randall didn't show up at the meeting,' Mrs Jeffries murmured. 'Anything else?'

'No.' Wiggins sighed, remembering Jane Malone.

He'd done some fast talking when she'd demanded to know why he was asking so many questions, and he feared his answers hadn't been clever enough for her. She'd looked at him like she thought he was lying. She probably wouldn't want to see him again.

All of them turned and stared at Smythe. He cleared his throat. 'Right then, I've learned a few things. First of all, let's not decide that Lester Hinkle were out lookin' for Jake Randall. He could've been lookin' for Rushton Benfield. According to one of his 'ousemaids—'

'Housemaid?' Betsy interrupted. 'You talked to a housemaid today?'

They all stared at her in surprise. Mrs Jeffries sighed inwardly, wondering what was the matter now. She'd so hoped that Betsy and Smythe wouldn't be so very competitive on this murder.

The maid blushed. 'I mean, that's a bit odd. Smythe usually talks to hansom drivers or butlers or street Arabs to get his information.'

The housekeeper fully expected the coachman to come back with some clever comment, but instead Smythe looked oddly pleased.

'This time I talked with a 'ousemaid,' he said. 'Nice girl she was. Very pretty. Her name's Lydia Stivey.'

'We don't need to know her bloomin' name,' Betsy muttered. 'Just get on with it.'

Smythe grinned widely. 'Accordin' to Lydia, Rushton Benfield left on the afternoon of March seventh for his meeting with the other shareholders. But he never come back. No one's seen 'ide nor 'air of the man.'

CHAPTER FOUR

'I SAY, MY NAME'S not going to be mentioned in the newspapers, is it?' Edward Dillingham asked anxiously.

'Er, I'm not really sure,' Inspector Witherspoon replied. He could hardly assure the gentleman his name wouldn't be in the press. It simply wasn't a guarantee the police could give, not with so many enterprising and aggressive reporters snooping about. 'This is a free country, Mr Dillingham, and as such, we do have a free press.'

'Well, it's rather important that I be kept out of it, you see.' The tall, blond-haired man drummed his fingers on the top of the inspector's desk. 'I mean, I've done my duty. I've come along here of my own free will because I was sure you'd want to speak with me. Not that I was all that familiar with Mr Randall, of course. He was merely a business acquaintance.'

'Yes, sir, we do appreciate your coming round,' the inspector said.

'Actually, I didn't have to come here at all.'

'We're aware of that, sir,' Witherspoon said patiently.

'Now, if you'll just answer a few simple questions, you can be on your way.' His mind went utterly blank. For the life of him, he couldn't think of how to begin. To give himself time to gather his scattered thoughts, he stared at the pale spring sunshine streaming in through the small windowpanes of his office.

After several moments he heard Constable Barnes, who was sitting behind Dillingham in a chair by the door, clear his throat. Witherspoon pushed some papers to one side and straightened his spine. Best to plunge straight in, he thought.

'You are one of the major shareholders in the Randall and Watson Mining Company.'

Dillingham nodded. 'Yes, but that won't be in the papers, will it? I mean, I shouldn't want anyone to know about my involvement.'

'Why not, sir?' the inspector asked curiously. 'A silver mine is a perfectly respectable enterprise.' Gracious, he thought, the man was acting like he'd been accused of running a white slavery ring.

'Yes, yes, of course it is. It's just that one doesn't like to have one's private business matters made public.' Dillingham gave him a weak smile, shifted in his seat, and crossed his legs. 'At least, not someone in my position.'

'I quite understand, Mr Dillingham,' Witherspoon replied. 'But we are investigating a murder.'

'I know, Inspector,' Dillingham said defensively. 'That is why I've come. Please, go on with your questions.'

'Do you have any idea where Jake Randall had been staying since he left his lodgings the first of this month?'

'Why would I know that?' Dillingham asked as he drummed his fingers on the top of the desk again. 'The man wasn't a friend of mine; he was a business associate.'

'Yes, but people frequently know their business associates' addresses.'

'I do business with my grocer, Inspector.' He uncrossed his legs and leaned back in his chair. 'But I hardly know where he lives. Nor do I care. And that was my attitude towards Mr Randall. I invested in his silver mine. I didn't see him socially.'

Witherspoon wished the young man would stop fidgeting. 'When was the last time you did see Mr Randall?'

Dillingham's pale eyebrows drew together in thought. 'Let's see, I'm not really sure . . . I know. It was last week. I saw him walking in Hyde Park.'

'Was he alone?'

'He was with a woman.'

'Did you speak to him?'

'No,' Dillingham stated. 'I was in a hurry.'

'Do you know who this woman was?' Witherspoon desperately hoped he did. He was tired of investigating a victim that no one seemed to know very well.

'Hardly.' He gave a nervous high-pitched laugh, then stopped abruptly as the inspector continued to stare at him. 'I mean, I didn't know the lady's name, but she did look awfully familiar.'

'Familiar,' the inspector repeated hopefully. 'You mean you'd seen her before?'

'I shouldn't say that I'd seen her before,' Dillingham said slowly. He leaned forward and gave the inspector a knowing smile. 'It was more that I'd seen her kind before. Do you know what I mean?'

Witherspoon hadn't the faintest idea what the man was talking about. A person was either familiar because you'd seen them before or they were not. 'No,' he said honestly. 'I'm afraid I don't.'

Dillingham blinked and drew back. 'Well, Jake was a bit of a ladies' man, if you get my drift. In the six months I've known him, I've seen him with several young women. They're always the same type. Small, blond and', he coughed delicately, 'a tad flashy.'

Witherspoon was disappointed. Drat. Why couldn't people just say what they meant? 'So you're saying that in your judgement, this woman wasn't well-known to the victim?'

'I'm not sure,' he said hesitantly. 'I mean, how could one possibly know such a thing?'

'I wouldn't expect you to be certain,' the inspector replied, 'but one does occasionally hear rumours or gossip. That sort of thing.' He had no idea where this line of inquiry would lead, but perhaps it would lead somewhere.

'Actually, now that you mention it,' Dillingham said brightly, 'I have heard gossip – not that I ever really listen, of course. But still, one can't help what one hears.'

'Of course. Now what was it that you'd heard about Mr Randall?' Witherspoon's hopes soared. Finally, someone was going to tell him something useful about Jake Randall.

'Rumour has it that he's quite smitten with someone.'

'Where did you hear this rumour, sir?' Barnes asked softly.

Dillingham jerked at the constable's words. He swivelled in his chair and stared at the man sitting by the door. 'Oh, I'd forgotten you were back there. I don't quite remember where I heard about the girl.'

'Do you know the woman's name?' the inspector asked.

'I'm afraid not.' Dillingham shrugged.

Barnes looked up from his notebook. 'Who would have been likely to know about Mr Randall's personal life?'

'The only person who would really be in a position to know would be Rushton Benfield. But it's no good your asking him. He's gone.'

'Maybe Benfield's been murdered, too,' Mrs Goodge said.

'Nah.' Smythe shook his head. 'Accordin' to Lydia, this in't the first time 'e's taken off. Rushton Benfield may be Sir Thaddeus Benfield's son, but 'e's not known for 'is good character. Seems like this in't the first time 'e's played fast and loose with someone else's money. Not that anyone ever proved anything against 'im, but Lydia claims there's people who cross the road when they see 'im comin'.'

'But I thought it was Randall that was the crook,' Luty said. 'He's the one with a bullet in his heart.'

Smythe shrugged his massive shoulders. 'I told you, it didn't make much sense. You'd think if a man 'ad a reputation as bad as Benfield's, 'e couldn't raise enough money to buy a drink, let alone 'elp swindle people out of fifty thousand pounds. But that's exactly what 'e did. Benfield is the one that got everyone else to invest in the mine. 'E give these big fancy parties and introduced Jake Randall to the others.'

Mrs Jeffries gazed at Luty speculatively. 'I think', she said slowly, 'we've just found the perfect task for you and Hatchet.'

Luty smiled brightly. 'You want us to try and find Benfield?' she asked excitedly.

'That shouldn't be so difficult,' Hatchet muttered.

'Partly,' Mrs Jeffries said. 'But I don't want you to merely find the man; I also want you to find out why someone like him would form such a close association with a man like Jake Randall in the first place.'

'Has anyone found out where Randall was stayin'?' Wiggins asked.

'No.' The housekeeper frowned. 'And that's also something we need to do. It's imperative not only that we locate his lodgings, but also that we find out as much as we can about him.'

'That's not gonna be easy.' Betsy shook her head. 'It's not like we've got much to go on. We don't know where he was stayin', we don't know who he were with, and we don't know for sure why he was even killed.'

'Precisely my point,' Mrs Jeffries said firmly. 'I suddenly realized that until we learn more about the victim, we won't get anywhere. So let's not worry about what we don't know and concentrate on what we do know. Jake Randall was a close associate of Rushton Benfield.'

'Who is now missin',' Mrs Goodge pointed out.

'True. But even if he's missing, that shouldn't stop us learning what we can about him.' Mrs Jeffries looked directly at the cook. 'Benfield is a member of a very prominent family. It should be easy for you to pick up quite a bit of information about him. Find out what his habits are, which club he belongs to, who his other friends might be.'

Wiggins scratched his chin. 'But I thought you said we should concentrate on learnin' about this Randall fella?'

'We will.' The housekeeper smiled. 'I think we'll find out all about Mr Randall by finding out about Mr Benfield.'

'Birds of a feather flock together,' Luty muttered. She gave Mrs Jeffries an admiring glance. 'I've got to hand it to ya, Hepzibah, that's right good thinkin'. Randall and Benfield had to meet somewhere, and they had to get to know each other well enough for Benfield to agree to front fer Randall in this here mining swindle.'

'What do you want the rest of us to do?' Betsy asked.

'We need to find out who among the shareholders at that meeting might own a Colt .45,' she said carefully. 'And we also want to independently confirm that the meeting broke up early in the afternoon and that all the shareholders have alibis.'

'You don't want much, do ya?' Smythe grinned. 'So we've got to find out all we can about Randall and Benfield, locate Randall's hotel and see which stockholder owned a gun, is that it?'

'I know it sounds difficult,' Mrs Jeffries said firmly, 'but I've complete faith in you. By the way, did you have any luck when you went to the river? Had anyone seen or heard anything?'

Smythe shook his head. 'No. But then again, I weren't askin' the right questions. We weren't even sure what time the bloke was killed. Now that I know

Randall was probably murdered close to where he floated up, and since we've narrowed down the time he was shot, I might be able to find somethin' out.'

'Listen.' Mrs Goodge crossed her arms over her ample bosom. 'Now, we all don't want to be runnin' about gettin' in each other's way, so I'll do as Mrs Jeffries suggested and find out all I can about Benfield. I think Smythe and Wiggins ought to take on findin' Randall's lodgin's and Betsy would be best for checkin' up on the shareholders on the evenin' of March seventh. But it seems to me that Luty and Hatchet are the best ones for tryin' to find out who owned the gun. Luty's an American, and it's an American gun.'

They all stared at her blankly.

The cook sighed loudly. 'Don't you get it? Luty can pretend it's an old family heirloom or somethin' that she's tryin' to track down.'

'That'd be kinda difficult,' Luty said dryly. 'The Peacemaker ain't been around long enough to qualify as anyone's heirloom. But I agree with ya about me tryin' to find the gun. I think that'll suit Hatchet and me jus' fine. Course, while we're at it, we'll try and find Benfield, too.'

Mrs Jeffries wasn't certain this was a particularly good idea. Luty had an inordinate fondness for firearms. She glanced at the bright peacockblue muff the elderly American had in her lap. Hatchet caught her eye.

'Don't worry, Mrs Jeffries,' he said calmly. 'Madam has left her own weapon at home today.'

'I only carry it when I think I'm gonna need it,' Luty said tartly.

'True, madam,' Hatchet replied. 'But your

opinion and my opinion about when it is necessary to arm oneself are decidedly different. As I recall, you seemed to think it perfectly reasonable to take a weapon to Lady Fitzwaller's garden party last week.'

'Course I did,' Luty agreed. 'We had to drive over fifty miles to get there. Nobody back home would ever take off on the trail without takin' a gun of some kind.'

'Agreed, madam,' he said, 'but I hardly think one needs to worry about bear attacks, rattlesnakes, or stagecoach robbers in Essex.'

Luty snorted. 'You'd be surprised. But that's neither here nor there. The point is, you and I'll have a sniff round for the gun.'

'By two-thirty, we realized that Randall wasn't coming,' Lester Hinkle said calmly. He was a grey-haired portly gentleman with a ruddy complexion and anxious brown eyes. 'The meeting was called for one o'clock, so it wasn't just a matter of him being a few moments late. When it became apparent he wasn't going to show, we all left.'

'I see,' the inspector said. He wished he could think of something else to ask. Both of the other shareholders had told him essentially the same thing. 'Were you upset?'

'Upset.' Hinkle smiled sadly. 'Of course. Wouldn't you be if you thought you were losing a great deal of money? And not just your money, but other people's as well.'

'Naturally. How did you meet Mr Randall?' the inspector asked.

'Through Rushton Benfield.' Hinkle sighed and turned to stare at the fire burning in the grate. 'He introduced us last year.'

'Were you one of the original investors in the mining operation?' Witherspoon thought that sounded quite good. 'I understand this was the second time investment money was raised.'

'That's correct,' Hinkle said. He gazed around his study. 'We were first approached six months ago. I invested over ten thousand pounds of my money in the venture at that time. Then, a few weeks ago, Benfield contacted me and claimed they needed more capital. Said the original estimates of the cost of equipment were underpriced. I wasn't happy about it, but I didn't want to lose my original investment, you see. So I came up with another ten thousand pounds. I also bought more shares for a group of smaller investors that I represented.' He smiled bitterly. 'That is what bothers me the most. I'm not a wealthy man, gentlemen,' he said to Witherspoon and Barnes, 'but I can weather a loss. The people who trusted me to look after their money, well, what can I say? I failed them and I'll never forgive myself.'

Witherspoon felt a wave of sympathy wash over him. Poor man. 'Was anyone other than the four of you gentlemen present during the meeting?'

'Only Mrs Cubberly.'

'Mrs Cubberly sat in on the meeting?' Witherspoon was quite surprised.

'Not really, but she was sitting in the drawing room sewing, and we were right next door in the study. I daresay, tempers began to get a bit hot when we realized

Jake wasn't coming. I expect we owe Mrs Cubberly an apology. I must remember to do that. Language was used that shouldn't have been used in the presence of a lady.'

'Where did you go after the meeting?' Constable Barnes asked.

Hinkle jerked his gaze away from the fire. 'Home,' he said quickly. 'I went straight home to bed.'

'Is there anyone who can confirm that?' the inspector asked.

'No.' Hinkle got to his feet. 'There isn't. My wife wasn't home that day. She was in the country visiting relatives.'

'What about your servants, sir?' Barnes asked.

Hinkle looked confused. 'Well, I suppose one of them heard me come in,' he mumbled, 'but I was so distressed, I went right up to my bedroom and lay down. I fell asleep and didn't wake up till late in the evening.'

'So no one saw you come home?' Witherspoon thought that most odd. He glanced around the beautifully furnished study. The mahogany desk was polished to a bright gloss; the late sunlight sparkling through the windows revealed not a speck of dust anywhere. The Hinkle home was large, elegant, and exquisitely furnished. When he and Barnes had arrived, a butler had let them inside. As they'd walked past the stairs he'd seen a tweeny polishing the carpet railings, and there'd been a parlour maid in the drawing room as they'd passed. This was obviously a large household. Yet Mr Hinkle was claiming that no one saw him come home.

'Not that I'm aware of.' Hinkle coughed. 'I know that sounds odd. But it was past three when I came in.

The servants were in the kitchen having their tea, my wife was gone and, as I said, I was most distraught. I went right up to my room and lay down.'

Witherspoon stifled a sigh. This wasn't going well at all. So far he'd interviewed three men who knew the victim, yet he didn't think he'd learned anything at all useful. He pulled his watch out and glanced at the time. If he hurried, he and Constable Barnes could probably get over to the London and San Francisco Bank before it closed for the day. Drat, he should have done that right after lunch. But it had started to rain and the bank was some distance away. And there was still Dr Bosworth to see before he went home for the evening. He rose to his feet and smiled politely at Lester Hinkle. 'Thank you for your cooperation, sir.'

By the time the inspector arrived home that evening, he was in a much better mood.

'I say, Mrs Jeffries,' he said to his housekeeper as she picked up the decanter of sherry, 'I do believe I'd prefer a brandy tonight.'

'Oh dear, sir,' she said, 'is the sherry not to your liking? Is there something wrong with it?'

'Oh no, no,' he said quickly, not wanting to admit that he found the vile stuff undrinkable. 'Not at all. But with this cold, well, brandy is so much more, more . . .'

'Medicinal,' she finished. She turned so he wouldn't see her pleased smile and pulled out a bottle of brandy from beneath the cupboard. 'How was your day, sir? Any progress on the case?'

'The day didn't start out particularly well, but I must say, it improved enormously late this afternoon.'

Mrs Jeffries handed him his brandy. 'In what way, sir?'

'As you know, I spent the morning at the inquest.' He paused and took a sip. 'Well, you know how Dr Potter is. The only thing he'd say for sure was that Jake Randall was dead.'

She clucked her tongue in sympathy. 'How very trying for you, sir. I suppose Dr Potter wouldn't speculate as to the time of death?'

'Does he ever?' Witherspoon asked. 'But not to worry, we got round old Potter. Constable Barnes and I had a word with young Dr Bosworth. And he told us some very useful information. Very useful indeed.'

As Mrs Jeffries already knew what Dr Bosworth had found, she kept her expression carefully blank. 'Really, sir?'

'Oh indeed. Dr Bosworth is certain Randall was killed on the evening of the seventh.' The inspector frowned. 'I'm not exactly sure how he knew this; something to do with the gases in the corpse.' He shuddered delicately and took another sip from his glass. 'But the most interesting thing was Bosworth is equally certain that Randall's wound was made with an American gun. One of those nasty firearms that are so very popular in the western part of the United States. Now, what is the name of it?'

'The Colt .45, sir?' she asked casually.

'Why yes, that's it.'

Mrs Jeffries patiently listened to the inspector as he told her the details of his day. She already knew much of the information, and it wasn't until they'd made their way into the dining room that he said something that made her ears tingle.

'The bank confirmed that Jake Randall had withdrawn the money on the morning of the seventh?' she repeated, staring at the inspector.

Witherspoon barely heard her question. He was too busy staring at his plate. 'Er, Mrs Jeffries, exactly what is this?'

'Hash,' she said quickly. 'Mrs Goodge is quite proud of this dish, sir. It's most economical. Now, sir, what were you saying about the money?'

'Is there any potato to go with this uh . . . hash?' he asked hopefully.

Mrs Jeffries turned to the sideboard and took down a covered bowl. Lifting the lid, she dumped the two tiny new potatoes onto the inspector's plate. 'Mrs Goodge says hash is so filling you don't need many vegetables to go with it,' she announced. She knew she'd never get the inspector's mind back on the case until he was fed.

He glanced sadly at his plate, picked up his fork and tentatively took a bite of the ground meat. 'Actually, this isn't too bad.'

'I do hope you like it, sir,' Mrs Jeffries said.

What he'd like was some nice steak, but he could hardly complain. The cook was merely following his instructions.

'About the money, sir,' Mrs Jeffries prompted.

'Oh yes, the bank manager was most cooperative. It seems there are only two people who had access to the investment money. Jake Randall and Rushton Benfield.' The inspector smiled. 'And as I said, Randall withdrew it all the morning of the meeting.'

'Goodness, sir,' Mrs Jeffries mused. 'Do you think that means Randall had found out the other investors were getting suspicious of him?'

'Oh, I expect so, Mrs Jeffries. And of course, things are so much clearer to me now. The money is gone and Randall is dead. I think, perhaps this case isn't going to be as difficult as I'd first thought.'

Alarmed, Mrs Jeffries stared at him. 'What do you mean by that?'

'Randall's dead. Benfield and the money are missing.' Witherspoon chewed eagerly. 'Now, if one man is dead and the other is missing, there's really only one conclusion one can draw.'

'Which is?'

'Benfield killed Randall and stole the money.' Witherspoon smiled happily. 'It's so very simple. Benfield found out Randall had taken the money, so he tracked him down, took the money for himself, and shot his partner.'

'But, sir,' Mrs Jeffries said, 'how could Benfield have done it? How did he know that Randall had withdrawn the money from the bank? And how did he find Randall? All the other stockholders claim that no one knew where Randall was staying.'

'Perhaps they didn't know. But I bet Mr Benfield did.' The inspector shook his head. 'Furthermore, the bank manager also told us that Rushton Benfield had been into the bank on that very same morning. The chief clerk had told him about Randall withdrawing the money. So you see, Benfield knew the money was gone. Oh no, Mrs Jeffries. This is a very simple case. Benfield is missing and the money is missing. Find one and you find the other. Why, I'll turn this city upside down. I'll have bloodhounds looking for the man. I'll comb the darkest alleys and the most dangerous neighbourhoods, but find Benfield, I will.'

'I don't think it's fair,' Betsy complained. She glanced pointedly at the clock on the mantel. 'They promised they'd be back by half eight and they're not here.'

'They're only two minutes late,' Mrs Goodge said as she placed a pot of cocoa on the table. 'Go easy on the lads.'

'Well, it weren't fair that they got to go out again and ask questions,' the maid continued petulantly. 'I've got to wait until the morning.'

Mrs Jeffries came in just as Betsy was speaking. 'Now, you mustn't let that worry you,' she said to the girl as she took her seat. 'You'll have plenty of time for your own investigations tomorrow.' She smiled at Mrs Goodge. 'Tonight's dinner was a success. Where on earth did you find that recipe?'

'The inspector liked it, did he?' the cook said innocently. Then she grinned. 'I found the recipe in Mr Francatelli's book, *A Plain Cookery Book for the Working Classes*. Had that one for years, but I've never used it much. But seein' as how the inspector got us all on this new household management scheme, I'll have to see what else I can cook for him.'

Remembering the inspector's expression as he'd doggedly ploughed through his dinner, Mrs Jeffries nodded. 'Oh, I think that's a very good idea.'

From behind them they heard the door open. Fred was the first one into the room. Tail swishing madly, he bounded toward the table. 'Hello, Fred,' the cook muttered. 'There's a nice bit of mutton over in your dish.'

Smythe and Wiggins hurried toward the table and took their seats. 'Sorry we're late,' the footman said. 'But Smythe's had the best bit of luck.' Wiggins pulled a pair of gloves out of his pocket and slapped them on the table.

'What's that, then?' Betsy asked suspiciously.

'Rushton Benfield's gloves,' Smythe announced casually. 'I found the driver that picked him up on the day of the meetin'. That's why we're late. We were over near Chester Square.'

'So you've found out something?' Mrs Jeffries said. 'Good, so have I.' She then proceeded to tell them everything the inspector had told her.

'So you see,' she finished, 'the inspector is convinced that Rushton Benfield shot Randall and stole the money. He's going to be combing the city for the man. He even said he'd use bloodhounds, but I do think he was joking about that.'

'What's 'e need bloodhounds for?' Wiggins said earnestly, ''E can use Fred here. 'E's as good as any bloodhound.' He reached down and patted the dog.

'Don't be daft, Wiggins,' Smythe snapped impatiently. 'Fred's a right good dog, but he ain't trained for trackin'. Besides, Mrs Jeffries has already told us that the inspector was only joking. Now, I've got a lot to say—'

'Just a minute, 'ere,' Wiggins interrupted. 'I don't see that the inspector is so far off the mark. Why couldn't you use dogs to track someone? And just because Fred's no bloodhound, don't mean he couldn't do it.'

Mrs Jeffries was tired of wasting time. 'Yes, Wiggins, I'm sure you're right. But why don't we discuss it later?'

'Right,' Smythe agreed. 'Let's get on with it. We went over to Chester Square, and I started askin' some of the hansom drivers a few questions. Didn't think I was goin' to learn anythin' 'cause no one could remember pickin' up a fare on the afternoon of the seventh.'

'Maybe all the shareholders come in their own carriages,' Betsy suggested.

'Nah, before I started on the drivers, I asked one of the street Arabs that 'angs about that area if he'd seen any private carriages going to the Cubberly 'ouse last Monday. The boy said he seen hansoms going down Davies Street.'

'There's a lad with a good memory,' Mrs Goodge muttered. 'Did ya part with any money for that bit of information?'

'Don't be so suspicious, Mrs Goodge,' Smythe explained. He grinned. 'The lad remembers 'cause he was runnin' an errand for someone on Davies Street 'imself.'

'Go on, please,' Mrs Jeffries prompted. Really, she thought, all this competitiveness between them must stop.

'Anyhows, like I said, I decided to start lookin' for the drivers.' He paused and poured himself a cup of cocoa. 'Well, I didn't have no luck findin' the cabs that brought any of the three there before the meeting, but I did find two drivers that brought two of 'em back late that evening.'

'What do you mean, brought them back?' Betsy asked. 'No one said anything about them goin' back to the Cubberly house that night.'

'They may not have said it,' Smythe continued. 'But that's what they did. All three of 'em. Everyone but Rushton Benfield returned to Davies Street around nine-thirty that night.'

'And I talked to the cabbie that picked Benfield up that afternoon,' Wiggins interjected proudly. 'That's where I got these gloves. Benfield was in such a rush he left them in the cab. Cost me a bit, too, I can tell you.' Suddenly his eyes widened. 'You know, I bet Fred 'ere could find that Benfield fellow.' He grabbed the gloves and knelt down beside the table. 'Come on, boy, take a good sniff now.'

Fred trotted over and dutifully sniffed the gloves.

'Don't be such a fool, boy,' Mrs Goodge admonished. 'That dog's no bloodhound. It takes years to train a dog to track someone.'

''E can do it, I tell you,' Wiggins insisted. 'That's right, boy, get the scent.'

Fred jerked his head away from the gloves and looked at the footman. 'Leave off, Wiggins,' Smythe commanded. 'We've got a lot to talk about. Put them ruddy gloves down and pay attention.'

'You all go on with your talkin'. I'm not givin' up.' He kept stuffing the gloves under the dog's nose. Poor Fred looked really confused by now. He'd sniff the gloves and then stare at Wiggins as though asking him what in the world he was supposed to do.

'Wiggins,' Mrs Jeffries said gently, 'Smythe is right, we really must get on with this.'

'I'm listenin',' Wiggins promised, 'Just let me 'ave a few more minutes.'

Betsy opened her mouth to protest as well, but Mrs Jeffries raised her hand for silence. 'Leave the boy be,' she ordered quietly.

Suddenly they heard the knocker on the front door. Before any of them could move, Fred suddenly leapt for the stairs.

''Ere, where you goin',' Wiggins yelped. But the dog ignored him and kept on going. He barked noisily as he went.

Smythe and Mrs Jeffries joined in the chase.

They hurried up the stairs and down the hallway to the front door. The knocking was louder now. Fred arrived there first. He began scratching on the door and whining.

Mrs Jeffries quickened her steps. She reached for the doorknob, but Smythe stopped her.

'Let me answer it,' he said. 'It's almost nine o'clock and we don't know who is out there.'

Fred howled.

'Quiet, boy,' Wiggins hissed as he grabbed the dog by the collar and pulled him back. But Fred broke off and rammed into the door again.

'Cor,' Smythe whispered. 'The animal's goin' mad.' He shoved the dog out of his way and Wiggins grabbed him. He yanked the door open.

Constable Barnes and another gentleman were standing there.

'Good evening, Constable,' Mrs Jeffries said loudly. She had to shout. Fred had started barking again.

The man with Barnes took a step back. Even the constable regarded the barking animal uncertainly.

'Sorry to be disturbing you, Mrs Jeffries,' he said, never taking his gaze off Fred. 'But I'd like to see the inspector. It's important.'

Mrs Jeffries had no doubt about that. 'Certainly, Constable. Do please come in.' She smiled at the thin, sandy-haired man standing next to him.

'This gentleman is Mr Rushton Benfield,' Barnes began.

From behind her, she heard a gasp.

'And he'd like to make a statement to the inspector.'

'I say, is something wrong?' Witherspoon's voice came from the top of the staircase.

'Nothing's wrong, sir,' Mrs Jeffries called back. 'But Constable Barnes is here. He's got Mr Benfield with him. I believe they'd like to speak with you.'

CHAPTER FIVE

'I TOLD YOU 'E could do it,' Wiggins hissed at Smythe.
He patted the dog approvingly. Fred bounced up
and down a time or two, basking in his master's praise.

''E didn't do nothing,' Smythe whispered back.

Inspector Witherspoon came slowly down the stairs
and into the hallway. He wore an old wool dressing
gown over his clothes, his hair was mussed, and his feet
were clad in slippers. Fred broke away from Wiggins
and dashed over to greet him.

'Er, hello, boy,' the inspector murmured, reaching down to scratch the animal behind his ears. He
straightened and stared in confusion at the group of
people standing by the front door. 'Er, I say, did I hear
correctly? Goodness, indeed I did. Constable Barnes is
here and the gentleman with him is Rushton Benfield,
I take it.'

'Yes, sir.' Mrs Jeffries stepped forward. She decided
she'd better take charge of the situation.

'I see,' he replied. He glanced at Smythe and
Wiggins. 'Er, there does seem to be more than just
Constable Barnes and Mr Benfield, though. Is some-
thing wrong?'

'Smythe and Wiggins escorted me to the front door,' Mrs Jeffries explained. 'We were downstairs having a cup of tea when we heard them knocking.'

'We didn't think Mrs Jeffries ought to be answerin' the door on her own,' the coachman said quickly. 'Not with it bein' after dark, sir. So Wiggins and I come up, too.'

'Ah.' The inspector smiled in approval. 'Jolly decent of you, and you even had the presence of mind to bring Fred up as well. Good boy.' He patted the dog again. 'That's right, guard the household.'

Constable Barnes cleared his throat. 'Excuse me, sir, I didn't mean to intrude on your evenin', but Mr Benfield here would like to talk to you. He come by the station right before I was leavin'. Knowin' how anxious you was to have a word with him, I took the liberty of bringin' him round.'

Witherspoon blinked. 'Yes, yes. Of course, Constable.' He glanced at the man standing behind Barnes. 'How do you do, Mr Benfield.'

Benfield nodded and looked nervously behind him at the open door.

'Would you like some tea brought up, sir?' Mrs Jeffries inquired softly.

'That would be nice,' he replied. 'And some buns perhaps,' he added, 'if that wouldn't inconvenience anyone.' The inspector realized he was quite hungry.

Mrs Jeffries, Smythe, and Wiggins went down the hall towards the kitchen stairs. Fred stayed with the inspector.

As soon as they'd reached the kitchen, Wiggins grinned triumphantly. 'I told you Fred could do it,' he announced to Betsy and Mrs Goodge.

'Do what?' Betsy asked. 'And what's goin' on up there? We heard voices.'

'Constable Barnes has brought Rushton Benfield here to talk to Inspector Witherspoon,' Mrs Jeffries explained.

'Benfield! Here?' Mrs Goodge exclaimed.

'Yes, here. Now. Upstairs and talking his head off to the inspector,' Mrs Jeffries said. 'Quick, Betsy, you know what to do.'

'Right.' The girl shot to her feet and started for the stairs. 'Should I try the study?'

'No, they'll be in there. Use the dining room. I'll pick up what I can as I serve the tea, but mostly we'll be relying on you.' She turned to the cook. 'We'll need a pot of tea and some buns.'

'What's she up to?' Wiggins asked, his gaze following Betsy as she disappeared up the stairs. He was depressed that no one else was as delighted with Fred's tracking ability as he was.

'She isn't goin' up to dust the chairs,' Smythe snapped. 'She's gonna be eavesdroppin' again.'

Mrs Goodge muttered mutinously as she gathered the tea things on the tray. She stalked to the cupboard and pulled out a cloth-covered plate. 'How did he know I had these baked? I was savin' them for tomorrow. Got lots of people droppin' by, and now I'll have to get up extra early and bake another batch.'

She glanced up as she poured the boiling water into the pot. 'What was you on about, Wiggins?'

'I was talkin' about Fred.' The footman grinned from ear to ear. 'He tracked that Benfield feller just like I told you he would.'

The coachman rolled his eyes heavenward. 'Don't be daft. Fred did no such thing. 'E run up the ruddy stairs 'cause 'e 'eard someone at the front door.'

'Fred's never done it before,' Wiggins insisted. 'I tell you, he 'ad the scent. He were trackin'.'

'Why don't we discuss this later?' Mrs Jeffries said as she placed the sugar bowl on the tray. She gazed at Smythe. His brows were drawn together in a worried frown, and his eyes were glued to the stairs. 'Don't worry about Betsy,' she said. 'She's smart enough not to get caught.'

'Are you sure, Mrs J?' Smythe gave her a long, hard stare. 'The inspector's a kind man, but if 'e catches the girl, even 'e wouldn't put up with 'er spyin' when 'e was talkin' official police business. I don't want to see 'er lose 'er position.'

'She won't lose her position,' Mrs Jeffries promised softly. 'I give you my word.'

He continued to stare at her for a long moment, then he grinned. 'All right. Now, do you want me to 'ang about 'ere or go out and try to see if I can learn anythin' from the pubs near Waterloo Bridge?'

Mrs Jeffries picked up the loaded tea tray. 'Stay here. We don't know what Benfield is going to tell the inspector. Let's see what he has to say before we do anything. His information may lead us up a completely different avenue of inquiry.'

'Maybe I should get up to the dinin' room, too,' he said. 'I might 'ear somethin' that needs action right quick.'

Mrs Jeffries thought about it. She shook her head No, it's too dangerous to have both of you hovering in there. At least if someone spots Betsy, she can always claim she's laying the table for breakfast.'

Inspector Witherspoon couldn't help but notice Rushton Benfield's hand shaking as he lifted the teacup to his mouth. The man was slender, below average height, and had a weak chin and long nose. His attire, though of excellent cut and quality, was a mess. His black silk cravat was askew, two buttons were missing from his waistcoat, his shirt was wrinkled, and there was a long, dark stain on the lapel of his coat.

Inspector Witherspoon regarded him with a mixture of curiosity and despair. The man hardly looked the part of a murderer. Perhaps this case wasn't going to be as simple as he'd hoped. Drat. Rushton Benfield had seemed such a likely candidate as the killer. But unless he'd come here tonight to confess, and the inspector suspected that wasn't going to happen, then this case was just as muddled as it had been from the start.

'Mr Benfield,' he began hesitantly. He wasn't sure exactly what to ask the man.

'Inspector.' Benfield put his cup down and reached for a bun. 'I thank you for seeing me at such an unorthodox hour. But I had to talk to you about Jake Randall.'

'Yes, I gathered that was why you came.' Witherspoon wondered what was so urgent that it couldn't wait until the morning. But perhaps it would be best simply to let the fellow talk as he would. Obviously, Benfield had something to tell him. Something important. He decided to let the man have his say in his own good time. Besides, Benfield was stuffing that bun in his mouth like he hadn't eaten for days.

'I know I should have waited until tomorrow morning,' Benfield mumbled around a mouthful of food. 'But I couldn't stand another night of hiding, another night of constantly looking over my shoulder and wondering if they'd found me.'

'If who found you?' Witherspoon asked. Fred plopped his head on the inspector's knees and stared at his roll.

'The killer, of course,' Benfield exclaimed.

'Someone is trying to kill you?'

'Yes,' Benfield said earnestly, his eyes darting to the door. 'That's why I came here tonight. Whoever killed Jake Randall is going to kill me, too.'

'Why should anyone want to kill you?'

'Why?' Benfield cried shrilly. He threw his hands out and gestured wildly. 'Because they think I stole their bloody money, that's why. And I didn't. I didn't have a thing to do with that. That was all Randall's doing. But you can't expect a madman to be reasonable. You've got to give me protection, Inspector. You've got to.'

Alarmed, Witherspoon stared at the agitated man. 'We'll give you all the protection you need,' he promised. And he meant it, too. The inspector knew his duty. Though sometimes, like tonight, he was a bit confused as to how to perform that duty. 'Now please, calm yourself and sit down. Why don't you start at the beginning and tell us where you've been and why you're afraid.'

Benfield closed his eyes and took a deep breath. 'I'm sorry,' he murmured. 'I'm not myself.'

'We understand, sir,' Barnes said kindly. 'Now, why

don't you take a few minutes to pull yourself together? We already know about the meeting last week, and we've heard the rumours about Mr Randall defrauding the investors out of their money. So why don't you tell us why you're so frightened? Take your time.'

'All right, I'll start at the beginning. Last week, Lester Hinkle contacted me and told me that he'd heard from a source in America that none of our investment money had actually been put into the mine operations.' He shook his head. 'I was shocked, utterly shocked. I couldn't believe it was true.'

'Why couldn't you believe it, sir?' Witherspoon asked. He broke his bun in two and gave half of it to the dog.

'Because I trusted Jake Randall. He may be a lot of things,' Benfield said earnestly, 'he certainly isn't a gentleman, but I didn't think he was an out-and-out thief.' He paused and smiled bitterly. 'I was wrong. But I didn't know it at the time. I assured the other investors that Randall would have a perfectly reasonable excuse for why the mine wasn't being operated, why there weren't miners being hired and equipment being purchased. Until Monday morning, I believed it myself.'

Barnes glanced at the inspector and then asked, 'What caused you to change your mind?'

'I went to the bank that morning, for another matter entirely. The chief clerk called me over. He was in a state. He kept asking me if there was something wrong with their service or if we were displeased. I told him no. They handled our business very well, and I asked him why he was so concerned.' Benfield stopped and took another deep breath. 'He told me that Mr Randall had been in that very morning and withdrawn every penny from our account. Naturally, I told the clerk he'd made a mistake. Surely, Mr Randall had merely transferred, via a letter of credit, the funds into the American branch of the bank. That's the way we'd done it before. But the clerk assured me that wasn't the case. Randall had made a flat-out cash withdrawal. Fifty thousand pounds! They'd had to open the vaults to pay him off.'

'Excuse me,' Witherspoon said, 'but are you saying you weren't really concerned until you found out the money was gone? Surely, you must have been upset when you heard the rumours about the mine?'

'But they were only rumours,' Benfield insisted. 'And there could have been dozens of reasons why Jake hadn't started the mining operation.'

'Really,' Witherspoon said. 'Such as?'

'It could have been the weather. The mine's in Colorado, in the Rocky Mountains. There's been one blizzard after another in that part of the world since last October. So, naturally, I didn't panic until after I'd talked to the bank clerk.'

'So you knew the money was gone when you arrived at Mr Cubberly's house for the meeting with the other investors?' Witherspoon said. He found himself believing Benfield. They already knew that Benfield had been to the bank that day and learned the truth about the money being gone.

Benfield nodded. 'Yes. I kept praying that Randall would show up. That he'd have a legitimate reason for his actions.'

'Were the other investors unduly alarmed at that point?'

Benfield pursed his lips in thought. 'Not exactly alarmed,' he said, 'but they were concerned.'

'Only concerned, sir? One of them had already contacted the police,' the inspector pointed out. 'Mr Hinkle asked Inspector Nivens to look into the matter for him.'

'Hinkle's inquiry was very casual, I'm sure. The only reason he went to Nivens was because he knew the man. If he hadn't known a policeman, he wouldn't have brought the matter up at all.'

Witherspoon wasn't sure he believed that. According to Nivens, Hinkle had been most upset. And it had been one of Hinkle's relations that had raised the alarm in the first place. 'I see.'

'At first the meeting was convivial,' Benfield continued. 'Everyone assumed that Jake would show up. They kept assuring one another that everything was all right, that it was just a mistake of some sort. John Cubberly insisted we all have a drink while we waited. He got out a bottle of whisky and we started drinking to pass the time. But the minutes ticked by and Randall didn't come.'

Witherspoon poured himself another cup of tea. 'Did you tell the others about the money being gone?'

'Not at first. I didn't want them to panic. But by two o'clock, I realized Jake wasn't coming. So I told them about the money being withdrawn from the bank.'

'And what was their reaction?'

'They were furious. They accused me of covering up for Jake. Said I'd known since I walked into the

93

house that the money was gone and hadn't told them.' Benfield's hands curled into fists. 'By this time, they were all drunk. They'd been drinking steadily since half past one. Cubberly started ranting and raving about what he'd do when he got his hands on Randall, Hinkle kept moaning that he was ruined, and Dillingham was almost hysterical.'

'And what did you do, sir?' Barnes asked.

'Me? I kept trying to reason with them, but it was no good. At about two-fifteen, I offered to try and find Jake. Dillingham immediately accused me of being in on the swindle with Randall. Said he'd go find him himself. The minute he spoke, everyone jumped on the idea of looking for Jake Randall.'

'So all of you knew that Randall had moved out of his lodgings?' The inspector was quite proud of himself for thinking of that question.

'Randall hadn't made a secret of it,' Benfield said. 'Of course, looking back, I realize he very carefully never told us where he was staying.'

'Then how did any of you know where to look for him?' Barnes asked.

'We didn't,' Benfield said flatly. 'But that didn't stop anyone. We all knew Jake's haunts and habits.'

'So all of you decided to go out and look for the man? Is that correct?'

'No,' Benfield said fiercely. 'They went out looking for Randall. I left when John Cubberly started to get physically violent. He shoved me against a wall and said he'd kill me if I didn't tell him where Randall and the money were. Hinkle and Dillingham pulled him off. By this time, Mrs Cubberly had come into the room and demanded to know what was going on. I took the opportunity to get out of there. I left so fast I almost knocked a maid down. And I've been in hiding ever since. I tell you, Inspector, one of those three men found Jake that day and killed him. Whoever did it is going to try and get me next.'

'But why should they do that, sir?' Witherspoon was genuinely confused. 'Presumably, if one of them killed Mr Randall, they also got their hands on the missing money.'

'But that's just it,' Benfield moaned. 'What if Jake didn't have it with him? You don't understand. They were screaming and yelling that I was in on it. If Jake didn't have that money on him when one of them caught up with him, then I'm a dead man.'

'Why would you think Randall didn't have the money with him?' the inspector queried.

Benfield gave a short, harsh bark of laughter. 'Because I know the bastard. He was a sly one. Thinking back, I realized he'd planned the whole thing all along. Take my word for it, the first thing he did when he withdrew that money on Monday morning was to hide it. He wasn't stupid enough to carry it around with him, not when he knew the game was up.'

'How would Randall have found out the other investors were suspicious of him?' Witherspoon asked. 'Did you tell him?'

'No, I haven't seen him since last week.' Benfield scratched his chin. 'I don't know how he found out. Hinkle was blabbing his suspicions all over town, though. Jake's got a lot of acquaintances. I'm sure he heard about it from one of them.'

An hour later Mrs Jeffries closed the door behind Constable Barnes and Rushton Benfield. She glanced over her shoulder and saw Betsy slipping out of the dining room. Nodding at the maid, she hurried into the study.

She stopped just inside the room. Inspector Witherspoon sat slumped in his chair, his gaze on the carpet and his expression glum. 'Why, Inspector,' she said, 'whatever is wrong?'

He looked up at her. 'What isn't wrong?' he said. 'This case is getting more and more difficult. I don't think I'm any closer to solving it. I was sure that Rushton Benfield had murdered Randall and stolen the money.' He sighed. 'But I don't think that's what happened after all. According to Benfield, he's been in hiding since last Monday.'

Mrs Jeffries immediately grasped the implication of the inspector's words. 'But sir,' she said, 'that doesn't sound right. According to Dr Bosworth, Jake Randall wasn't killed until Monday evening at the earliest. It wasn't reported in the press until Thursday, so why would Mr Benfield be in hiding? He couldn't have known Randall was dead until Thursday morning.'

Witherspoon shook his head. 'At that point, he wasn't hiding from the killer; he was hiding from the other investors. It seems they got most upset when he told them about Randall withdrawing their investment money from the bank. Benfield told me he decided to lay low for a day or two, to give their tempers time to cool off, but when he saw the newspapers on Thursday morning, he got genuinely frightened. He thinks one of the three of them did it. He's convinced that one of them found Randall and shot him.' Witherspoon moaned. 'I tell you, Mrs Jeffries, it's all a terrible muddle. Now I've got three suspects and no clues. If Benfield's story is correct, any one of them could have murdered Randall. According to him, the other shareholders were so furious about the money, they decided to go and look for Jake Randall when he didn't show up for the meeting. If Benfield's telling the truth, that means all three of them were lying in their statements to me.'

'Now, now, sir.' She clucked her tongue sympathetically. 'You mustn't get discouraged. It's late and you're tired. But come the morning, you'll be refreshed and ready to take on the hunt.'

'Hmmm.' Witherspoon absently patted Fred on the head. 'I hope you're right. Actually, I'm not precisely sure what to do next—'

'Come now, sir.' She laughed. 'You're teasing me again. I know precisely what you'll do and so do you.'

'I do?' He looked at her hopefully.

'Of course you do, and just to prove to you that I'm finally learning your methods, I'll tell you.'

'Oh, please do.'

'You'll go back to the Cubberlys, of course! If Cubberly, Hinkle, and Dillingham went out to look for Randall, they probably agreed to meet back at the Cubberly home sometime that day to compare notes. Obviously, if one of them found him, the others would want to know about it.' She laughed again. 'You see, sir. I'm onto you. I know how you like to pretend you're totally in the dark as to what do next, and then you like to surprise us all by coming up with something absolutely brilliant.' She paused and beamed at him.

Her words cheered him enormously. Witherspoon sat up straight and lifted his chin. Come to think of it, he told himself, he was jolly good at solving murders. Perhaps it didn't matter that he hadn't quite figured out how he solved them. 'I wouldn't say I was brilliant,' he tried to say modestly. 'But as it happens, you're absolutely right. Naturally, it had struck me that if they went out looking for Randall, they'd probably agreed to come back to the Cubberly residence sometime that day.' His eyebrows drew together, and he got to his feet. 'Now the thing is, I really must find out if indeed they did come back that day. And more importantly, which one of them found Jake Randall.'

'And I presume you'll be looking for the gun?'

'Oh, I don't think there's much point in that, Mrs Jeffries.'

'Why ever not?'

Witherspoon smiled confidentially. 'Randall was murdered by the river. Obviously, no one would be stupid enough to hang on to the murder weapon, not when they could so easily chuck it into the Thames.'

Mrs Jeffries sighed and glanced at the sleepy figures around the table. All of them were dead tired. Betsy's eyes were half-closed against the bright spring sunshine coming in through the window, Mrs Goodge's chin was propped on her hand, Wiggins was rubbing the sleep out of his eyes, and Smythe was hunched over a cup of tea.

They'd been up very late. They'd spent a good hour listening to Betsy and Mrs Jeffries tell what they'd learned. Then they'd spent another hour arguing over what it all meant.

'What do we do next?' Betsy asked half-heartedly. 'Seems to me the inspector's doin' all right on this case on his own. We certainly haven't been much help.'

'That's not precisely true,' Mrs Jeffries said.

'Oh yes, it is,' Mrs Goodge declared. 'So far the only thing we've found out before the inspector was that they all come back to the house late that night.'

Mrs Jeffries thought she really ought to argue the point, but she couldn't. It was true. So far they hadn't learned anything useful. Still, she wasn't going to let them give up. 'Nevertheless,' she declared stoutly, 'you must all buck up. We've a lot to do today.' She turned her gaze to the coachman. 'Smythe, you must continue talking to the hansom drivers near Chester Square.'

'What good will that do? Already I found two of the drivers that brung 'em back that night, and I didn't find out anythin'. Findin' the third one won't help any. We still won't be any closer to figurin' out who shot the bloke.'

'We won't know that until you try,' Mrs Jeffries said stoutly. Really, it wasn't like them to be so very down in the mouth. 'You can find out where all the men were picked up that evening. See if any of them came from the vicinity of Waterloo Bridge. And after that, try going back to the bridge again. As you said yesterday, now that we've established the place and time of the murder, you may have better luck.'

'All right,' Smythe said tiredly. 'But I don't think it'll do much good.'

'You're doing better than I am,' Mrs Goodge

grumbled. 'I haven't had hardly anyone through this kitchen that's even heard of any of the suspects, let alone known any gossip about them.'

'Well, at least I've found out that Fred's a good trackin' dog,' Wiggins declared.

'Yoo-hoo, anyone home?' Luty's voice came from the back passage.

'We're right here, Luty,' Mrs Jeffries called out.

A moment later Luty and Hatchet emerged into the kitchen. 'Good mornin', everyone. Lovely day, isn't it?' She stopped near the table. 'For land's sake, you've all got faces longer than an undertaker's apron. What's wrong?'

'We're not doin' too well with our inquiries,' Smythe volunteered.

'We're not findin' out much of anythin',' Mrs Goodge grumbled.

'Oh, feelin' sorry for yourselves, huh?' Luty flounced into an empty chair. Hatchet bowed formally and took the one next to her. 'Well, nell's bells, that's okay,' she continued. 'We all got a right to feel sorry fer ourselves once in a while.'

'It's not really a case of self-pity,' Mrs Jeffries explained. 'We're all a bit tired, too. Rushton Benfield was here last night.' She went on to bring Luty and Hatchet up to date on everything they knew. 'So the point is, we're not really certain what to do next.'

'I know what you should do next,' Luty declared.

They all stared at her.

'You can figure out a way to get your inspector to have a word with Zita Brown.'

'Who's that?' Wiggins asked.

Luty grinned. 'John Cubberly's housekeeper. Me

and Hatchet had quite a nice chat with her last evenin', didn't we, Hatchet?'

'Yes, madam, we did.' He shuddered.

Luty laughed. 'Hatchet's got his nose out of joint 'cause we spent the evenin' at a tavern. Zita Brown talks more when ya wet her whistle.'

'Hmmph,' Hatchet snorted in derision. 'I would hardly call that particular establishment a tavern. The place was disgusting. Utterly filthy. It was filled with the most disreputable band of people I've ever seen. For once, I was glad that madam had her gun with her.'

'The place wasn't very nice,' Luty admitted. 'But I've seen worse. Still, you ain't interested in hearing about the gin swillers at the White Rose. Let me tell ya what Zita told us. It'll make your hair curl.'

The air of apathy around the table abruptly vanished.

'First of all, I know who owned the gun that killed Randall.' Luty paused dramatically.

'Please, madam.' Hatchet sighed. 'Do get on with it.'

Luty shot her butler a disgruntled frown. 'Oh, all right. You won't even give a body a chance to build up to a good story. John Cubberly owns a Colt .45.'

Mrs Jeffries gazed at the elderly American with admiration. 'Gracious, that's excellent, Luty. How on earth did you find that out?'

'Let me tell ya what else I heard first,' she answered. 'Otherwise Hatchet here will have a hissy fit.'

'I've never had a "hissy fit", whatever that is, in my entire life,' the butler mumbled. 'But do, please, finish your story. We can fill them in on the nefarious details later.'

'Not only does Cubberly own the gun,' Luty

continued, 'but he was wavin' it around and threatenin' to kill Randall with it, too.'

'Why didn't Benfield tell the inspector that Cubberly had a gun?'

'I ain't sure.' Luty shrugged. 'But let me finish before you start askin' questions. There's more. Zita said she was standin' in the kitchen washin' out some tea towels when all of a sudden the maid come runnin' in like the hounds of hell was after her. Zita asked the girl what was wrong, and the girl said that Mr Cubberly was wavin' a gun around and threatenin' to shoot someone. Before Zita could stop her, she'd grabbed her coat and run out the backdoor.' She paused and laughed. 'Poor girl, she ain't been back since. Accordin' to Zita, though, that ain't the first time someone had run off from that household and not come back. Seems they was always losin' servants.'

'Did Zita Brown actually see the gun?' Mrs Jeffries asked.

'Yup.' Luty nodded. 'Saw it with her own eyes. She said she stood there fer a few minutes wonderin' what she ought to do when she heard footsteps in the front hall. Zita went up and had a look. Cubberly and the other two were strugglin' into their coats. She watched them stagger out the front door, then she went upstairs and stuck her head into the drawing room. That was when she saw the gun. It were layin' in plain sight.'

'Bloomin' Ada,' Smythe exclaimed. 'If it were still there when those three went out lookin' for Randall, then none of them could 'ave shot the bloke.'

'Maybe one of them came back and got it?' Betsy suggested.

'Maybe,' Luty replied. 'Maybe not. There's no way to know fer sure. Right after that, Mrs Cubberly started yellin' fer the maid. Zita told her the girl had gone and went back to the kitchen. Said Mrs Cubberly was right put out about it.'

'All right, then.' Smythe regarded Luty speculatively. 'Tell us 'ow you got the woman to talk.'

Hatchet snorted again. Luty ignored him 'That were' easy.' She withdrew her gun from her muff and laid it on the table. Everyone except Hatchet stared at the weapon. 'It's a Colt .45,' Luty explained. 'I took it with me yesterday evening. When I got to the Cubberly house, I went round to the kitchen door and told Zita Brown I'd heard there was a gun in their house. Told her it was the mate to this one and that I'd pay a right good price to git it fer myself. Told her I was a collector.'

Wiggins frowned. 'I don't understand. Why should this Zita Brown have anything to do with Mr Cubberly's gun?'

'She shouldn't,' Smythe replied. He looked at Luty with grudging admiration. 'What Luty was doin' was lettin' the woman think she'd be willin' to pay to get the gun for her collection.'

Wiggins was truly shocked. His eyes grew round as saucers. 'You mean, you wanted her to steal if for you?'

Hatchet snickered. Luty had the grace to look embarrassed. 'I wouldn'a really bought the danged thing,' she said defensively. 'But I had to come up with some story to find out who of 'em owned a Colt. It didn't take more'n two minutes of talkin' to the woman to figure out that she drank like a danged fish and that she'd tell ya anything ya wanted to know as long as you kept pourin' gin down her throat. So we took her to her local waterin' hole and let her talk her head off. And it worked, too.'

'Indeed it did, Luty,' Mrs Jeffries said. She wasn't sure she approved of Luty's methods, but then again, she was in no position to be judgemental. She'd bent the truth herself a time or two when she was ferreting information out of someone.

Luty picked her gun up. 'Nice, ain't it?' she muttered as she ran her hands over the handle.

'Really, madam,' Hatchet said. 'I think you ought to put that thing away before someone gets hurt.'

'Quit yer fussin',' she said, making no move to put the gun away. 'Do ya think I'm a fool? The gun's not loaded.'

'I say.' Witherspoon's voice floated down from the stairwell. 'Hello. Is anyone home?' They froze as they heard his footsteps clambering down the stairs.

Luty hastily tried to stuff the gun back into her muff, but the barrel got caught in the loop of a tassel.

The inspector came into the kitchen. 'Oh, I am sorry to disturb your tea break,' he began. He stopped, his expression surprised when he saw Luty Belle and Hatchet. 'I say, it's so very nice to see you again. Do forgive the intrusion, but I was wondering if there were any of those buns left. Constable Barnes and I were so close I thought I'd pop in and have one with a cup of tea.'

'There are plenty of buns left,' Mrs Jeffries said as she leapt to her feet.

But she was too late: Witherspoon had spotted the gun in Luty's lap. I say, is that a . . . a . . .'

'Gun,' Luty finished. She grinned at him. 'Yep, it's a Colt .45. You know, the strangest thing has happened. Hepzibah tells me you think a gun like this was used to shoot that Randall feller. I read about it in the newspapers — took kinda a special interest, on account of him bein' a countryman of mine.' She glanced at Mrs Jeffries.

The housekeeper nodded slightly and hoped that Luty knew what she was doing.

'Er, yes,' the inspector said uncertainly. 'We think he may have been shot with a weapon like yours. But that's not the sort of information we want spread around.'

'Don't worry, Hatchet and I can keep our traps shut,' Luty assured him. 'But what I'm tryin' to tell ya is I think I might have run across some information that might help ya. I don't know if you know it, but I'm a gun collector.'

'Er, no. I didn't.'

'Been collectin' them fer years, but that's neither here nor there.'

Mrs Jeffries held her breath.

Luty smiled confidently. 'The point is, Inspector, us collectors are always on the lookout for addin' one or two good pieces to our collection. Now, there ain't that many guns like this in London.' She held the weapon up and Witherspoon stepped back a pace. 'And this one's got a scratch on the handle. Here, have a look and you'll see what I mean.'

'Oh, that's all right.' Guns made the inspector very nervous.

'Anyways, I had my sources puttin' feelers out tryin' to find me a Colt for my collection so I could get shut of this one. I want my collection to be as perfect as I can get it. Well, I run across the name of a man who might have one for sale.'

'Really?' Witherspoon wished she would get to the point. He was dying for a cup of tea and a bun.

'Really.' Luty grinned. 'And after talkin' to Hepzibah here, I suddenly realized it was a name you might be interested in.'

Witherspoon forgot about his stomach. 'Who is it?'

'John Cubberly. I believe he's one of the people involved with that murder you're investigatin'.'

CHAPTER SIX

CONSTABLE BARNES HURRIED to keep up with the inspector. 'You say you heard that Mr Cubberly had a gun from this American friend of yours?'

'She's really more a friend of Mrs Jeffries, my house-keeper,' Witherspoon replied as they turned the corner onto Davies Street. 'Rather eccentric woman. But I like her. I'm not so sure I like her pastime, though. Whoever heard of collecting guns!' He clucked his tongue in disapproval 'These Americans do the oddest things. But as I said, she'd heard through one of her sources that John Cubberly bought a Colt .45 from a dealer last spring. Goodness knows why, but he did. Mrs Crookshank, who, of course, knew nothing of our investigation, happened to mention Mr Cubberly's name to my housekeeper, who immediately informed her that she ought to have a word with me.'

'Bit of a coincidence,' Barnes muttered. They'd reached the gate to the Cubberly house.

'True,' Witherspoon agreed. 'But then coincidences happen all the time.' He pushed the wrought-iron gate open and stepped onto the paving stones. 'That's why they're called coincidences.'

Barnes shot his inspector a startled look and followed him up to the door. 'Do you think Cubberly will admit to ownin' it?'

'I certainly hope so. You know, one does get so tired of people who think they can pull the wool over our eyes. I must say, I think his not mentioning the gun earlier puts a very black mark against him. Leads one to believe Cubberly's got something to hide.' Witherspoon banged the knocker against the door. 'We'll get the truth this time, Constable. Even if we have to question the servants again.'

Barnes smiled cynically. 'There aren't any servants, sir. At least none that I've seen, exceptin' that old harridan who calls herself a housekeeper.' He clamped his mouth shut as the door cracked open and a pair of suspicious brown eyes stared out at him.

'Oh, it's you again.' A fat, grey-haired woman wearing a dirty apron over a black dress grudgingly opened the door.

'Hello, Mrs Brown,' Constable Barnes said politely.

She ignored his greeting. 'I suppose you want to see 'im.'

'We'd like to have a word with Mr Cubberly, please,' the inspector replied.

''E's in the study.' She jerked her head down the hall and stepped back to let them pass.

Witherspoon noticed a strong scent of spirits as he passed the woman. He wondered why on earth a respectable businessman like John Cubberly would have such slovenly household staff.

Mrs Cubberly stepped out of the drawing room as they walked down the hall. She stared at them coolly, her chin tilted to one side. She didn't appear to be surprised to see them.

'Good day, Mrs Cubberly,' Witherspoon said. 'We're sorry to disturb you, but we'd like a word with your husband.'

'What about?' Her voice was as cool as her expression.

Startled by the blunt question, Witherspoon blinked. 'Why, our investigation, of course.'

She continued to stare at him as though she were deciding whether or not to comply with his request. Then she raised her hand and waved at the drawing room. 'Go in and sit down,' she ordered brusquely. 'My husband is in the study. I'll get him.'

'There's no need for that,' a voice said from behind them. 'I'm right here.' John Cubberly, a frown on his face, came down the hallway and stopped in the door. He glanced uneasily at the police and then turned to his wife. 'This doesn't concern you, Hilda. Why don't you go upstairs?'

'Just a moment,' the inspector said. 'I would like to have a word with Mrs Cubberly, if you don't mind.' He hadn't a clue what he'd ask the woman, but her behaviour was so peculiar he decided he really should ask her something.

'I do mind,' Cubberly replied. 'Presumably you're here about Randall's murder. My wife has nothing to do with my business affairs. She barely knew the man.'

'It's all right, John,' Mrs Cubberly said. 'I'll answer their questions.' Ignoring her husband's frown of displeasure, she turned and walked back into the drawing room.

The three men followed her. Barnes, who apparently didn't think he was going to be invited to sit down, took the initiative and headed for one of the matching armchairs next to the fireplace. As soon as he was seated, he whipped out his notebook and then looked inquiringly at his boss. Witherspoon followed his example and sat down next to him, the leather creaking as he settled himself. The Cubberlys sat rigidly on the faded velvet settee.

The inspector decided to get right to the point. 'Mr Cubberly, we have it on good authority that you own a gun.'

Cubberly gaped at them, his small eyes widening in shock. 'Rubbish,' he replied, recovering quickly. 'I've no idea where you heard such nonsense, but I assure you—'

Mrs Cubberly interrupted. 'Many people own guns, Inspector.'

'For God's sake, Hilda,' Cubberly snapped, glaring at his wife. 'Do be quiet and let me handle this.'

'I was merely pointing out a fact,' she replied tartly.

'Thank you, Mrs Cubberly,' the inspector replied. 'We're aware of the fact that many people in London possess firearms. The question is, does your husband?'

'There's no need to be impertinent,' Mrs Cubberly reprimanded.

Cubberly said quickly, 'I'll admit that I do own a weapon.'

'You don't have to tell them anything, John,' she said. 'They've no right to come here asking their silly questions. You've told them everything you know.'

'Hilda, please,' he pleaded. 'Let me take care of this.'

'Let you take care of this!' She snorted.

Cubberly clamped his lips together in a flat, grim line.

Witherspoon cringed inwardly. He was dreadfully embarrassed. Arresting people for murder was one thing, but watching a domestic disagreement was quite another kettle of fish. He didn't like it at all. But he knew his duty. 'Where is your gun now, sir?'

Cubberly closed his eyes briefly and took a long, deep breath of air. 'It's locked in the drawer of my desk.'

'What kind of weapon is it, sir?' Barnes asked.

'A Colt .45.' Cubberly's voice was barely audible.

'You realize, sir,' Witherspoon said seriously, 'that is the same kind of weapon we believe Jake Randall was murdered with.'

'How on earth could you possibly know what kind of gun the man was killed with?' Mrs Cubberly charged.

'How we know is completely irrelevant,' the inspector replied. He wasn't about to tell her that they only had Dr Bosworth's word for the kind of gun that had been used in Randall's murder and that it wasn't admissible as evidence. 'Could you please fetch the gun? We do, of course, need to examine it.'

Cubberly didn't seem to hear him; he was staring at the carpet.

'This is absurd,' Hilda Cubberly snapped. 'We don't have to show you anything unless you've a warrant.'

Gracious, the inspector thought. Mrs Cubberly certainly seemed well informed about the law. And she was determined to protect her husband.

'Actually, madam, I believe you do.' Witherspoon wished he'd paid a bit more attention to all those lectures and notices about Judge's Rules. He wasn't sure whether she had to show him the weapon or not. After all, they had allowed him into the house without a warrant. For a moment the inspector racked his brain, trying to remember Justice Hawkins's foreword to the Police Code. That had explained everything about those tedious rules. And they were so very complex.

Goodness, how on earth was anybody supposed to remember every little detail? It wasn't as if he hadn't read them – he had. Five years ago. Drat. Judge's Rules. He really must make a point of reading them again. It would be so very helpful in a situation like this.

'No disrespect intended, Mrs Cubberly,' Barnes said, 'but the inspector's right. Your husband's already admitted he owns a gun. Now you don't have to show us, but we've a right to station a man here or to detain the both of you at the police station while we do get a warrant.'

'Oh, all right,' Cubberly said, his tone resigned. He turned and smiled weakly at his wife, his expression unexpectedly tender. 'Hilda, dear, stop worrying. I know you think you're protecting me, but I've nothing to hide,' he told her softly. 'I haven't done anything wrong. The gun's safely locked in my desk.'

He got up and left the room. Witherspoon and Barnes followed him into the study.

The inspector stood beside a dusty table and absently took off his spectacles. He watched Cubberly take a small gold key off his watch fob. Sitting his spectacles down, he stepped closer to the desk.

Cubberly inserted the key into a locked drawer. His hands were steady as he pulled it out. He looked inside and gasped. 'Oh, my God,' he said, his expression stunned.

Barnes edged Cubberly out of the way, glanced inside and looked at the inspector. 'There's no gun here, sir,' he said.

'But this is impossible,' Cubberly muttered. Wild-eyed and pale, he shook his head in disbelief. 'It's got to be here, I put it here myself. But it's gone. The bloody thing is gone.'

'This is very serious, Mr Cubberly,' Witherspoon stated. 'Very serious, indeed.'

'When was the last time you saw the weapon, sir?' Barnes asked.

'I . . . I . . . I'm not sure,' Cubberly said weakly.

'But you just admitted you locked it in there yourself,' the constable continued, his voice hardening in suspicion.

'That's because I had to have put it away,' Cubberly cried, 'The drawer is always locked, and I'm the only one with the key.'

'Was it Monday, the day of the meeting?' Witherspoon asked. 'Was that when you locked the gun away? Was that the last time you saw it? We know that you and the other investors were furious when Jake Randall didn't show up for the meeting. We know that you went looking for him. Did you take the gun with you?'

'Of course I didn't take it with me.'

'Are you sure, sir?' the inspector pressed.

'I'm bloody certain,' Cubberly yelled. 'Who told you we went looking for Randall that day?'

'Never mind how we acquired that information,' Barnes put in. 'Just answer the inspector's questions. And while you're at it, we'd like to know where you went that afternoon.'

Witherspoon suddenly remembered his conversation with his housekeeper. 'And we'd also like to know when you all came back here, please.'

'They left here at half past two and they returned that evening at half past nine,' Hilda Cubberly said. She was standing in the doorway. 'Furthermore, any of them could have taken that gun. John left it lying here in plain sight.'

'Hilda,' Cubberly whimpered. 'Are you trying to put a noose around my neck?'

'Don't be ridiculous,' she said bluntly, 'I'm trying to save you. My husband had the gun out that day. Everyone saw it. I did, the housekeeper did, the maid saw it, the other shareholders. Anyone could have taken it.'

'It was probably that damned girl,' Cubberly cried.

'What girl?' Barnes asked suspiciously.

Cubberly turned to his wife, his expression beseeching. 'Tell them, Hilda, tell them how the maid disappeared without a word. In the middle of the day.'

'Excuse me, Mr Cubberly,' Witherspoon interjected, 'but what has your maid got to do with a missing gun?'

'What's she got to do with it?' he replied, his voice trembling. 'It's bloody obvious what happened. She saw the gun, waited till the room was empty and then snatched it up. She probably planned to sell it.'

Witherspoon thought that sounded a bit farfetched. He'd noticed that when trouble brewed, people of Mr

114

Cubberly's station always tried to blame a servant. But really, this was a bit too much. Yet he was duty bound to look into it. 'What's the girl's name?'

'Lottie Grainger,' Mrs Cubberly replied.

'That would explain why she left so suddenly,' Cubberly added hastily. 'It's so obvious. You'd best start looking for her right away. I'm sure she stole the gun.'

'What would she want with a weapon, sir?' Barnes asked wearily. From the tone of his voice, the inspector was fairly certain the constable had come to the same conclusion as he himself.

'I've already told you,' Cubberly said impatiently, 'She wants to sell it. A Colt .45 is quite valuable, you know. And of course, her sort think nothing of stealing.'

The constable's eyebrow's rose. 'Her sort, sir?'

'What my husband means is that she was completely untrained,' Mrs Cubberly explained. 'She comes from the East End. Her references weren't very good. I only took her on because I felt sorry for her. She'd only worked for us for a few months. She'd previously worked for some actress. But my husband is right – she did disappear that day. Left without a word. You can verify that by talking with our housekeeper.'

Witherspoon tried to keep everything straight, but it was getting difficult. And he still had so many more questions he needed to ask. He didn't think for one minute that the maid had stolen the gun. But he didn't know for sure. There was always the possibility that the Cubberlys were telling the truth. What if the maid really had taken the gun? That would probably mean it wasn't the weapon that had killed Jake Randall. But if the gun was left lying out for anyone to see, someone else could have taken it. Drat.

By the time Witherspoon and Barnes left the Cubberly residence a half hour later, the inspector's stomach was growling and his head hurt.

Barnes hailed a hansom cab, gave the driver the address, and they climbed inside. 'Do you think he was tellin' the truth, sir?' he asked the inspector.

'I've no idea, Constable, no idea at all. But I do know, if that gun was lying about, any one of them could have nipped back and taken it.' He sighed. 'Mrs Cubberly's admitted anyone could have gained entrance to the house. She was upstairs lying down, and her room is at the back. The housekeeper had gone down to the kitchen and the front door was unlocked. Really, you'd think people would have more sense than that, leaving a loaded weapon out where any fool could get his hands on it.'

'They were drunk.'

'True,' Witherspoon mused. 'But Mrs Cubberly wasn't. She should have made sure the gun was put away.'

'But she didn't. Silly woman took to her bed with a headache.'

'That's understandable, Constable,' the inspector said. 'She told us she was dreadfully upset. First her husband acting like a madman and then finding out the maid had run off. We'd better send some lads over to the East End to see if they can find this young woman . . . what was her name again?'

'Lottie Grainger.' Barnes sighed deeply. 'We can

116

send 'em over there, but the chances of us findin' this girl are pretty slim. Especially if she don't want to be found.'

'But why wouldn't she want to be found?'

'It's been my experience, sir,' Barnes explained, 'that there's lots of people that don't think of the police as friends. Especially them from that part of London. But that doesn't mean she's a thief. When she saw Cubberly wavin' that gun around, she probably got scared and ran.'

'Yes, I think I know what you mean. But we've got to try. That's not to say that I believe Cubberly's accusation. From the sound of it, three drunken men and a loaded gun, I've no doubt you're right and she ran because she was frightened.' Witherspoon pursed his lips and frowned. 'We've no evidence she even knew Jake Randall. So why would she want to shoot him?'

'Well, we do have Mrs Cubberly's statement that she caught the girl makin' eyes at Randall once when he was round there,' Barnes said thoughtfully. 'But I don't put much store by that. Jake Randall sounds like the kind of man who'd flirt with any pretty lass who crossed his path. And the girl bein' a thief is just a tad too convenient, if you get my meanin', sir.'

'Hmmm, I'm afraid I do.' Witherspoon's stomach roared. Embarrassed, he shuffled his feet on the bottom of the cab to try to cover the noise.

'Course, we don't know it was Cubberly's gun that was used to kill Randall,' Barnes continued.

'I've a feeling it was,' Witherspoon said. He firmly quashed his earlier doubts. 'How many weapons of that sort are there in London? There can't be all that many.'

He rubbed the bridge of his nose and tried to think. 'It all fits, Constable,' he announced.

'What does, sir?'

'Whoever took the gun must be the killer.' The inspector was suddenly sure of it.

They had independent confirmation that the weapon hadn't been in John Cubberly's possession when he left the house that day. Therefore, Witherspoon reasoned, someone else could have taken it or Cubberly could have come back and gotten the Colt himself.

'If we believe their story, sir,' Barnes pointed out. 'We've only the Cubberlys' word that the gun was left lying in the drawing room.'

'The housekeeper confirmed it. Said she'd poked her nose into the room after the maid had gone running out of the kitchen.'

'Yes, but I'm wonderin' about that. Seems to me Zita Brown is the type to say anything the Cubberlys want her to. She don't want to lose her position.'

Witherspoon thought Barnes had a point. The Cubberlys were hardly the most benevolent of employers. But then again, from the looks of the housekeeper, she wasn't the most competent of servants either.

Grrr . . . He grimaced as another embarrassing sound erupted into the confines of the quiet cab. Unfortunately, they were stopped in traffic, and the horrid noises from his stomach were perfectly audible.

'Sounds like you're hungry, Inspector,' Barnes said cheerfully. He glanced out the window. 'We're right close to your house, sir. Why don't I drop you off for a bite of lunch? I'll nip on down to the station and get the lads off to the East End. I'll also get them started on checkin' Cubberly's whereabouts on the afternoon of the murder. Not that I think we'll have much luck there, but you never know.'

'Oh no, that won't be necessary,' the inspector protested. He thought longingly of the police canteen. Visions of pork pies, steak-and-kidney pudding, and sausage and chips floated into his head. He licked his lips. 'The canteen will do for me.'

'Come now, sir,' the constable said. 'You don't want to be eatin' that greasy muck when you can have a nice hot meal in your own home.'

Witherspoon shuddered at the thought of the meals he'd had at home lately. But he didn't wish to appear ungracious. 'That's quite all right, Constable. Dropping me off is too much trouble. I don't want to delay your inquiries.'

'Not a bit of it, sir,' Barnes assured him. He rapped sharply on the roof and stuck his head out again. 'Turn up the next street', he ordered the driver, 'and cut on over to Upper Edmonton Gardens.'

Mrs Goodge grinned from ear to ear when Mrs Jeffries hurried into the kitchen after lunch. 'Did the inspector enjoy his meal, then?'

'He didn't eat much of it,' Mrs Jeffries said innocently. 'When he left here, he was muttering something about the police canteen.'

'Good. A few more days of this and maybe we can get back to our usual way of doing things.' Her smile faded and she flushed guiltily. 'Did he eat anything at all?'

'He had a few bites of mutton and some mint sauce.'

'I don't like feedin' the poor man such wretched meals, Mrs Jeffries. My conscience is startin' to bother me over it.'

'Don't worry, Mrs Goodge,' the housekeeper assured her. 'The inspector isn't really suffering. Besides, I do believe this is the only way we can make our point. The inspector isn't in any real financial danger. Some of his investments aren't doing as well as they used to, but that's no reason to stop enjoying life entirely.' She glanced around the empty kitchen. 'When are the others coming? I've so much to tell them.'

'Smythe and Wiggins are upstairs washin' up, and Betsy's not back yet. Should we wait for her?'

'No, we don't have time,' Mrs Jeffries was aware of a vague sense of unease with this case. Despite everything she'd learned from the inspector at lunch, they were still no closer to a solution. She hoped that the others had something to report. Something that made sense, something that would give her the one piece of the puzzle that would make the rest of it fall into place.

She turned at the sound of heavy footsteps coming down the kitchen stairs. Smythe appeared first, with Wiggins right on his heels.

The coachman took his customary place at the table. 'Isn't Betsy back yet?'

'Not yet,' Mrs Goodge replied. 'And Mrs Jeffries said we can't wait. If she comes back this afternoon, I'll catch her up on everythin'.'

'What do you mean "if". Of course she'll be back,' Smythe interjected.

'Don't snap my head off, man.' The cook shot him an impatient frown. 'I didn't say she wouldn't. I'm only sayin' I'll tell her everything, so there's no reason we can't get on with it now. I've found out a few things,' the cook said proudly. 'And seein' as we're behind on this case, we'd best get crackin'.'

Smythe looked like he was going to protest, so Mrs Jeffries intervened. 'Mrs Goodge is right,' she said firmly. She smiled confidently at the coachman. 'We had best get on with it. Wiggins, would you like to sit down?'

The footman had wandered over to the sideboard. 'What's 'appened to Fred's bone?' he asked as he moved to the table.

'I gave it to the inspector,' Mrs Goodge said, her voice defensive. 'And it weren't a bone. It was a decent piece of mutton.'

'But you were savin' that for Fred,' Wiggins protested. 'You told me so this mornin'.' Fred, who'd followed him over to the table, raised his head at the mention of his name.

'I know what I told you, but I changed my mind. I've got some nice stew bones for Fred,' the cook snapped. 'Now, please, let's stop ditherin' about and let me have my say.'

Everyone stared at her.

Mrs Goodge took a deep breath. 'Well, I don't know if it has anything to do with Randall's murder, but I've found out that Mr and Mrs Cubberly weren't exactly a match made in heaven. And both Hinkle and Dillingham had money trouble.'

'Goodness, you have been busy.'

'We've got to catch up,' the cook said seriously. 'I got up at half past four this mornin' to do my bakin'.

I've had half of London through this kitchen today and fed 'em good, too. Like I told you, if you feed people, they talk.'

Smythe sighed impatiently, but kept his mouth shut.

'Tell me about Cubberly first,' Mrs Jeffries commanded. So far, he was the most likely suspect.

'I couldn't find out much about his past so I don't know if he had any connection with Jake Randall before he invested in his silver mine, but I did hear that he married Hilda Cubberly for her money.'

Smythe smiled cynically. 'Half of London marries for money.'

Mrs Jeffries hid her disappointment well. If Hilda Cubberly had been found with a bullet in her chest, then the information would have been useful.

'Yes, but the reason Mrs Cubberly married Mr Cubberly is what's interestin',' Mrs Goodge continued. 'She did it to keep her father from leavin' all his wealth to charity. The butcher's boy has a sister who used to work for Eammon Enright – that's Hilda's father. He said there was a right old dust-up when John Cubberly was courtin' Hilda. Hilda didn't want to marry him. Didn't want to marry anybody, from what I heard. But Mr Enright, who was in poor health and gettin' older, wanted to see her married and settled. He told her if she didn't accept John Cubberly's proposal, she wouldn't get nothing. As it is, he left John control of all of Hilda's money.'

'That was rather unfortunate,' Mrs Jeffries said dryly. 'John Cubberly doesn't seem to be doing all that well with his wife's inheritance.'

'Oh yes, he is,' Mrs Goodge countered. 'Not that you can tell it by the way the Cubberlys live. He's a right miser. Now Hinkle's not a miser, but he's not much of a businessman either. He's lost more money the last two years than any of us'll see in a lifetime. His creditors are pressin' him, too.'

'And Dillingham,' Mrs Jeffries prompted. 'What kind of trouble was he having?' This information was indeed very useful. If two out of the three suspects were desperate for money, that would explain Randall's murder. Providing, of course, that Jake Randall had the money with him when whoever killed him caught up with him.

Mrs Goodge laughed. 'Oh, Dillingham don't have the kind of money trouble that Hinkle's got. There's no real creditors on him, least not the respectable kind. But he does have a straitlaced old Methodist as a father.'

'What's that got to do with money trouble?' Wiggins asked.

'Edward Dillingham likes to gamble.' The cook winked slyly. He needs the money he invested in Randall's silver mine to pay off his gaming debts. His creditors may not be respectable, but they're pressin' him for payment. Losing money in business is one thing – the old man probably wouldn't get too angry about that – but he isn't going to want to pay off his boy's gamblin' debts.'

Mrs Jeffries looked thoughtful. 'I wonder why Dillingham invested his money in a silver mine if he owed money elsewhere?'

'He didn't owe no one at that time. He'd been doin' pretty good at his gamin' until he hit a run of bad luck a few months ago,' Mrs Goodge explained. 'He's twenty thousand pounds in debt. His father thinks gamblin's a sin. If he finds out about his son, he'll toss him out on his ear. And you'll never guess who it was that introduced Dillingham to his first card game neither.'

Smythe gave her an exasperated glance. 'Well, who was it, then?'

'Rushton Benfield.' Mrs Goodge smiled triumphantly.

'Does Dillingham owe Benfield money?' Mrs Jeffries asked quickly.

The cook's smile faded. 'I don't know. But I'll keep on diggin'. It may take a day or two to find out.'

'What else did you learn about Benfield?' Smythe asked.

'Not much more than what you told us before,' Mrs Goodge admitted. 'But like I said, I'm still workin' on it. Give me a day or two.'

Mrs Jeffries nodded in satisfaction. The cook's information did provide a motive for at least two of the three men who'd been looking for Jake Randall that afternoon. Unfortunately, it didn't provide a motive for John Cubberly. If Hilda Cubberly had brought money into their marriage, then he was the only one of the three that wasn't desperate to get his investment back from the murdered man. 'You've done an excellent job, Mrs Goodge.' She turned to the men. 'Do either of you have anything to report?'

Smythe yawned. 'Not much. No luck gettin' anythin' more out of the cabbies and no one near the bridge heard or saw anythin'.'

'Oh dear.' Mrs Jeffries smiled sympathetically. 'Perhaps you ought to try a different approach.'

'Let me keep workin' on them hansom drivers,'

Smythe said. 'Whoever shot Randall didn't walk to Waterloo Bridge that night.' He snorted. 'Toffs never walk anywhere, so someone had to take 'im.'

''E could 'ave taken the train,' Wiggins suggested. 'The station's right close.'

'I don't think whoever did it took the bloomin' train.' Smythe clamped his mouth shut and glared down at the tabletop. A moment later he looked up and smiled sheepishly. 'Sorry, but I hate to give up.'

Mrs Jeffries stared at him closely. Something was bothering the coachman. Something about this case. 'Well,' she said cheerfully, 'I don't blame you. I, too, hate giving up. Furthermore, I may have some information that can help you.'

She went on to tell them everything she'd learned from the inspector over lunch. 'So you see,' she finished, 'Cubberly admitted the three of them left the house at around half past two and shared a hansom cab to their various destinations.'

'Where did they get out at?' Smythe asked sharply.

'Unfortunately, Cubberly got out first. He wasn't sure where the others were going. Either that or he was too drunk to remember. All he knows is his assignment was to go to the Strand. It seems Mr Randall was fond of the theatre. He used to hang about in the district. Cubberly was going to have a look around that area, check the pubs and the hotels and talk to a few of Randall's associates. He'd been known to be well acquainted with several young women from the district. Actresses, I believe.'

'Maybe I'd better have a run over there,' the coachman mused.

'I think that would be a very good idea. We want to confirm Mr Cubberly's movements, if we can. And remember, he was quite drunk,' Mrs Jeffries emphasized. 'I'm sure someone will remember him.'

'Too bad he wasn't able to tell us where the other two went,' Mrs Goodge said.

'We should have that information by tonight,' Mrs Jeffries replied. 'The inspector is interviewing Dillingham and Hinkle this afternoon. But there's something else we must do as well. I think it's imperative that we find Lottie Grainger.'

'The maid that run off?' Wiggins said. 'But why? She heard the old boy wavin' a gun around, got scared and left. What's she got to do with Randall's murder?'

'Probably nothing,' Mrs Jeffries agreed. 'But remember, if she saw Cubberly waving that gun around, as you put it, then she was close enough to the drawing room to hear and perhaps even see everything that happened during the meeting. I want to know exactly what went on that day. We've only Cubberly's word to the inspector about what was said and done. There could be a great deal more.'

Smythe propped his chin on his hand. 'Did the inspector talk to the Cubberly housekeeper?'

'He spoke with her, but I'm not sure he asked the right questions,' Mrs Jeffries said bluntly. 'But don't worry. He left his spectacles at the Cubberly house.'

'And you're goin' back this afternoon to get 'em.' The coachman grinned. 'Good. Maybe you can get the woman to tell us somethin' really useful.'

'Should I get over to the East End, then?' Wiggins

asked. 'I could take Fred with me. I bet if I could find somethin' that belonged to this Lottie Grainger, Fred could track her. Just like he did that Benfield feller.'

Mrs Goodge moaned, Smythe rolled his eyes heavenward, and even Mrs Jeffries felt a rush of impatience. 'No, Wiggins,' she said firmly. 'I think it best if you leave Fred here this afternoon. By the way, you haven't told us what you've learned today.'

Wiggins blushed. 'That's because it weren't all that much. I hung about Davies Street and talked to a few people. But no one said anythin' useful. Exceptin', I don't think that Mrs Cubberly is as mean a miser as Mr Cubberly.'

'And why not?'

''Cause she's a woman,' Smythe interrupted. 'Wiggins never likes to think ill of a female.'

'That's not true,' the footman protested. 'It's just that Agnes told me that she saw Mrs Cubberly giving some money to a beggar boy once. So if she was givin' away money, she can't be as mean as her husband.'

'Who is Agnes?' Mrs Jeffries asked gently. She didn't want Wiggins feeling that his contribution was worth less than the others'. But really, there were times when she wished that Wiggins wasn't so easily distracted by a pretty face.

'She's a housemaid at the Brompton place,' Wiggins said. 'Across the street from the Cubberlys. She's a right nice girl, told me lots about the Cubberlys. Said they had a 'ard time keepin' servants.'

'We already know that, boy,' Mrs Goodge snapped. She pushed away from the table and stood up. 'Now, if it's all the same to the rest of you, you'd best be gettin' on. I've got a coal delivery comin' in a few minutes, and I want to see what he can tell me.'

They all stood up. Wiggins and Fred wandered off, and Mrs Goodge disappeared down the hall toward the pantry. Mrs Jeffries turned to Smythe. 'Is something bothering you?'

His heavy dark brows drew together. 'I guess you could say that,' he muttered. 'It's probably nothing, not the sort of thing I want to talk about in front of the others.'

'Will you tell me?'

'Course I will.' He gave her a smile that didn't reach his eyes. 'But you've got to promise you won't think I'm goin' daft or gettin' fanciful.'

CHAPTER SEVEN

M RS JEFFRIES STARED at Smythe in surprise. He was the most practical of men. Despite his rough appearance and his heavily accented speech, he was very intelligent. She smiled kindly. 'I don't think there is anything you could tell me that I wouldn't take seriously. Regardless of how farfetched your ideas about this case may seem, I want to hear them.'

He relaxed visibly, 'Fair enough, Mrs J. But I warn ya, I don't have any real reason for what I'm thinkin'. It's just a feelin' I've got.' He broke off and gave her a sheepish grin. 'Cor, I sound like one of them daft old women who sit around stirrin' up 'erbs and potions and claimin' they've got the sight.'

'You have excellent instincts, Smythe,' Mrs Jeffries assured him. 'You should learn to trust them. Now tell me what's on your mind.'

'It's the case, Mrs J.' He brushed a lock of hair off his forehead. 'I've got a feelin' we're goin' about it all wrong. Do you know what I mean?'

She knew exactly what he meant. She had the same feeling herself. In all honesty, she had to admit that so far they'd learned practically nothing of any real value. Or at least if they had, she couldn't make sense of it yet. And time was running out.

'Yes, I do,' she admitted. 'And I'm not sure what to do to remedy the situation. What do you think we're doing wrong? And please, be honest. Don't worry about my feelings. I realize I'm the one that tends to send everyone off in certain directions, but that doesn't mean I'm infallible.' She gave him that speech because she knew perfectly well that he'd tiptoe around the truth for hours if he thought she'd be hurt by his words.

Smythe stared at her for a long moment before speaking. Finally, he said, 'I don't think it's anythin' we've done. More like it's what we 'aven't done.'

'But what haven't we done that we should be doing?' she asked earnestly. 'That's what I want to know. Why aren't any of our usual methods working in this case?'

'Because I think it's the case itself that's throwin' us off the scent,' he replied. 'It's not like most of the others. We've got no real scene of the crime, no witnesses, and we've convinced ourselves that Randall was done in because of that bloomin' silver mine. But what if that ain't the way it 'appened? What if the bloke were murdered for an entirely different reason? We don't know nothin' about this Jake Randall. It's like we're trying to find a straw man.'

Mrs Jeffries suspected he might be correct. There was something decidedly peculiar about this murder and the victim. Maybe they were approaching it all wrong. But she couldn't for the life of her see any other way to go about finding the killer.

'I agree with everything you've said,' Mrs Jeffries

replied. 'But I don't know what else we can do. Jake Randall is turning out to be the most elusive of victims. The police still haven't found out where Randall was staying between the first of the month and the time he was killed. Furthermore, neither the porter nor any of the other tenants at his former residence knew anything about the man. For that matter, no one seems to know much about him either.'

'Benfield probably knows a fair bit.'

'Quite possibly,' she agreed. 'But we haven't heard from Luty or Hatchet yet, and they were the ones trying to find out what they could about Benfield. Perhaps they'll come up with something useful soon.' Mrs Jeffries tried to make her voice hopeful, but could tell by the expression on the coachman's face that she hadn't succeeded. He didn't think Luty and Hatchet would have any better luck than the rest of them had. For all any of them knew, after Benfield had spoken to the inspector, he'd disappeared off the face of the earth. She made a mental note to ask the inspector if the police had verified his movements on the day of the murder.

'Let's look at what we do know about the bloke,' Smythe suggested. 'He was an American. He liked women and he had Rushton Benfield frontin' for 'im.'

'No,' Mrs Jeffries interrupted, 'we're only assuming Benfield was, er, fronting for him, as you put it. It could well be that Benfield is entirely innocent.'

He looked sceptical. 'I don't believe that, and I'm not sure I believe that tale 'e told the inspector that 'e were 'idin' out from the other investors.'

'Why not?' she asked curiously.

Smythe smiled faintly. 'Remember that conversation we 'ad a few days back? The one where Betsy tried to tell us that rich people don't settle their problems by killin'?'

'I remember.'

'Much as I hate to say it, the lass was right. Now, maybe Benfield is the kind to settle a score with a gun or a knife, but you can bet your last farthin' that none of the others are.' Smythe shook his head. 'Can you really imagine Cubberly or Hinkle or that twit Dillingham beatin' Benfield to a pulp?'

'But Benfield claimed that Cubberly did get violent,' Mrs Jeffries pointed out. 'He said he was pushed against the wall.'

'But Cubberly was soaked!' Smythe exclaimed. 'They'd been drinkin' whisky. Bloomin' Ada! Benfield knew that the other three weren't goin' to stay snozzled forever. He knew that once they sobered up, the first thing they'd all do was get their solicitors. They weren't gonna come after 'im. Yet he stayed in hidin' for days! Why?'

Stunned, Mrs Jeffries stared at the coachman. He was absolutely right. Why hadn't she thought of it herself? And more importantly, what else had she overlooked? 'That's a very good question.'

'And another thing,' he continued, warming to his subject. 'We've got to learn more about the victim. For all we know, Randall might 'ave been a nasty piece of work that 'ad 'alf of London lookin' for 'im with murder on in their 'earts.'

'But we've already tried to do that,' Mrs Jeffries reminded him. 'Luty and Hatchet are still attempting to learn what they can about both Benfield and Randall. But so far, we haven't had much success.'

'No disrespect meant to either of 'em,' Smythe said earnestly. 'But they may not have the right sources to do it. Luty knows a lot of people, but I'd wager that she don't know many of the sort that'd be able to deliver the goods on Randall and Benfield. They're crooks, Mrs J. I know. I can feel it.'

Surprised by his certainty, she was taken aback for a moment. She stared at the determined expression in his brown eyes and her stomach tightened. 'And what do you suggest we do to rectify the situation?'

Smythe regarded her evenly. He hesitated briefly before he spoke. 'Let me start workin' on it. There's no point in me hotfootin' over to the Strand today. The inspector'll have the lads in blue confirmin' Cubberly's statement.'

'That's true,' she agreed. 'All right, but what are you proposing to do this afternoon? Continue with the hansom drivers?'

'Nah, I'll do that later. I want to take a crack at findin' out more about Benfield and Randall. But it would mean lookin' up some blokes I 'aven't 'ad much to do with for a long time.'

'I see,' Mrs Jeffries said slowly. She had a horrible feeling that Smythe was trying to tell her something. 'I take it the people you're referring to aren't particularly respectable.'

He nodded, but continued to meet her gaze. 'Right.'

For a moment she didn't know what to say, so she just stared at him. She'd trust Smythe with her life, yet suddenly she realized how little she knew of his past.

All she knew for certain was that he'd worked for the inspector's late aunt, loved horses, and was a very good man.

But except for Wiggins, she knew little more about any of the servants of Upper Edmonton Gardens. Chance had brought them together. Or perhaps it was something else, something other than pure chance. In the months they'd lived with the inspector, they'd forged a strong bond. A true bond of respect and friendship for one another, a bond strengthened when they'd all begun working together on Witherspoon's cases.

But despite their closeness, their sense of family, there was something else as well. An unspoken and tacit agreement between them not to ask one another questions. Not to nose about in each other's past. She knew little of Mrs Goodge save that she'd cooked for some of the finest families in London. There were many gaps in her life, gaps that she didn't share with anyone. Betsy was the same. She'd shown up half-starved and ill on Witherspoon's doorstep soon after Mrs Jeffries came to work for him. And she never spoke of her past either. Wiggins was the only one they really knew much about. He'd come to work for the inspector's late aunt Euphemia when he was a lad of twelve. He had no family.

And now Smythe was revealing something about himself. About his past. Mrs Jeffries realized he was watching her carefully, waiting to see her reaction. She smiled calmly and forced her speculations to the back of her mind. 'Are you trying to tell me that some of the people you may need to question have criminal associations?'

Smythe smiled sadly. 'I'm afraid I am,' he admitted honestly, 'But I swear, Mrs J, I'll be careful. I can take care of myself. I won't do anything that's against the law and I won't put our inspector in an embarrassin' situation. But if I could get a few feelers out, I know I could find out the goods on both Randall and Benfield.'

'But what if your, er, former associates don't know anything about either of them?' Mrs Jeffries asked anxiously.

'They'll know about 'em,' he replied confidently. 'Take my word for it.'

Lester Hinkle was just finishing luncheon when the inspector and Constable Barnes were ushered into the dining room.

'Sorry to bring you in here,' Hinkle mumbled as he shoved a dessert plate with half a treacle pudding on it to one side, 'but my wife has guests. They're in the drawing room, and I don't want them to be disturbed.'

'This will do fine, sir,' Witherspoon said. His mouth was watering. The air was filled with the lingering scent of roast beef. On the buffet, next to the huge cherrywood dining table, the rest of the pudding sat in solitary splendour.

'As long as you don't mind,' Hinkle said. He waved his hand towards the empty chairs. 'Sit down.'

The policemen pulled out chairs and took a seat. Witherspoon watched Lester Hinkle closely. The man looked small and defeated. He was hunched forward over the dining table, his elbows resting on the white damask tablecloth, his gaze locked morosely on the far wall as though he were looking for the meaning of life in the pattern of pink climbing roses on the wallpaper.

The inspector felt a surge of sympathy for him. But he ruthlessly squashed the feeling. This man might very well be a murderer. 'Mr Hinkle,' Witherspoon began. Hinkle continued to stare at the wall.

'Mr Hinkle,' he tried again, and this time Hinkle turned vacant, uncaring eyes in his direction. 'I should like to know exactly where you went on the afternoon of March seventh.'

'So you know,' Hinkle replied. 'I suppose it was Cubberly who talked, not that it matters. I would have told you the truth eventually.'

The inspector wasn't sure he believed him.

'I suppose Cubberly also told you we'd been drinking,' Hinkle said. He tossed his linen napkin onto the table. 'That's why we acted so stupidly.' He laughed harshly. 'When Randall didn't show up, we thought we could find the bounder.'

'Did you locate Mr Randall?' the inspector asked softly.

Hinkle slowly shook his head. 'No. I was so drunk I couldn't have found my way home, let alone Jake Randall.'

'You're not trying to tell us, sir, that you were so drunk you don't remember what you did or where you went?' Witherspoon asked in alarm.

'It's a bit hazy,' Hinkle replied. 'But not so much that I don't recall my movements.' He paused and took a deep breath. 'The three of us left Cubberly's house sometime after two. I don't know when exactly. I didn't look at my watch. We sent a beggar boy who was hanging about the front of the house to get us a hansom. Cubberly got off at the Strand. I can't exactly remember why, but I suppose he had a reason.'

'He was looking for Randall in the theatre district,' the inspector said, hoping the information would help the man remember.

Hinkle nodded. 'That's right. It's starting to come back to me.'

The inspector silently congratulated himself. 'Can you recall what you talked about in the hansom?' It would certainly be helpful if one of them had pulled out the gun and shown it to the others. Perhaps even talked of shooting the man! Then the inspector remembered that both Mrs Cubberly and the housekeeper had claimed the gun was still in the study after the men had left. Drat.

'What did we talk about?' Hinkle laughed harshly. 'Why, we talked about what a scoundrel Randall was. How we couldn't wait to get our hands on him and make him give us our money back. I believe Cubberly was muttering about prosecuting him for fraud. I'm not sure, but I do recall him going on and on about some high-priced solicitor he used.'

'And where did you get off, sir?' Barnes asked.

Hinkle seemed to shrink into his chair. 'Waterloo Station,' he whispered.

Witherspoon went still. Hinkle was admitting that he was less than two hundred yards from where Randall's body was found. 'Why were you going to the station?'

'I thought I might find Jake there,' he admitted ruefully. 'Stupid thing to do, really. But I knew that

Randall had spent some time in South America. I had the notion that if I hung around the station and watched the trains leaving for Southampton, I might spot him.'

'You were thinking he'd get a ship from Southampton, were you?' Barnes asked. He didn't look up from his notebook.

'Why Southampton?' the inspector asked. He was getting confused. 'Why not Liverpool or the London docks? Ships leave from all those places.'

'Randall had talked about how he'd taken the Royal Mail Steam Packet to Brazil once. That line leaves from Southampton. I don't know why I thought Jake might show up there, but I did. Whisky will do that to you. Makes any silly idea you come up with seem reasonable.'

'Was that your only reason for going to Waterloo?' Witherspoon pressed.

Hinkle took his spectacles off and rubbed the bridge of his nose. The inspector was sure he was trying to give himself time to think.

'What other reason would there be?' Hinkle shrugged. 'I realize how absurd my actions seem in the cold light of day, but remember, Inspector, I wasn't my usual rational self.'

'Did anyone see you at the station?' the inspector asked.

'Lots of people saw me,' Hinkle replied wearily. 'But they were all strangers. I didn't run into anyone I know, if that's what you're getting at.'

That was precisely what Witherspoon wanted to know. By his own admission, Hinkle was in close proximity to the scene of the crime. 'How long did you stay at the station?'

'Several hours. It was getting dark when I left.'

Witherspoon remained silent. He tried to get his thoughts in order. He had more questions to ask and he wanted to make sure he didn't forget any of them.

Barnes asked, 'What did you do then, sir?'

Hinkle sighed. 'I walked. By late that afternoon, the whisky had worn off, and I was sober enough to realize how ridiculous it was to be hanging about the railway station on the off chance that I might spot Jake Randall. But it was too early to go back to the Cubberly house. We planned on meeting there at half past nine that night.'

'Did you stop anywhere and have a meal?' the constable asked.

'I wasn't hungry, and I didn't fancy going to my own home, so I just walked the streets.'

'So you claim you spent the afternoon at the station and then walked aimlessly until it was time for all of you to meet again at the Cubberly house. Is that correct?' Witherspoon thought Hinkle's explanation was quite weak. But weak or not, it might stand up in a court of law. A good barrister would see to that. Drat. Hinkle had one of those wretched alibis that couldn't be proved or disproved.

'That's correct.' Hinkle looked at him with beseeching eyes. 'I don't suppose you believe me, Inspector, but I swear it's true. I didn't see Jake Randall that day. And I didn't murder him.'

'What happened after you returned to the Cubberly house?' The inspector wanted to see if Hinkle's version matched the one Cubberly had given him.

'Nothing really,' Hinkle replied. His shoulders slumped and his mouth turned down in a pathetic frown. 'Of course we'd all sobered up by then. Neither Dillingham nor Cubberly would admit to finding Jake, and I certainly hadn't had any luck. So we met back at the house, said a quick good night, and I left.'

'You were the first to leave?' Witherspoon asked carefully. Cubberly had claimed that Dillingham left first.

'No, Dillingham went off right before I did. He was in a state. He wanted us to keep looking for Randall. Poor blighter, he kept insisting he had to find the man and get his money back.'

Witherspoon looked at Barnes. 'Are you saying, Mr Hinkle, that Dillingham went off to continue the search?' Cubberly hadn't mentioned that.

'I can't say for certain. But that's definitely the impression I got.'

The inspector felt certain he was learning something important. He decided to plunge boldly forward. Sometimes, as his housekeeper had once said, a surprise question will yield unexpected results.

'Did you see Mr Cubberly's gun when you arrived back that evening?'

Hinkle wasn't in the least surprised. He shook his head. 'No, the gun wasn't anywhere to be seen. I assumed that John had put it away.'

Mrs Jeffries tapped softly at the backdoor of the Cubberly house. She held her breath. There were so few servants in the household, she prayed that Mrs Cubberly wouldn't be answering the door.

The door cracked open, and a pair of suspicious, red-rimmed eyes glared out at her.

She smiled warmly. 'Mrs Brown?' she queried.

'Who wants to know?' The door opened an inch wider.

'My name is Hepzibah Jeffries. I'm Inspector Witherspoon's housekeeper.' Her smile softened. 'I do so hate to trouble you, but the inspector's left his spectacles here, and I've come to fetch them.'

'Might as well come in, then.' The woman turned and trudged down a darkened hallway. 'Mind you slam the door behind you,' she called over her shoulder.

'Yes, of course,' Mrs Jeffries said brightly. 'I do so hate to put you to any trouble. It's so very good of you to help me.'

She heard a grunt in reply. Oh dear, this woman is not going to be easy to talk with, Mrs Jeffries thought as she followed her into the kitchen.

The room was dark, the light streaming in through the two windows over the open scullery dulled by the dirt on the panes. The grey stone floor was streaked with dust and grease, several of the wooden slats on the standing pallet next to the sink were broken, and there was a thick line of rust on the edges of the kitchen range.

'Wait here,' Mrs Brown instructed her. She jerked her head toward one of the rickety chairs by the fireplace. 'You can have a seat if you like. It might take me a few minutes to find them spectacles. Do you know where he left 'em?'

'I'm not really sure,' Mrs Jeffries replied. 'Perhaps Mrs Cubberly knows where they are.'

'Not bloody likely,' the housekeeper replied as she left.

As soon as she disappeared, Mrs Jeffries tiptoed back into the hall. There were two doors along the corridor leading to the backdoor. She hurried to the nearest door, cocked her head towards the kitchen stairs and heard the housekeeper's slow footsteps as she mounted the stairs. Mrs Jeffries could tell by the woman's progress that she wouldn't be back in a hurry. She turned the knob and stuck her head inside the room.

A meat larder. The walls were lined with slate shelves and the floor was glazed tile. There were hooks for hanging joints dangling from a cross beam, a table, and a chopping block. But the only meat stored was a small, brown-wrapped parcel, which she thought was probably a joint of some kind.

Mrs Jeffries backed out, closed the door, and dashed to the next one. Opening it, she peeked inside and saw that it was a dry larder. But the shelves that should have been bulging with bread, flour, and other staples were surprisingly bare. There were a few tins of vegetables, a jar of preserves, and half a loaf of brown bread. There was very little food in this household, she thought. As she turned to close the door she noticed a housemaid's box, almost identical to the one Betsy and she used at Upper Edmonton Gardens to carry their cleaning supplies, stuck in the far corner. Mrs Jeffries went back to the kitchen. She thought about having a quick search through the house when she heard Zita Brown's heavy footsteps on the stairs.

'It took me a bit o' time to find 'em,' the woman

announced sourly as she plonked the inspector's spectacles on the table.

'Thank you so very much for looking,' Mrs Jeffries replied. 'I must say, I'm so sorry to have put you to any trouble.'

The only reply was a grunt.

Mrs Jeffries tried to think of what to do to get the woman talking. Normally, she had no difficulty engaging people in conversation, but this woman was a horse of a different colour. 'Excuse me for asking,' she began, 'but might I trouble you for a cup of tea? It's a long way home, and once I get back there, I won't have time to do anything but work, work, work. The inspector is quite a nice man, but he is demanding.'

It was precisely the right thing to say.

'Demanding!' Zita Brown shuffled towards the stove. 'I can tell you all about that. Do this, do that, cook the meals, do the bleedin' laundry.' She snorted as she put the kettle on to boil. 'House this big and I'm the only one here. You'd think that old bastard would hire more staff, but no, not him. He's too bleedin' tightfisted to pay fer any more help.'

Mrs Jeffries jumped right in. 'Gracious! You don't mean to say you're expected to do everything? But that's absurd. Why, it's positively criminal.'

'Course it is.' Zita shuffled back to the table and plopped in her chair. 'But he don't care how hard I work, and she don't notice what the bloomin' house looks like. All she cares about is shuttin' herself up in her bleedin' room and readin' them ruddy books of hers.'

Mrs Jeffries assumed the housekeeper was referring to the Cubberlys. But she didn't dare ask. The woman needed a few more moments to vent her rage. 'Have you always had to do it all?'

'Sometimes they have a housemaid,' Zita admitted grudgingly. 'But they never stay.'

'Really? How very dreadful? Why do they leave? Is Mr Cubberly a . . . well, you know. One who takes liberties?'

Zita threw her head back and laughed. 'Him! Not likely. The only thing he uses his pole for is takin' a piss. He don't even take liberties with his missus, much less anyone else. But the girls don't stay 'cause the old fart won't pay a decent wage.' She suddenly leaned forward. 'You wouldn't believe how much they give me. Full housekeeper, I am, and the bastard won't pay more then twenty quid a quarter.'

'That's shocking.' Mrs Jeffries was horrified. That was less than half what a proper wage was. 'But doesn't the mistress of the house object? Surely, she'd need a ladies' maid. Why, who does her hair? Who helps her undress?'

'No one. She does it herself.' Zita broke off and cackled with glee. 'Last maid we had run off in the middle of the day. Mind you, I don't much blame her, what with that lot upstairs drinking like there was no tomorrow and wavin' a gun about.'

'A gun!' Mrs Jeffries wished she'd offered to take the woman out for a drink. At this rate, she was going to be here all day. 'How dreadful.'

The kettle whistled and the housekeeper went to the stove. 'It weren't that bad,' Zita replied. She poured boiling water into the pot. 'It were just Mr Cubberly and some of his friends playin' about. But Lottie weren't used to that kind of nonsense, and she took it into her head to run off. Mrs Cubberly was mad as a wet cat over it. Silly cow. Do the mistress good to turn her hand to something once in a while.'

'Does Mrs Cubberly help you?' Mrs Jeffries asked as Zita placed a cup of tea on the table. There was a piece of dried food on the bottom saucer.

'Her? Not bloody likely. Screamed like a banshee 'cause she had to answer the door herself the day Lottie run off. But I didn't pay her no mind.' Zita settled herself into her chair. 'These old legs can't take climbin' all them stairs every time someone comes to the ruddy door. There's too much to do down here. Cookin' and cleanin' and polishin'. When she started screaming about it, I told her I only climbs them stairs once a day when I do the sweeping and dustin' upstairs.'

'Who takes care of the upper floors?' Mrs Jeffries asked.

'I do.' She picked up her teacup and slurped greedily. 'I do everything around here.'

Mrs Jeffries realized she wasn't going to get anything worthwhile out of the housekeeper. 'How very awful for you,' she murmured sympathetically.

Zita slurped her tea. 'Ah, I'm used to it.'

'It's unfortunate that Mrs Cubberly is an invalid,' Mrs Jeffries said. She wanted to get the housekeeper talking about the Cubberlys again.

'She's no invalid,' Zita exclaimed.

'I'm sorry. Perhaps I misunderstood, but I thought you said she spends all of her time in her room.'

'That's 'cause she's always got her nose stuck in one of them silly books of hers.'

'Ah well, I suppose she isn't all that different from most women of her station,' Mrs Jeffries said casually. 'Many of them spend so much time sitting, it's surprising their limbs still function.'

Zita threw back her head and howled with laughter. 'Right enough,' she agreed. 'Last time her nibs got off her backside was the day Lottie run off. Made Mrs Cubberly so bleedin' mad she grabbed her cloak and announced she was goin' for a walk.'

'I'll bet she didn't walk far.' Mrs Jeffries smiled cynically, hoping to keep the woman talking.

'Don't know how far she walked, but she didn't come back till almost a quarter to seven that night.'

'Gracious, you've a good memory.'

'Not too hard to remember,' Zita said dryly. 'As she were leavin' she yelled at me to have her dinner ready by seven o'clock. Put me in a right old pickle, that did. What with Lottie takin' off, and me havin' to do it all that day. But I did like she wanted. Her bleedin' dinner was waitin' fer her when she come down to the dining room. Seven o'clock right on the nose. But did she thank me? Not bloody likely. Just tucked in without a word, stuffin' her face and givin' me orders to leave a cold supper fer Mr Cubberly.'

'Still no word from the uniformed lads?' Witherspoon asked as he and Barnes waited in the library of the Dillingham home. 'About what?' Barnes dug out his notebook.

'Oh, confirming Benfield's story or locating Randall's lodgings, er . . .' The inspector paused and shifted on the stiff horsehair settee, trying to find a comfortable position. But it was impossible. The seat was as hard as a wooden plank. The other furniture in the large, sparsely furnished room looked equally miserable, too. The only colour was a white-fringed shawl draped across a tabletop. A thick Bible sat smack in the centre of it. Witherspoon thought it an odd spot to keep a Bible. There were oak bookcases along one wall and all the shelves were empty, save for a few books on one of them. Witherspoon would hardly have called this room a library, but that's what the butler had called it, so he supposed it must be one.

'They've found out Benfield was where he claimed to be, hidin' out at that woman's empty flat. The porter confirmed he'd seen him come in on the Monday afternoon around three. Benfield didn't leave the flat until the night he come to the station. The porter's certain of it 'cause Benfield paid him to fetch him food and drink.' Barnes shrugged. 'Mind you, that don't mean that Benfield was there the whole time. The porter's an old man. Benfield could have slipped in and out without him seein' him.'

'Hmmm . . .' the inspector muttered. That alibi was really no better than Lester Hinkle's or John Cubberly's. 'And Randall's lodgings?'

'They haven't found Randall's lodgings yet, sir. Nor the murder weapon.' Barnes glanced at the closed double oak doors. 'What did you think of Hinkle's statement? Do you think he was tellin' the truth?'

'One hates to think that citizens lie to the police on a regular basis,' Witherspoon replied, 'but, honestly, I've almost reached that conclusion. Hinkle's information about Dillingham became much more damaging after he'd learned we knew about the gun. I think perhaps he was trying to throw suspicion on Mr Dillingham because his own position is so precarious. But frankly, Constable, I don't know what to make of it yet.' He stopped, realizing that he sounded as unsure of himself as he felt. And that would never do. He cleared his throat and straightened his spine. 'But like I always say, jumping to conclusions without the facts is useless.'

'True, sir,' Barnes agreed. He kept his eyes on the door. 'But we don't have any facts in this case. All we've got is Hinkle claimin' he was wanderin' around Waterloo Station or walkin' the streets and practically accusin' Dillingham of killin' Randall.'

'Not to worry, Constable,' Witherspoon replied firmly. 'The truth will out.' He thought that sounded rather good.

'Specially if we send a few men over to the station to verify his story,' the constable said grimly. 'If he was wandering around drunk as a lord, someone's going to remember him.'

That wasn't what the inspector meant, but he didn't bother correcting Barnes.

The double doors opened and Edward Dillingham rushed inside the room. Closing them quickly, he turned and dashed across the room towards the two policeman. He skidded to a stop right in front of them.

'What on earth are you doing here?' he hissed softly. He glanced towards the closed doors.

'We'd like to ask you a few more questions,' Barnes replied. He stood up and Dillingham stepped back a few feet.

'But I've already answered all your questions.'

There were footsteps outside in the hallway. Dillingham jerked his head around, a panicked look in his eyes.

'Not all of them, sir,' Barnes said.

Dillingham didn't appear to hear. His gaze was locked on the door and his ear was cocked that way too.

'Mr Dillingham,' the inspector prompted.

He turned at the sound of the inspector's voice, 'You really must go,' he beseeched them softly. 'I'll be happy to come down to the police station, but you must leave.'

The footsteps stopped outside the door. The knob began to turn, Dillingham made a strangled noise of pain just as the door opened.

'Oh God,' he muttered frantically. 'Now I'm done for.'

Luty tossed her cloak over the back of her chair and sat down. 'Hatchet'll be here soon,' she said. 'But he said fer us not to wait.'

'In that case,' Mrs Jeffries said, 'we won't. We've much to report.'

'We only met a few hours ago,' Wiggins muttered. 'I ain't 'ad time to get out and 'ear nuthin'.' He stopped and frowned at the lone plate of bread and butter sitting in the centre of the table. 'Is this all there is?' he asked, his tone outraged. 'What 'appened to them scones you were bakin' this mornin'?' he asked the cook.

'I'm savin' them for tomorrow,' Mrs Goodge said firmly. 'This is the third time we've met today, and I'm not wastin' any more sweets on you lot. Got to save 'em for my sources. Besides, this is plenty. Nothing wrong with a good bread-and-butter tea.'

'It'll be enough fer me,' Luty announced. 'And we don't need to bother savin' Hatchet any. He eats too much anyway. Come on, let's git started.'

Smythe glanced at the empty chair next to the cook. 'Cor, blimey, isn't Betsy back yet? The lass has been gone all day. Where'd she go anyway?'

'I'm not certain,' Mrs Jeffries said. 'But I'm sure she'll be along any minute. In the meantime, we've much to discuss.' She was eager to tell them what she'd learned from Zita Brown, and she also wanted to talk about Smythe's ideas on the case. 'Now, does anyone have anything to report?'

'Hatchet and I found out that Benfield's been disinherited,' Luty volunteered. 'But I don't think it means much. It happened seven years ago.' She turned accusingly to the housekeeper. 'And I'm still waitin' fer you to tell me what part of Colorado this here mine is in.'

'I'm sorry, Luty,' Mrs Jeffries said apologetically. 'I keep meaning to tell you. The inspector told me the mine is located in a town called Pardee. It's near a place called Leadville.'

'Well, well,' Luty muttered thoughtfully. 'That's interestin'.'

'Yes, I'm sure it is,' Mrs Jeffries said quickly. 'But I don't think it has much bearing on Jake Randall's murder.' She was interrupted by the slamming of the backdoor.

Betsy, breathless and with her cheeks flushed, ran into the kitchen. 'Thank goodness you're all 'ere,' she exclaimed. 'I've not got much time.'

'Why are you in such a bloomin' 'urry?' Smythe asked.

'I've learned all sorts of things today,' she announced proudly. She stripped off her gloves and reached around the coachman for the teapot. 'But the most important thing I learned was where Lottie Grainger might be.'

'Betsy, do sit down and have a rest,' Mrs Jeffries ordered. She wondered how in the world Betsy had found out about the missing maid. She hadn't been here for either of the two other meetings they'd had today.

'A quick cuppa and then I've got to run,' Betsy replied. She looked at the housekeeper, her expression serious. 'You see, Lottie Grainger is very important and we've got to find her.'

'Why's she important?' Luty demanded.

Betsy smiled triumphantly. 'Because she was carryin' on with Jake Randall.'

CHAPTER EIGHT

INSPECTOR WITHERSPOON HOPED Edward Dillingham wasn't going to faint or go into fits or something
awkward like that. But really, he thought, the man was
breathing so hard he sounded like a steam engine, and
he'd gone a funny colour. 'Er, are you all right?' he asked.

Dillingham gave a strange, high-pitched squeak as
the library doors opened. A strangled giggle slipped
from his throat as the butler stepped into the room.

'Excuse me for interrupting, sir,' the servant said,
addressing Dillingham, 'but your father has gone out.
He asked me to give you a message.'

Witherspoon could hear Dillingham trying to catch
his breath.

'Thank you, Livingstone.' Dillingham's voice trem-
bled. 'What is it?'

'Mr Dillingham would like you to join him tonight
for dinner, sir. Eight o'clock.'

'That'll be fine, Livingstone.'

Witherspoon and Barnes looked at each other as the
butler left, quietly closing the door behind him. The
inspector decided to wait until Dillingham's colour

returned and his breathing slowed before he would start asking questions. Gracious. He didn't want the fellow to peg out on him.

'I say, I'm dreadfully sorry about that.' Dillingham laughed awkwardly.

'Who were you expectin' to come through that door, sir?' Barnes asked softly.

The inspector threw the constable a grateful look. Trust Barnes to get right to the heart of the problem. Edward Dillingham had clearly been frightened of someone seeing him being interviewed by the police. Not just apprehensive or nervous. Scared. Of course, it might be difficult to get the man to admit to such a thing. What could one say? 'Excuse me sir, but were you terrified your mother was going to catch you talking to the police?' Thank goodness for constables. So much less inhibited about some things.

Dillingham contrived to look offended. 'I've no idea what you mean,' he blustered.

'Come now, sir,' Barnes persisted. 'When you saw that door openin', you looked like you were gettin' ready to lose your stomach. Turned white as a sheet, you did.'

'I've had a spot of indigestion,' Dillingham said doggedly. Then he suddenly threw his hands into the air. 'Oh, what's the use? I was scared. Terrified, if you must know.'

'Would you mind telling us why?' Witherspoon asked. It might have nothing to do with the case, but then again . . . For all he knew, Dillingham might have been afraid it was the murderer. In which case, it meant that he knew more than he'd led them to believe.

'I was afraid it was my father.'

Witherspoon could understand that. Most young men wouldn't want their parent to know they were a suspect in a murder. But that hardly explained Dillingham's state. Surely there was more to it than that. 'I take it you wish to spare your father any needless worry.'

'Worry! Believe me, he won't be worried. Livid, aghast, horrified. The very idea of my being involved in a murder will make him furious,' Dillingham cried. 'He knows nothing about this . . . this wretched murder. And I want to keep it that way. I won't have my father bothered with your questions.'

'We'd no intention of asking your father anything,' Witherspoon said. 'Unless, of course, we find out that he had something to do with Jake Randall.'

'He's never even met the man.'

'Does he own any shares in the Randall and Watson Mine?' Barnes asked.

'Of course not,' Dillingham snapped. He'd recovered completely from his fright. 'Now, why don't you say what you've come to say and leave. I'm a busy man, I've no time to stand about chatting.'

'Could you tell us where you were on the afternoon of Monday, March seventh?' the inspector asked.

'March seventh?' Dillingham murmured. 'You mean' the day we had the meeting?'

'Yes, sir,' Witherspoon said patiently.

'But I've already told you what I did that afternoon,' Dillingham exclaimed.

'Would you tell us again?' Barnes prodded.

'Oh, all right,' he said impatiently. 'After I left the Cubberly house, I had a late lunch at the Crown Hotel, then I walked down Oxford Street to Marble Arch. I went into the park and took a walk. Then I went to a pub.'

'And what time did you leave the park, sir?' the inspector asked. He sighed silently. Why did people persist in lying to the police?

'Inspector,' Dillingham said, 'I don't know what you're getting at. But as I told you yesterday, I've no idea what time I left the park. It was getting toward evening. That's all I can remember.'

'Have you remembered the name of the pub you went into when you left the park?' Witherspoon prodded. 'You weren't able to recall it when you gave your statement yesterday.'

'It was a common public house, Inspector, somewhere near Notting Hill Gate. There's no reason why I should remember what the place was called.' He pulled a pocket watch out of his waistcoat. 'Now I really must ask you to leave—'

'Too bad your memory hasn't improved none, sir,' Barnes interrupted. 'But then again, not many people have good memories. Take for instance the waiters at the Crown Hotel. None of them can recall you coming in at all.'

'That's hardly my fault,' Dillingham snapped.

Witherspoon was tired. It was late, he was hungry, and he wasn't going to waste any more time giving this chap the opportunity to tell the truth on his own. 'That's most unfortunate,' he said. 'Because a confirmation of your story from another person would have been most helpful. As it is, we'll have to assume you did not tell us the truth yesterday.'

'Now, see here . . .'

'Come now, Mr Dillingham, Let's not waste any more time. Both Mr Hinkle and Mr Cubberly have admitted that the three of you did not simply go your own separate ways after the meeting. You went looking for Jake Randall. We also know you were all three drunk and that instead of going home the night of the seventh, you returned to the Cubberly house.' He paused to take a breath. Dillingham was staring at him with wide, frightened eyes. 'We'd like to know exactly where you went that afternoon and, more importantly, did you find Mr Randall?'

'They told you everything?' Dillingham whispered.

Witherspoon nodded.

'Oh God,' he moaned. He stumbled to the settee and sat down. 'I know what you're thinking,' he murmured. 'But I swear, I didn't kill Randall. I didn't even see him. The hansom dropped me on the Pall Mall. My task was to go to the clubs round there. I've a membership at the Carlton, and I've friends at most of the other ones.'

'Was Randall a member of the Carlton or any other club?' Barnes asked, scribbling busily in his notebook.

'No, but he had friends and acquaintances who were.'

'Did anyone you know see you that afternoon?' the inspector asked.

'Not that I recall,' Dillingham said hesitantly. 'Oh no, wait. Richard Sedwick saw me at the Carlton. He invited me for a game of cards. I declined, naturally.'

Barnes glanced up from his writing. 'What time was that, sir?'

'I think around four o'clock.'

Teatime, Witherspoon thought. He wished Mr Dillingham would offer them a cup of tea. But he didn't think that was very likely. 'Who else, other than this Mr Sedwick, saw you? We'll need some additional confirmation of your whereabouts.'

Dillingham's mouth gaped open. 'But I don't know who saw me. There must have been dozens of people milling about the Carlton, but I can't remember who—'

'What about the other clubs?' Witherspoon asked. 'Where else did you go besides the Carlton?'

'Nowhere,' Dillingham admitted.

'Then it should be easy to check your story,' the inspector said softly. 'If you were at the Carlton all afternoon, someone on the staff is bound to remember you.'

Dillingham covered his face with his hands. 'No, they won't,' he groaned.

Egads, the inspector thought as he stared at the distraught man, was he still lying? 'Why ever not?'

'Because no one saw me.' He looked up. 'I wasn't feeling very well. Right after I ran into Sedwick, I went into a back room and curled up in an armchair. It's a room that's not used much. I don't think anyone goes in there. I slept for several hours.'

'When did you wake up?' Barnes asked patiently.

Dillingham began to wring his hands. 'It was almost nine o'clock.'

'Did anyone see you leaving the Carlton?' Witherspoon prodded. 'The porter, perhaps, or the doorman?'

Dillingham smiled bitterly. 'No, I crept out a side

157

door. I didn't want to risk running into anyone I knew. To be perfectly honest, I was a bit of a mess.'

'That's most unfortunate.' Witherspoon also thought it very odd. Surely, if one were searching for someone, one made oneself known to the staff and asked questions. But Dillingham claimed all he did was crawl off into an overstuffed chair and fall asleep. Really, he thought, his story doesn't make any sense. 'Tell me, sir, did you go back to the Cubberly house anytime during the day?'

Dillingham looked genuinely surprised by the question. 'Why should I do that?'

Witherspoon tilted his head to one side and watched the man closely. 'To get John Cubberly's gun.'

'Who told you that?' Dillingham demanded. 'I never went near the house until that night. Until everyone came back.'

The inspector noticed he hadn't denied knowledge of the weapon. 'No one's accusing you of anything, Mr Dillingham.' He paused. 'Did you know Mr Cubberly's gun is missing? We believe it's the weapon that killed Randall.'

'I don't know anything about a gun,' Dillingham cried.

Witherspoon held up his hand for silence. 'Please, sir, we know quite well that you do. John Cubberly got the gun out earlier – he was waving it about and threatening to kill Randall. We also know that you and Mr Hinkle were angry as well, so angry, in fact, that Rushton Benfield felt his life was in danger.' He paused and looked Dillingham straight in the eye. 'Benfield, in fact, has told us everything. We know that the three of you knew that the money was gone and that Randall had taken it.'

'Benfield's a liar.' Dillingham leapt up from the settee and began to pace the room. 'I didn't threaten him. John Cubberly did. Hinkle and I had to pull him off the fellow. He was trying to choke him.'

Witherspoon recalled that Benfield had merely said that Cubberly had shoved him up against the wall.

'We were drunk, Inspector,' Dillingham persisted. 'We didn't know what we were doing. But I assure you, Cubberly may have gotten his gun out, but it was still sitting there when the three of us left. Right on the table. I noticed as I left the room. You can't seriously believe that men of our position would go out and murder someone over a stock swindle.'

'But someone did.' Witherspoon smiled sadly. 'It's been my experience that desperate people commit desperate acts.'

'Have you asked Rushton Benfield what he was doing that afternoon?' Dillingham charged.

'Yes, sir. We have,' Witherspoon replied. 'And we're quite satisfied with his statement.' Actually, they still needed additional confirmation of Mr Benfield's statement. 'Let's get back to you, sir. By your own admission, you've no witnesses as to where you really were that afternoon.'

'You could easily have gone to the Cubberly house and gotten the gun,' Barnes added.

'That's absurd,' Dillingham yelled. 'Mrs Cubberly and the servants were there. Ask them if I came back.'

'Mrs Cubberly was in her room and there aren't many servants. It would be an easy matter to have

159

slipped back to Davies Street, nipped into the house, and picked up the weapon,' Witherspoon said.

'But why would I do that?' Dillingham's voice took on a whining tone. 'I'm not a murderer.'

'Mr Hinkle claims you were still terribly angry when you came back that night,' the inspector persisted.

'Hinkle said that?' Dillingham's eyes flashed angrily. 'He's just trying to save his own skin. How do you know he didn't go back and get the gun?'

'We don't,' the inspector replied. 'But someone did. According to Mr Hinkle, even after the three of you had sobered up, you were the only one who wanted to continue looking for Randall. Cubberly and Hinkle were ready to give up. But you, on the other hand, kept insisting you'd continue the search.'

Dillingham flushed angrily. 'That's a damned lie. I'll admit I wanted my money back, but no more than the other two did. What else did that fool Hinkle tell you? Whatever he says is a pack of lies. He's trying to make it look like I'm the only one with a reason for killing Jake Randall. But that's ridiculous. They wanted their money back as much as I did.'

'Really?' Witherspoon smiled coolly. 'Mr Hinkle claims that Cubberly talked of hiring a solicitor to retrieve his funds and Hinkle himself said he can weather the loss.'

'Hinkle can no more take the loss than I can,' Dillingham said with a sneer. 'He's in debt up to his ears, and John Cubberly's too tightfisted to hire a solicitor. Good Lord, the man's so cheap he won't even offer you a cup of tea. I almost died of shock when he opened that bottle of whisky before the meeting.

You've seen that household of his. And if anyone's got something to hide, it's Cubberly.'

'What do you mean by that?' Witherspoon asked.

Dillingham's sneer turned into a mirthless smile. 'If I were you, Inspector, I'd go back to the Cubberly house and ask John about the overcoat he had on that night. Ask him why it was wet and covered with mud.'

Witherspoon blinked in surprise. 'His overcoat, sir?'

Dillingham nodded. 'I noticed it hanging on the coatrack when I went in that night. You see, Inspector, I'm quite observant. It was damp, dripping in spots, actually, and covered with mud.'

'Carryin' on with Jake Randall,' Mrs Goodge repeated. 'Are you sure?' She looked offended, as though she were annoyed that she hadn't heard this bit of gossip.

Betsy nodded. 'I'm sure.'

Smythe got up and yanked out Betsy's chair. 'Sit down, girl. You'll not be goin' out again tonight. It's gettin' dark.'

Betsy glared at him. 'Fat lot you know. I've got to go out again.' But she sat down.

'Do have some tea and bread, Betsy,' Mrs Jeffries offered. 'I daresay Smythe is right. It is getting far too late to go out.'

'But Mrs Jeffries,' Betsy protested, 'I've got to find Lottie Grainger. I think she might know more about Randall's murder than anyone.'

'What did you find out today?' Mrs Jeffries asked.

'Let me start at the begginin',' Betsy said, taking a quick sip of tea. 'This mornin' I decided to go back over to Chester Square and do a bit of snoopin' about

161

on my own. Didn't have much luck findin' out any-thin' useful at first. There weren't no activity around the Cubberly house, and I saw the inspector goin' into Mr Hinkle's house when I nipped over that way.' She paused and took another quick sip of tea.

'Get on with it, Betsy,' Mrs Goodge said irritably.

Wiggins suddenly started to sniff the air. 'What's that smell?'

'Stock,' the cook replied. She glanced at a huge copper pot on the stove. 'I'm boilin' up some bones for stock. Now come on, Betsy, don't keep us in suspense.'

'Give the lass a chance to drink her tea,' Smythe said.

Mrs Jeffries cast an anxious glance toward the clock. Time was getting on. It was well past the tea hour.

'Ah.' Betsy put down her cup. 'That was good. Any-ways, like I was sayin', I didn't want to 'ang about the Hinkle house in case the inspector or Constable Barnes come out, so I dashed up the road and went into a tea shop.' She leaned forward on her elbows, her blue eyes sparkling with excitement. 'Had the best bit of luck. I was sittin' there when the waiter brought me my tea. Well, we started chattin'. I was askin' him about the Cubberlys just on the off chance he might have seen or heard something, when all of a sudden, the woman sittin' at the table next to mine happened to say she didn't know much about the Cubberlys, exceptin' that they was tightfisted, but she used to be good friends with Lottie Grainger, the maid.'

'Very good, Betsy,' Mrs Jeffries said.

'Sometimes ya git lucky,' Luty added, 'and some-times ya don't. Looks like you hit it good.'

Betsy smiled. 'I did. Wait'll you hear. Anyways, I

changed tables and sat down with the woman. Her name was Dolores Singleton. Her uncle owns the grocer's round the corner from Davies Street. That's how she met Lottie. They become friends 'cause Lottie did the shoppin' for the household. Dolores told me that Lottie Grainger and Jake Randall were sweethearts. Claimed that Randall was mad over the girl. Said he give 'er money, bought her nice clothes, and even took her to the theatre. That's where Lottie and Jake met, you see. Lottie was workin' for some actress, and Jake took a fancy to her.'

Mrs Jeffries thought that a very interesting piece of information. 'You don't, by any chance, happen to know if Randall got her the position with the Cubberlys?' she asked.

'That's just what I asked Dolores. She said Lottie had once mentioned that it were Jake who told her about the job.' Betsy shrugged. 'But she didn't know if he 'ad anything to do with her gettin' the post.'

'But Cubberly's a miser,' Wiggins protested. 'Everybody knew that. Why would Randall want his sweetheart workin' at such a horrible place?'

Mrs Jeffries looked at the footman. Sometimes Wiggins surprised her. 'That's an excellent observation, Wiggins,' she said approvingly.

'If Randall were givin' her money and clothes and takin' care of the girl,' Smythe said, 'maybe he didn't care if she worked for a miser. It looks like he wasn't plannin' on hangin' about London forever, so maybe he saw Lottie workin' at the Cubberlys' as just a temporary position. Besides, Randall may have had other reasons for wantin' her inside the Cubberly house.'

'What reasons?' Mrs Goodge asked.

'The girl could have warned him if the investors started gettin' suspicious about their money,' the coachman replied. 'That would explain why Randall disappeared from his lodgings at the first of this month and didn't tell anyone where he was stayin'. Lottie probably got wind of what was goin' on and warned 'im.'

'But we don't know that,' Betsy cried. 'And I don't think we're going to find Randall's killer until we talk to Lottie.'

'I quite agree,' Mrs Jeffries said cautiously. 'But I don't think it's urgent that you find her tonight.'

'But what if the killer finds 'er first?' Betsy cried.

'Don't be so dramatic, lass,' Smythe retorted. 'You don't know that the killer 'as any interest in findin' Lottie Grainger. For all you know, Lottie might have shot 'im.'

Betsy shook her head. 'She couldn't. Dolores told me she was as mad about Jake as he was about her. He treated her like a queen. Jake was always doin' special little things for Lottie. Buyin' her sweets and flowers and callin' her by her middle name 'cause the initial matched 'is.' She shook her head vehemently. 'He took her to the theatre and the music hall and dozens of other places. Why, he once took her to the Criterion Restaurant. Dolores said it made Lottie laugh 'cause Jake had to give the snooty feller that run the place an extra guinea to get a table. Lottie wouldn't've killed him. She loved 'im too much.'

'Then she's our most likely suspect,' Luty said tartly. 'Hell hath no fury like a woman scorned. Seems to me, if Lottie Grainger was so in love with this rascal and she found out he were fixin' to steal a trunk load of money and run off somewhere, she'd be mad enough to kill him.'

'How would she get hold of a gun?' Betsy asked.

'She could easily have slipped back to the house and stole Mr Cubberly's,' Mrs Jeffries said. 'But all of this is sheer speculation. Though I agree with Luty that it's possible Jake's murder could have been a crime of passion and not of greed, as we've all assumed. We've no evidence whatsoever that Lottie Grainger had a motive or an opportunity to murder Randall. Furthermore, Betsy, before you go dashing off to look for Miss Grainger, we'd better bring you up to date on everything we've found out today.'

By the time she'd finished telling Betsy what they'd learned and reporting the results of her visit to the Cubberly housekeeper to the rest of them, it was quite late.

Hatchet had come in halfway through the recital. He was the first one to speak. 'I do beg your pardon for asking, madam,' he said to Mrs Jeffries, 'but are you sure this Zita Brown was telling you the truth?'

'Why in tarnation would she lie to Hepzibah?' Luty demanded, giving her butler a puzzled frown.

'Because, madam,' he replied, looking down at his employer, 'we know for a fact that Mrs Brown drinks to excess. It's been my experience that people who imbibe to the extent that she obviously does frequently get confused.'

Wiggins scratched his chin, Smythe's brows drew together, and even Mrs Jeffries wondered what Hatchet was trying to tell them.

'Oh, for land's sake, man,' Luty exclaimed impatiently.

'What are you tryin' to say? Was the woman lyin' or are you tryin' to tell us she's just plain loco.'

'Let me put it in very short, simple sentences, madam,' Hatchet said pompously. 'Mrs Brown may not have been lying. From the circumstances that Mrs Jeffries described, the housekeeper would have no reason to fabricate falsehoods—'

'I thought you claimed you was goin' to keep this short,' Luty interrupted.

Hatchet ignored her. 'However, the woman is a drunkard. For all we know, her account of Mrs Cubberly going out for a walk on the day of the murder could have happened another time.'

'Huh?' Wiggins looked really confused now.

Exasperated, Hatchet leaned forward. 'Look,' he said impatiently. 'I once worked for a drunkard. Someone very much like Mrs Brown. He was so far gone with drink that he couldn't tell you what day it was, let alone what he'd done that morning. He was always getting his activities confused. Sometimes, on a Monday evening, he'd insist he'd been to church that morning. Do you understand what I'm saying? Mrs Cubberly may have indeed taken a walk. But she could well have taken that walk on the day before the murder or the day after or even two weeks earlier! You can't take the word of a drunkard,' Hatchet said earnestly. 'They simply cannot be trusted.'

Mrs Jeffries was the first to speak. 'Your point is well taken,' she said. But she wasn't sure that he was right. Zita Brown had been very definite.

Betsy pushed her teacup to one side. 'I really think I ought to get over to the East End.'

Smythe frowned. 'Don't be daft. Only a fool would go out that way at this time of day. It's almost dark now.'

'But it's important. . . .' Betsy protested.

'Of course it's important,' Mrs Jeffries said gently. 'But, that's a very huge area of the city, my dear. How will you ever begin to find the girl?'

'It'll be like lookin' for a needle in a 'aystack,' Smythe snapped.

'But we've got to find 'er,' Betsy insisted.

'And we will,' Smythe promised. 'First thing tomorrow mornin', I'll 'ave a go at it myself. It's too dangerous for you.'

'You'll have a go at it,' Betsy said indignantly. 'That's not fair.' She turned to Mrs Jeffries. 'Listen, Mrs J, I know you're thinkin' I shouldn't be goin' over that way, but take my word for it, I'm a lot more likely to find Lottie than anyone else. I know that area. I grew up there and I can take care of myself and . . . and . . .'

The coachman snorted. Mrs Jeffries held up her hand, her gaze fixed on Betsy's face. 'Go on,' she ordered. 'And what?'

'And there's somethin' else I've got to do. Somethin' I've been puttin' off for a long time.' Betsy paused and took a deep breath. 'Please don't ask me about it; it's something private.'

Mrs Jeffries studied the pretty housemaid carefully. She was again assailed by the same speculations she'd had earlier. Only this time it wasn't the coachman who was revealing his past. It was their own sweet Betsy. She may not have wanted to reveal why she wanted to go to the poorest part of London, but the very fact that she was so insistent about going told Mrs Jeffries much.

'Besides,' Betsy continued doggedly, 'I've got a pretty good idea where to look for Lottie.'

Mrs Jeffries came to a decision. 'Where?'

'Dolores told me that Lottie's mum is at the Limehouse Work House. I know that place.' She broke off and hastily looked down at her lap. 'I know it real well,' she said softly.

'All right, Betsy,' Mrs Jeffries said calmly. 'Why don't you leave first thing tomorrow morning.'

'Cor blimey, Mrs J,' Smythe protested. 'That place is filled with pickpockets and cutthroats. The kind o' people that'd kill ya for your shoes. You can't let Betsy go, not by 'erself, anyways. I'll go with 'er. Least with me along, I can make sure she don't get 'er throat sliced.'

'I don't know, Hepzibah,' Luty added. 'I ain't one for thinkin' that just 'cause you're female, you can't take care of yerself, but that's a right nasty part of town. I ain't sure that a pretty girl like Betsy should be over there on her own. I reckon Smythe's right. He should go, too.'

Wiggins looked utterly horrified. 'You can't do it, Betsy,' he said incredulously. 'You go over there, and we'll never see you again.'

'Don't be foolish, girl,' Mrs Goodge said brusquely. 'Let Smythe go lookin' for this girl. Why take them kind of risks when you don't have to?'

'Smythe can't go,' Mrs Jeffries replied calmly. 'He's got other matters to attend to. Besides, I think Betsy is right.'

'You can't mean that,' the coachman protested. 'And I can put off gettin' the goods on Benfield and Randall until after we find Lottie.'

'What do you mean, "gettin' the goods on Benfield

and Randall"?' Luty interjected angrily. 'That's me and Hatchet's job.'

'Don't worry, Luty,' Mrs Jeffries said quickly. 'Smythe is referring to a different avenue of inquiry.' She glanced at the coachman and added, 'A very important avenue of inquiry.' She turned and smiled cheerfully at Luty. 'We'll still need you and Hatchet to continue with your own avenues of investigation.'

'Well, I should hope so,' Hatchet muttered.

'All right,' Luty said grudgingly.

'Listen,' Betsy said earnestly. 'I appreciate all your concern, I truly do, but I'll be fine.'

'At least take Fred with ya,' Wiggins pleaded.

Mrs Jeffries noticed that Betsy carefully avoided looking in Smythe's direction. That was probably just as well, she thought; the coachman looked like he was ready to spit nails. His brows were drawn together ominously, his jaw was rigid, and his hands were clenched into fists.

'Thanks, Wiggins,' Betsy said gratefully. 'But I really won't need 'im.'

'Hmmph,' Mrs Goodge snorted. 'I don't like it,' she mumbled. 'I don't like it at all.'

'Me neither,' Luty echoed.

'Pardon me.' Hatchet tapped the top of the table for everyone's attention. 'I do not wish to intrude upon a subject which is clearly not my concern, but—'

'You've never let that stop ya before,' Luty mumbled.

Hatchet took no notice of her. 'But, as I was saying, I may have a solution that will ensure Miss Betsy's safety without interfering with her investigation or delaying Mr Smythe with his.'

Witherspoon was so glad to be home that he didn't even mind the wretched taste of the sherry. He settled back in his chair and gave his housekeeper a wan smile. 'I say, today was rather remarkable.'

'How so, Inspector?' Mrs Jeffries asked. She knew she had to keep him talking as long as possible. They'd spent so much time arguing about Betsy and the case that Mrs Goodge had been very late in getting dinner started.

'Well, if I do say so myself, we made rather good progress.'

'That's wonderful, sir.' Mrs Jeffries smiled in approval. 'But I'm not at all surprised. You are, of course, a remarkable detective. Come now, I'm all ears. Do tell me what you've found out.'

Witherspoon swelled with pride. Talking to his housekeeper always made him feel so much better. 'We found out that none of the principals in this case have particularly good alibis. You know, of course, that Cubberly, Hinkle, and Dillingham went looking for Randall after the meeting on Monday.' He couldn't remember whether he'd told her this earlier.

'Yes, sir. You mentioned that at lunch.'

'Speaking of lunch,' the inspector asked hopefully, 'er, do you happen to know what Mrs Goodge is serving for dinner?'

'I'm afraid it's a simple supper tonight,' Mrs Jeffries replied. 'The household management scheme, you know. Mrs Goodge is doing her very best to follow your instructions and trim back a bit.'

'Simple supper?' Witherspoon repeated. Perhaps it would be eggs and chips or a nice piece of sausage.

'Barley soup. Now, sir, about those alibis?'

Witherspoon pushed the thought of food from his mind. What was the point in looking forward to barley soup? 'To begin with, all of the alibis are rather weak.' He leaned forward eagerly. 'You know what I mean.' He began to tell her about his afternoon.

Mrs Jeffries listened attentively. She wanted to make sure she didn't miss the details. Details that might later prove to be important.

'So you see, Mrs Jeffries' – the inspector relaxed and absently picked up his sherry – 'not one of the principals in the case, not even Rushton Benfield, can be eliminated as suspects.'

'Oh dear, sir,' she murmured. 'That is worrying, isn't it? And I'm afraid you may have to expand your list to include Mrs Cubberly.'

Surprised, the inspector stared at her, his glass halfway to his mouth. 'Whatever do you mean?'

'Well, sir. You did leave your spectacles at the Cubberly house,' she began, 'so naturally I went to fetch them. When I got there, I spoke with Zita Brown, the housekeeper. She told me the most extraordinary thing. She claimed that Mrs Cubberly went out for a walk after the men left to search for Randall.'

'But I questioned Mrs Brown,' the inspector said defensively. 'She said nothing like that to me.'

'What exactly did she tell you, sir?'

'She told me that Mrs Cubberly spent most of her time in her room,' Witherspoon replied. He frowned. Drat. Had he even asked Mrs Brown about Mrs Cubberly's movements that day? He wasn't sure. He'd been so busy getting the taciturn woman to admit to seeing the gun that he may have overlooked the most obvious question of all. 'Oh dear, I think I've made a mistake.'

Mrs Jeffries feigned surprise. 'You, sir? I'm sure that's not true.'

Dejected, he sagged in his chair. 'But it is,' he insisted. 'I've been so stupid. Mrs Brown didn't tell me about Mrs Cubberly's walk because I failed to ask her. Frankly, it took so much bother to get the woman to even confirm seeing Cubberly's gun in the house after the men had left that it completely slipped my mind. Stupid, really.'

'Don't be too hard on yourself, sir,' Mrs Jeffries murmured sympathetically. 'How did Mrs Cubberly claim she'd spent the afternoon?'

'She said that all the commotion had given her a headache,' Witherspoon replied morosely, 'and that she'd spent the rest of the day having a rest.' He paused and frowned. 'I can't believe I made such a mistake. I really should have asked the housekeeper the right questions!'

Mrs Jeffries stared at him in some alarm. Inspector Witherspoon had very little confidence in his own abilities. She didn't want him doubting himself now.

'I think, sir,' she said slowly, 'that you asked just the right questions.'

'That's very kind of you, Mrs Jeffries—' he began.

'I'm not being kind, sir.' She had no compunction about interrupting him. 'Remember how we've always said that your abilities as a detective are rather unique. Why, everyone talks about your methods and how very unusual they are.'

Witherspoon nodded. He was watching her with a

172

wary, hopeful expression. The kind that a child wore when you walked into the nursery with a bag of sweets.

'Well, sir . . .' Mrs Jeffries paused to give herself time to think. She was making this up as she went along. 'I think that one part of your mind deliberately made you leave your spectacles at the Cubberly house. You know what I mean, sir. Sometimes we all do things that we didn't think we meant to do, but we really did.'

'Er, yes,' he replied. He looked thoroughly confused now. 'I think I know what you mean.'

'And in leaving the spectacles at the house, you set up the situation so that you'd have a good excuse to go back and have a private chat with the housekeeper. Well, sir, it wouldn't be the first time you've done something like that. You've often told me that servants especially will speak more freely to you a second or third time.' She smiled apologetically. 'But unfortunately, I ruined things by fetching the spectacles myself. I am sorry, sir.'

'Think nothing of it, Mrs Jeffries,' Witherspoon replied.

'So you see, sir,' she continued, 'you've no reason to feel like you've made a mistake. Your actions were most correct. You probably didn't even realize it at the time, either. But that one part of your mind, that very clever part that makes you so very good a policeman, was guiding you all along.'

'Do you really think so?' he asked. Witherspoon couldn't remember any part of his mind acting as a guiding force. But really, there was so much about the mind that one didn't know. And he was a jolly good detective. He'd solved far more than his share of crimes. Perhaps there was something to what his housekeeper claimed.

'Absolutely, sir,' Mrs Jeffries said confidently.

CHAPTER NINE

B RIGHT SUNSHINE STREAMED through the dining-room windows as Mrs Jeffries entered. She set the silver-covered tray down on the sideboard and yanked open a drawer. Taking out silverware and a white linen serviette, she hastily laid the table for the inspector's breakfast.

Betsy usually did this task, but as the girl wasn't here, it fell to Mrs Jeffries. She paused and stared into space, thinking. Had she done the right thing? Betsy had looked so small and fragile this morning when she'd left.

Hatchet and Luty had arrived well before dawn, but all of them had been up to see Betsy off. As they'd hustled the girl into the waiting carriage, Mrs Goodge had mumbled a dark warning of pickpockets and white slavers, Wiggins had kept pressing Betsy to take Fred with her as a guard dog, Luty had volunteered to loan her a six-shooter, and even she had found herself calling out unnecessary warnings. The only one who hadn't put his tuppence worth in was Smythe. He'd stood by the carriage door, scowling at everyone and looking as though he'd like to wring all their necks.

'Good morning, Mrs Jeffries,' the inspector said cheerfully. He took his seat and poured himself a cup of tea. 'What do we have for breakfast this morning?'

'Good morning, sir,' she replied. She lifted the cover off the tray and smiled faintly. 'It's a lovely breakfast, sir. A fried egg and some toast.' She set the plate in front of him.

Mrs Goodge had outdone herself. The egg was the smallest one Mrs Jeffries had ever seen.

'Thank you, Mrs Jeffries.' He frowned faintly as he stared at his breakfast. 'You know,' he mused, 'I'm beginning to have second thoughts about my household management scheme.'

Mrs Jeffries smiled innocently. 'Really, sir?'

'Hmmm, yes.' He picked up his fork. 'I'm not sure saving a few pounds each month is worth all this effort. I mean, poor Mrs Goodge must be at her wit's end.'

'It has been difficult for Mrs Goodge, but she's managing.' It wouldn't do to be too enthusiastic about the end of the household management scheme. Not yet, at any rate. She poured herself a cup of tea and sat down next to him. 'Inspector,' she began, 'I'm afraid I've done something you may not approve of, but I really felt I had no choice.'

Witherspoon smiled around a mouthful of egg. 'I can't imagine you doing anything I'd disapprove of,' he said gallantly. 'But why don't you tell?'

'It's Betsy, sir,' she said. 'Last night after you'd gone to bed, a message arrived for the girl. It was from an old friend, a Mrs Delia Poplar. Unfortunately, Mrs Poplar is very ill. She may be dying.'

'How dreadful.'

'It was indeed. Betsy was most upset. She begged me to let her go to see Mrs Poplar. The woman is quite elderly. I gather she helped raise our Betsy. Well, as you've been working so very hard on this case, I didn't want to disturb you, so I gave her permission to go. She left early this morning. I do hope you don't mind.'

'Not to worry, Mrs Jeffries,' Witherspoon said. 'You did exactly as I would have done. How long will she be gone?'

'A day or two, sir.' She sincerely hoped that was true. None of them could stand the strain of worrying about Betsy's safety for more than that.

'Let us hope that Betsy's friend recovers.' He reached for the one piece of toast in the rack. 'Er, I say, is there any marmalade?'

Mrs Jeffries got a fresh jar out of the bottom of the sideboard. 'Here you are, sir. You'd best eat every crumb; you'll need your strength today.'

'Yes, indeed I will,' he agreed.

'What are you planning to do this morning?'

'Today?' He laughed. 'Oh, the usual. Poke about here and there and see what I can find. I say, though, Edward Dillingham made an odd statement yesterday. He claimed that when they all returned to the Cubberly home that night, he noticed John Cubberly's overcoat was wet and covered with mud.'

'Was Dillingham implying that Cubberly had been near water?' she asked. 'Someplace like the river or more specifically the river under Waterloo Bridge?'

'I believe so, Mrs Jeffries.' He clucked his tongue. 'But it's no good Dillingham telling us about the coat now. I mean, if he'd told the truth at the start, it might

177

have been useful information. We could have asked Cubberly about the coat, or questioned Mrs Cubberly or Mrs Brown. But as it is, the garment's probably been cleaned.'

'I doubt that, sir,' Mrs Jeffries replied casually. 'Unless, of course, Mr Cubberly cleaned the coat himself. Which, if he is your murderer, he would have done.'

'But surely Mrs Cubberly would have taken care of the coat,' the inspector insisted. 'From what I understand, wives are very insistent about that sort of thing. I daresay most women wouldn't want their husbands going about in a dirty overcoat.'

'Mrs Brown told me that Mrs Cubberly did very little around the house,' Mrs Jeffries countered. 'And after seeing the state of the Cubberly kitchen, I don't think cleanliness is one of Mrs Brown's greater virtues.'

'So you think I ought to take Dillingham's statement seriously? Perhaps pop around to the Cubberly house and have a look at it?'

She smiled confidently. 'Why, thank you, sir, for inquiring after my opinion. I'm most flattered. But we both know you've already made up your mind. Of course you're going to ask Mr Cubberly to show you his overcoat, and if I know you, you'll ask him to turn out his pockets as well.'

Wiggins suddenly stuck his head in. 'Sorry to interrupt your breakfast, sir,' he said to the inspector. 'But Inspector Nivens is here to see you. Shall I bring 'im in?'

'That's very good of you, Wiggins,' Witherspoon said. 'Please show the gentleman in.' He turned to Mrs

Jeffries. 'I say, it's jolly decent of the rest of the household to help out in Betsy's absence.'

'Yes, it is,' Mrs Jeffries agreed as she got up and shoved her chair under the table. She quickly picked up her teacup and placed it behind the covered tray. Composing her features, she turned and smiled politely as Wiggins ushered the odious Inspector Nivens into the dining room.

'Sorry to bother you, Witherspoon,' Nivens said. He nodded at Mrs Jeffries. 'But I wanted to drop round and see how you were getting on with this Randall murder.'

'Why, you're not bothering me at all,' the inspector insisted. 'Do sit down and have a cup of tea with me. Have you had breakfast?'

'I've eaten, thank you.' Nivens pulled out the chair Mrs Jeffries had just vacated. 'But I could do with some tea.'

'I'll get a cup,' Mrs Jeffries volunteered. She moved as slowly as she dared over to the sideboard. Inspector Nivens was about to be served the slowest cup of tea he'd ever had. She wasn't leaving this room until she had some idea what he was doing here.

'Now,' Witherspoon said cheerfully, 'what would you like to know?'

Mrs Jeffries opened the glass-fronted cupboard and got the cup. Closing that cupboard, she inched to her left and slowly opened the one containing the saucers.

'I'd like to know how close to an arrest you are,' Nivens answered the inspector.

Mrs Jeffries could feel his gaze on her back. But that didn't make her hurry.

'Oh, I'm not sure how close we are,' Witherspoon said. 'We've an awful lot of suspects. At least four of them.'

'Have you found the murder weapon yet?' Nivens asked. 'Forgive me for being so blunt, Witherspoon. But it's rather important to me that we find Randall's killer.'

'It's important to all of us,' Witherspoon replied.

'Yes, but I've a special interest,' Nivens said coldly. 'I invested a substantial amount of money in that silver mine. The only way I'm ever going to get it back is if we find the killer.'

Mrs Jeffries inched open the silver drawer and took her time finding a teaspoon.

'I say,' the inspector replied, 'I'd quite forgotten that. Of course you're concerned about the progress of the case, and well you should be. If you've got a few minutes, why don't I give you a full report—' He broke off as a loud, cracking noise filled the room. 'Egads, what was that?'

'I believe your housekeeper just slammed the drawer,' Nivens replied.

'I'm so sorry, sir,' Mrs Jeffries apologized. 'The drawer slipped. I didn't mean to close it so hard. It used to stick, you see. I'd forgotten that I'd asked Smythe to fix it last week. Well, as you can hear, he did a superb job.'

Barnes and Witherspoon took a hansom to the Cubberly house. John Cubberly answered the door himself. 'Oh, it's you. I suppose you want to come in?'

'That is why we've come, sir,' Witherspoon said politely.

'Hmmph,' Cubberly snorted. But he opened the

door. 'I'll thank you to keep your voice down. Hilda's not feeling at all well.'

'I'm sorry Mrs Cubberly is ill,' the inspector said. He shot a quick glance at Barnes. 'Is she well enough to answer a few questions?'

Cubberly led them down the hall and to the drawing room. 'No,' he replied quickly. 'She's got one of her headaches and she's lying down. Unless it's absolutely necessary, I won't disturb her.'

'It may be necessary,' Barnes said softly.

They'd decided on the way over that it would be wise for the constable to ask both Mrs Cubberly and Zita Brown about the condition of her husband's overcoat on the night of the murder.

'You'll have to convince me that it's necessary. What is it you want?' Cubberly snapped. His tone was brusque to the point of rudeness, but the inspector could see the fear in the man's eyes.

'We'd like to have a look at your overcoat,' Witherspoon said. He watched Cubberly's face for a reaction. A flash of guilt in those small eyes or a dark flush of shame creeping over that muttonchop beard.

But Cubberly only stared at him. 'My overcoat?'

'Yes, sir,' Witherspoon said patiently. From the corner of his eye, he saw Mrs Cubberly hovering near the door. 'Oh, I'm so sorry,' he apologized, turning to look in her direction. 'I do hope we didn't disturb you. Your husband said you weren't feeling well.'

'Do go back upstairs, Hilda,' her husband ordered softly.

Hilda smiled weakly. 'What is it they want this time? More questions?'

'No, dear,' Cubberly answered. 'They only want to have a look at my coat. Heaven only knows why. I certainly don't.'

'What coat?'

'My overcoat. It'll only take a moment, and then they'll be gone,' he assured her. 'You go upstairs and lie down.'

'I don't want to lie down,' she retorted. There were lines of strain around her eyes and mouth. She stared contemptuously at the two policemen. 'I've no idea why you want to look at an overcoat, but if you'll wait here, I'll get it.'

Cubberly moved toward the hall. 'Don't trouble yourself, Hilda, I'll get it.'

'You won't find it on the coatrack,' she told her husband, turning her back on him and walking into the hall. 'I took it upstairs to be brushed.'

Witherspoon's spirits sank. Drat. If the coat had been brushed, it was no doubt useless as evidence. Not that he'd had any serious hopes that it could be evidence.

Mrs Cubberly returned a few moments later, a heavy black overcoat in her arms. Constable Barnes took the coat from her and held it up for the inspector to examine.

Witherspoon couldn't believe his eyes. The coat was covered with dried brown mud. There was mud on the pockets, on the lapels, and there was one particularly nasty streak of it running down the back.

'I thought you said you were going to have it brushed, Hilda,' her husband complained. 'For goodness' sakes, it's a ruddy mess.'

'Mrs Brown has been busy, and we don't have a maid anymore,' she replied sullenly.

182

Witherspoon pointed to the stains. 'Mr Cubberly,' he asked, 'will you please tell me how this mud came to be on your coat?'

'I got splashed by a carriage,' Cubberly replied. He stared at the inspector for a moment. 'What's this all about? Why do you care if there are mud stains on my overcoat. They've been there for days.'

'Would you please empty the pockets, sir,' the inspector asked. He'd suddenly remembered what Mrs Jeffries had told him this morning.

'Empty the pockets?' Cubberly appeared stunned by the suggestion. 'Now, see here—'

'Would you rather empty them down at the station?' Barnes inquired softly.

Sputtering with rage, Cubberly snatched the over-coat away from the inspector. He shoved his hand in the front pocket and turned it inside out.

Empty.

'Now the other pocket,' Witherspoon prompted.

'Oh really, this is an outrage.' But Cubberly did as he was told. He yanked the pocket inside out. Three pennies and a farthing dropped onto the carpet, as did a small piece of folded white notepaper.

Witherspoon reached for the notepaper. He opened it, read the contents, and handed it to Barnes. 'Would you read it aloud, please, Constable.'

Barnes cleared his throat. 'It's dated March seventh and addressed to "J". It says: "Meet me tonight on the footpath by Waterloo Bridge at eight o'clock." It's signed "Jake".'

Hilda Cubberly gasped and stared at her husband with wide, horrified eyes.

'I've never seen that note in my life,' Cubberly whispered.

'Then how did it get into your pocket, sir?' the inspector asked. He thought that if Cubberly were faking his reaction, he should be on the stage. The man looked utterly stunned.

'Oh, John,' Hilda cried. 'How could you?'

'But I've done nothing, Hilda,' he beseeched her. 'I swear it. I've never seen that before, ever. I've no idea how it got into my pocket.'

Barnes stepped closer to the inspector. 'Should I get some lads round to search the house?'

'You'll do no such thing,' Mrs Cubberly yelped. 'Not without a warrant.'

Witherspoon dithered for a moment. He had no doubt that with this new evidence, they could obtain a warrant, but that would take time. And there was one part of him that wasn't sure it was the right course of action. Perhaps, he thought, the 'guiding force' that Mrs Jeffries had mentioned this morning was trying to tell him something.

'Not yet, Barnes,' he told the constable. He ignored Mrs Cubberly. 'But we will station a man outside the front and back doors of this house. Mr Cubberly, please don't try to leave town.'

'And what about me?' Mrs Cubberly asked. 'Am I a prisoner, too?'

The inspector could think of no reason for asking Mrs Cubberly to remain available for further questioning. 'No, Mrs Cubberly,' he said politely. 'And your husband isn't a prisoner either. That's not the way we do things in this country. We're merely asking him to make himself available for further questioning. As for you, you may come and go as you please.'

Betsy wished she'd never agreed to meet Hatchet at regular intervals. With his thick, white hair, straight erect carriage, and elegant black coat, he stood out in this district like a sore thumb. Holding her hand over her nose to keep out the smell, she darted around a stopped rubbish cart sitting smack in the middle of the Whitechapel High Street and hurried toward the tall man craning his neck in an effort to locate her.

'I'm right 'ere, Mr Hatchet,' she called. She giggled as she saw Hatchet step pointedly around a frowsy, middle-aged woman blocking his path and talking at him a mile a minute. Betsy was fairly certain what the woman was offering as well.

'Thank goodness you're all right, Miss Betsy,' Hatchet said. He glanced over his shoulder, saw the woman in hot pursuit and grabbed Betsy's arm. 'Let's walk,' he suggested quickly.

'What's yer hurry, ducks?' the woman called. 'We can talk about me price, you know.'

Hatchet pretended not to hear. 'I'm so glad to see you're safe,' he told Betsy. She practically had to run to keep up with his long strides.

'Of course I'm safe,' she panted as he steered her around the corner. 'This area used to be home to me. I know my way around.'

'Nevertheless' – he glanced over his shoulder again, saw that his pursuer had give up, and sighed in relief – 'I've been quite concerned. How are your inquiries going?'

'Lottie's mum is dead,' Betsy said bluntly. 'But one of the women at the lodgin' house where she used to live saw Lottie a couple of days ago. She thought the girl had gone over to her aunt's on Wentworth Street. That's where I'm 'eaded now.'

'Would you like me to accompany you?' Hatchet asked.

Betsy didn't have the heart to tell him that he'd just slow her down. 'No thanks, I'll be fine on my own.'

'As you wish,' Hatchet said formally. 'As per our arrangement, I'll be back here for you at five o'clock.'

Inspector Witherspoon pushed his empty plate to one side and burped delicately. Ah, sausage and chips, he thought, a repast fit for a king. He decided he'd seriously underestimated the pleasure of a good meal. Perhaps he'd have a word with Mrs Jeffries this evening when he got home. Enforcing thrift in a household was certainly wise but, really, he'd come to dread some of the ghastly concoctions Mrs Goodge had foisted upon him in the name of economy. He gazed around the busy police canteen for a moment, then leisurely reached for the mug of strong, sweet tea.

'Did you enjoy your food, sir?' Barnes asked. He sat down opposite the inspector. 'Mind you, I don't know why you want to eat this greasy muck when you can nip home and have a proper meal.'

Witherspoon smiled. This had been the best meal he'd had in days. 'Actually, Constable, I quite enjoyed my lunch. Have you eaten?'

'Yes, sir, I had a couple of sausage rolls while I was

talkin' to the lads. If you don't mind my askin', sir, why didn't we search Cubberly's house?'

The inspector sighed. 'I didn't think the time was right, Constable. Something about finding that note in Cubberly's pocket struck me as very odd. Before we violate a man's privacy and search his home, I want to be very sure that he's guilty.'

'And you think Cubberly isn't?' Barnes asked incredulously. 'But he was the only one that knew where Randall was going to be that evenin'. He had a message from the victim tellin' him the time and place to meet him.'

'Yes, but why did Randall want to meet Cubberly?' The inspector frowned thoughtfully. 'That's what I want to know.'

'Well, if you want my opinion, sir, I think Cubberly and Randall was in it together. I think they both planned to steal the investment money, split it and then go their separate ways. But Cubberly got greedy. He wanted it all. So he sent the other two out on wild-goose chases to make sure they was out of the way. Then he met Randall, shot him and stole the money. It's probably hidden somewhere in his house right now.'

'Yes, but doesn't it strike you as strange that he would be foolish enough to keep the evidence? Why didn't he burn the note?' Witherspoon asked. That detail bothered him greatly.

Barnes pursed his lips. 'I don't see that it's all that odd, sir,' he mused. 'We know Cubberly's a miser. He probably stuck that paper in his pocket out of habit. You know what I mean, sir. He's the kind that uses both sides on a piece of paper, keeps writing on the

187

bloomin' thing till it's completely covered in scribbles. My aunt Gemma used to do that. Used to send us letters that people had written to her, only she'd cross out their bit and cram her own news onto the top and sides. Horrible to read, they were.'

'I suppose it's possible Cubberly could have done so. Gracious, we're all creatures of habit,' the inspector said thoughtfully. Yet, still, there was something wrong with casting Cubberly in the role of murderer. Something that didn't fit. But he couldn't put his finger on what it was.

'I think that's exactly what he did, sir,' Barnes insisted. 'And our list of suspects is gettin' smaller. We know that the murder was done at around eight o'clock, so that means Mrs Cubberly couldn't have done it. Zita Brown says she was back at the house by seven forty-five. And Hinkle couldn't have done it either. While you was eatin' lunch he showed up 'ere with Lady Augusta Waddington.' He paused and took a breath. 'Lady Waddington claims she saw Hinkle walking near Holland Park on Monday the seventh. She called out to him from her carriage, but he didn't hear the lady.'

'What time did she see him?' Witherspoon asked.

Barnes smiled. 'A quarter to eight. She remembers because she was late gettin' to a dinner engagement over on Mortimer Street that was due to start at eight. So Hinkle couldn't have done the murder. I can't see someone like Lady Waddington providin' an alibi for Lester Hinkle just because she likes him.'

'Yes, but there's still Benfield and Dillingham,' the inspector insisted. 'Either of them could have done the murder.'

'We're still workin' on that,' Barnes admitted. 'If Dillingham were asleep and Benfield were in hidin', it might be hard comin' up with anyone who can confirm their story. But neither of them knew where Randall was goin' to be that night. Cubberly did.'

Witherspoon was sitting with his back to the room so he could look out the window at the pigeons in the police yard. Barnes was standing beside him. Neither of them had noticed Inspector Nivens coming up and standing behind Witherspoon's chair. 'I quite agree with the constable,' Nivens said softly.

Startled, the inspector swivelled around in his chair and stared at Nivens. 'I say, I didn't hear you. Gracious, you are a quiet fellow.'

'Treading softly is a most useful characteristic in a policeman,' Nivens replied. He walked around the table and pulled out a chair. 'I didn't mean to eavesdrop, but I couldn't help but overhear your conversation. You really ought to search the Cubberly house.'

The inspector drummed his fingers on the tabletop. Perhaps the constable had a point. Perhaps he was paying too much attention to his 'guiding force' and not enough to proper police methods. Yet, still, he wasn't sure. He did so hate violating a man's privacy without absolute, positive proof that it was necessary.

'Even with two men watchin' the house,' Barnes continued doggedly, 'if he wants to make a run for it, we might not be able to stop him. Cubberly made a mistake, but I don't think he's stupid. He might be able to give our lads the slip if he takes it into his head to leave while the gettin's good. We'd have egg on our

189

faces, then, sir. I don't fancy explainin' to the chief how we let our prime suspect get away.'

'The chief isn't known for his tolerance of mistakes,' Nivens added.

Witherspoon capitulated. He didn't relish the thought of explaining it to the chief either. 'All right, Constable. Get some uniformed lads. We'll search the Cubberly house.'

Tea was a dismal affair at Upper Edmonton Gardens. Everyone, including Mrs Jeffries, was thoroughly depressed.

Mrs Goodge slammed a plate of digestive biscuits on the table and shoved them toward the centre. They missed crashing into the teapot by a hairsbreadth. 'Uh, sorry,' she mumbled, 'but I've had a miserable day. Didn't learn anythin' worth repeatin'.'

'I'm sure that's not true,' Mrs Jeffries said soothingly. 'But let's have our tea before we begin our discussion.' She wasn't in any hurry to start talking about the case either. She'd achieved absolutely nothing today herself. She'd spent the whole day reviewing every possible aspect of this case and she was no closer to the solution.

Smythe picked up his mug. 'If you don't mind, Mrs J, I'd like to get started. I want to get back out.'

Mrs Jeffries brightened. 'Does that mean you have something interesting to report?'

'Nah, at least nothing that seems to 'ave anythin' directly to do with Randall's murder,' he replied. 'But I'm meetin' someone tonight who might be able to 'elp some. All I found out today was that Jake Randall and Rushton Benfield go back a long way. They was involved in some kind of property fiddle about seven or eight years ago.'

'That's better than what I heard,' Mrs Goodge muttered darkly. 'But it weren't my fault. I couldn't keep my mind where it should be, what for worryin' about the girl.'

'I'm sure Betsy will be just fine,' Mrs Jeffries said firmly. She wished she could believe it herself. 'After all, Hatchet is keeping a close eye on her.'

'Fat lot of good that's goin' to do,' Smythe snapped. 'No disrespect meant, Mrs J, but Hatchet's not exactly a spring chicken. The toughs over in that area could eat someone like 'im for breakfast.'

'Don't you be too danged sure of that,' Luty said tartly. She was standing in the kitchen door. 'I let myself in,' she explained as she hurried over to the table. 'And don't you be thinkin' that Hatchet can't hold his own with anybody. Take my word fer it, he can. He'll bring Betsy back safe and sound. Now, what was you sayin' about Benfield and Rushton pullin' some property fiddle?' she asked the coachman.

He shrugged. 'I weren't able to get the details. But I know that they didn't get away with any money. Randall ended up hightailin' it back to America, and Benfield got disinherited. There was talk of prison, but Benfield's father managed to pay off the victims and get everythin' hushed up.'

'That figures,' Luty mumbled. 'Goes along with what I found out, too.'

'Excellent, Luty.' Mrs Jeffries smiled brightly. Perhaps their luck was changing. 'Do tell us.'

'I heard the same story Smythe did,' she replied. 'And I couldn't get many details neither. But I think I figured out the reason Benfield took off and holed up after that meetin' broke up on the day Randall was murdered, and it weren't because he was scared of the other investors, neither.'

'Then who was he hiding from?' Mrs Jeffries asked curiously.

'No one. I think Benfield was tryin' to lay low, stay out of sight, so to speak. I think he was tryin' to distance himself from any scandal that might break because Randall was swindlin' the silver-mine investors.'

'Why would he do that?' Mrs Goodge asked. 'Surely he weren't daft enough to think the others would forget they'd been swindled out of fifty thousand pounds. There was bound to be a fuss.'

'Yeah, but I think he was hopin' to stay out of sight till the worst of it was past. Benfield's pa took sick a few months back and has had a change of heart about his boy,' Luty explained. 'Accordin' to Letitia Knowles – she's that neighbour of mine who knows everything that goes on in this town – Sir Thaddeus Benfield has put his baby boy back in the will. I reckon that Benfield panicked when he found out Randall was up to his old tricks. He probably wanted to stay out of sight till everything blew over. He sure as shootin' didn't want his pa to find out about the swindle. And the old man's dyin'. By the time the scandal becomes public knowledge, Sir Thaddeus may be six feet under. Course, Benfield hadn't counted on Randall bein' murdered. Unless he's the killer.'

★ ★ ★

'This is ridiculous,' Hilda Cubberly snapped. 'What on earth do you hope to find? I tell you, you've no right to be here without a warrant.'

Inspector Witherspoon sighed inwardly. 'Mrs Cubberly, I realize this is a most uncomfortable situation for you, but we're well within our rights. If you like, you may send for your solicitor.'

Witherspoon had taken the precaution of rereading the Judge's Rules and the Police Code before beginning the search of the Cubberly home.

'That won't be necessary,' John Cubberly said wearily. He looked at his wife, who was pacing angrily in front of the fireplace. 'Do sit down, Hilda,' he begged. 'You'll wear yourself out.'

She didn't answer him.

From upstairs, they could hear the sound of footsteps and the opening and closing of doors as the upper rooms were searched. The downstairs had already been done.

Mrs Cubberly stopped pacing and glared at the ceiling. 'Your men had better put everything back as they found it,' she cried angrily. 'And there'd better not be anything missing.'

'I assure, you, madam,' the inspector said, 'our police are not thieves.'

'Inspector.' Barnes's voice came from the top of the staircase. 'You'd better get up here, sir. We've found something.'

Witherspoon, with Hilda and John Cubberly on his heels, hurried toward the stairs.

'You couldn't have found anything,' Cubberly charged. 'There's nothing to find, for God's sake.'

'Shut up, John,' Mrs Cubberly said in a low, quiet voice. 'Don't say another word until we get a solicitor here.'

Barnes stood at the top of the staircase. He jerked his head to his left. 'Down here, sir. It's in Mr Cubberly's dressing room.'

They trooped down the hallway and into a large, monkish bedroom. The walls were a plain white and bare of ornamentation or pictures, the windows covered with cheap brown cotton curtains and the furniture scratched and old.

On the far side of the room was another door. A young uniformed police constable was standing beside it.

'In the dressing room, sir,' Barnes said. He led them into the small room and pointed down at a pair of boots covered with a polishing cloth. 'Have a look in there, Inspector.'

'Wiggins.' Mrs Jeffries smiled kindly at the footman. He looked dreadfully depressed. 'Have you had any success today?'

He shook his head. 'No. The whole bloomin' mornin' was a waste of time.'

'Exactly where did you go today?' she persisted.

Wiggins blushed. 'Over to Davies Street. I wanted to try and talk to Agnes again. Spent half the day 'angin' about the area, and the only person I talked to was that little street Arab that 'angs about lookin' for errands to run.'

'At least you didn't have to spend yer morning round a bunch of thieves and scoundrels,' Smythe said.

Mrs Jeffries gave the coachman a sharp look. Obviously, seeing his former associates and friends hadn't been a particularly happy experience for him. She wondered if Betsy would come back equally morose.

From outside, they heard the sound of a carriage. Smythe leapt from his chair and flew down the back hall to the backdoor. 'It's Betsy and Hatchet,' he yelled. 'And they've got someone with 'em. It's a woman. Bloomin' Ada, I bet it's Lottie Grainger.'

Witherspoon knelt down and pushed the cloth to one side. The handle of a gun protruded out of the boot. He swallowed and carefully reached for the weapon. Guns made him dreadfully nervous. Cautiously, he grasped the handle and pulled it out of the boot.

Barnes shook his head gravely. 'That's a Colt .45, sir.' He reached for the weapon. 'If you don't mind, sir, I'll have a look at it.'

'Er, do you know much about firearms, Constable?' He handed the gun over.

'A bit, sir,' Barnes replied. Holding the gun with the barrel pointed toward the floor, he cocked it open and peered into the chamber. 'Looks like we've found the murder weapon, sir,' he stated softly. 'One bullet's been fired.'

CHAPTER TEN

Lottie grainger, lovely, green-eyed, dark-haired and very nervous, twisted her hands together in her lap. She stared anxiously at the seven people gathered round the table.

'Betsy told me you was all 'elpin' to find out who killed my Jake,' she said softly. 'Is it true?'

'Yes, it is,' Mrs Jeffries said firmly. 'But we're going to need your help.'

'I don't know,' Lottie replied. 'I don't much like gettin' mixed up with the police and all that.'

'Do you want Jake's killer to go unpunished?' Mrs Jeffries prodded. The girl was as skittish as a kitten in a room full of bulldogs. One false move and she would probably bolt for the door.

'Of course I don't,' Lottie said. 'But Jake . . . Jake was doin' some things that weren't proper. I didn't really know all that much about 'em, but the police may not believe me.'

'If you are innocent of any wrongdoing,' Mrs Jeffries told her, 'then you needn't worry about being arrested. You have my word.'

Lottie stared at her for a few moments. 'All right. I don't want whoever killed Jake to get away with it. I'll do what I can to 'elp you.'

'Good. Now, we think the best way of going about our task is for you to tell us all you know about Jake.'

Lottie's eyes filled with tears. 'Jake were wonderful,' she murmured, brushing at her cheeks. ''E treated me like a queen.' She held her hand out. ''Ere, look it this, Jake give it to me less than a fortnight ago. It was our engagement ring.'

On her finger was a ruby set in an ornate gold setting. Mrs Jeffries was fairly certain the gem was real. Jake Randall had obviously thought enough of his sweetheart to give her an engagement ring of real value.

'It's lovely,' Luty said softly. She tilted her head to one side and gazed at the grief-stricken young woman. 'He musta loved you a lot.'

''E did,' Lottie whispered.

'Then if you want to see his murderer brought to justice, you gotta trust us. You gotta tell us the truth, even if it makes Jake look bad. Even if it makes you look bad, ya understand? You can't hold nothin' back. Tell us everything you know and answer all our questions,' Luty said earnestly. 'We'll make sure the no-'count varmit that put a bullet through yer man's heart swings from the gallows. You've got my word on it.'

Lottie wiped her eyes and straightened her spine. 'Ask me anything you want.'

'If it's all right with everyone,' Mrs Jeffries said, 'I'll ask the questions. If I miss anything, the rest of you be sure and speak up.' She glanced around the table, and one by one they nodded.

'Right, then.' Mrs Jeffries paused and took a breath. She really must get her thoughts in order. She must ask the right question. 'Where did you go after you left the Cubberly house?'

'I went to Jake's lodgin' house,' Lottie replied. 'I wanted to warn him.'

'Warn him about what?'

'About the gun. I'd already warned him they was gettin' suspicious about the mine, but this was different. They was out for blood. Mr Cubberly was wavin' that gun around and threatenin' to kill Jake. So I left as quick as I could and went to warn 'im. But Jake wasn't there. I waited all day. All day and 'e never come.' Her eyes filled with a fresh batch of tears, but she quickly wiped them away. ''E was already dead. Cubberly had found 'im.'

'Why do you think John Cubberly's the killer?'

''E were the one with the gun,' Lottie said earnestly. 'Who else coulda done it?'

Mrs Jeffries knew this wasn't the time to tell Lottie there were a host of suspects. She didn't want the girl to stop talking. 'When did you find out Jake was dead?' she asked softly.

'Same as everyone else,' Lottie said wearily. 'I saw it in the newspaper on Thursday morning.'

'How long did you stay at Jake's lodging house?' Mrs Jeffries thought this a most pertinent question. She wanted to understand the girl's movements on the day of the murder.

'Until late Monday night. I waited as long as I could, you see. But then I got scared.'

'Scared of what?' Mrs Goodge interjected.

'Jake and me was supposed to go off together, and

198

when 'e didn't show,' Lottie explained, 'I thought . . . I thought . . . Oh God, I'm ashamed to admit it now. But I thought 'e'd gone off without me.' She started crying again.

Smythe looked away from the weeping woman, Betsy reached over and patted the girl's arm, Luty rolled her eyes impatiently, and Wiggins fidgeted in embarrassment. Mrs Goodge had the good sense to refill the teapot.

Mrs Jeffries waited until the emotional storm had passed. But this was taking far too long, she thought. If they weren't careful, the inspector would come home and find them questioning the girl. She decided to try a different method. 'Lottie, I know this is most distressing for you, but I think it would be more efficient if you told us about Jake in your own words.'

'Where should I start?' Lottie sniffed. 'I mean, do you want to know 'ow I met 'im, or what?'

'Just start talking,' Mrs Jeffries suggested. 'And we'll see where that leads us.' She was an excellent listener. It had often been her experience that if one listened carefully, people opened up like a sieve.

'All right.' Lottie tilted her head to one side and her eyes took on a faraway look. 'I met Jake about six months ago when I was workin' as a ladies' maid for this actress. But I wasn't happy there, didn't much like the sort that 'angs about the stage, if you get my meanin'. Jake didn't like me being there either. Jake told me he'd 'eard of a position as a housemaid for the Cubberlys. He warned me right off the wages was poor, but he thought it'd be best if I went there anyway. I weren't that worried about the wages. Jake give me plenty of money.' She shrugged. 'Besides, it weren't goin' to be for very long. He'd asked me to marry 'im and we were plannin' to go to the United States together.'

'Did Jake ask you to do anything for him while you worked at the Cubberlys'?' Mrs Jeffries asked gently.

Lottie hung her head. ''E asked me to keep me ears open and to tell him if they ever started gettin' suspicious about Jake's business dealin's.' She lifted her chin. 'I know I shouldn'a done it for him. But I loved Jake. I didn't want anyone to hurt him. And I didn't know he was plannin' on stealin' the investment money, I really didn't. I found out about the money bein' gone from the bank when I was listenin' at the door when they was havin' their meetin'. That's the first I knew of it, I swear. I know Jake did some things that was wrong,' she said defensively. 'But 'e didn't deserve to be murdered.'

'No one does,' Hatchet murmured.

'Go on,' Mrs Jeffries prompted. 'Tell us the rest. What prompted you to be listening outside the door that day?'

'Because I knew somethin' was wrong. A few days before they had this meetin', Mr Hinkle come over to the Cubberly house. Now, I weren't listenin' at the door that time, but I did hear what Hinkle was tellin' Mr Cubberly. Blimey, I'm surprised the whole neighbourhood didn't hear Hinkle. He were shoutin' at the top of his lungs. He told Mr Cubberly he'd had a cable from some cousin of his about Jake's mine. Said the mine wasn't bein' worked. Said there might be trouble with their investment money, but he wouldn't find out for sure until he received his cousin's letter.'

'Did you tell Jake this?'

Lottie nodded. 'Oh yes, I 'ad to wait until Mrs Cubberly had gone up to her room for the day and Mr Cubberly had gone to the city, but as soon as they left, I nipped out to the front gate and waited till Harry showed up.'

'Who's 'Arry?' Smythe asked.

''E's the little street beggar that 'angs about Davies Street and Chester Square,' Wiggins answered. He smiled at Lottie. 'I'm right, aren't I?'

Lottie laughed. 'Yes, but 'ow do you know Harry?'

'Let's just say I've met 'im in the course of our inquiries,' Wiggins said proudly. ''E's a nice little nipper. 'E misses you, you know. Told me the other lady at the Cubberly house weren't near as nice as you.'

'What did you have this Harry do?' Mrs Jeffries asked. She was getting rather impatient.

'I sent the boy off with a note for Jake. Warnin' 'im,' Lottie replied. 'That's 'ow Jake and I used to stay in contact with each other. 'Arry was always bringin' me notes, tellin' me where to meet Jake or bringin' me some money from 'im.'

Mrs Jeffries pressed on. 'And then what happened?'

'Jake come around that night and I told 'im what I'd overheard. He wanted me to leave with him then. But I couldn't. So he moved out of 'is hotel and into a lodgin' house over near Westminster. Jake made sure none of the investors knew where 'e was stayin'.'

'So that explains why Jake Randall moved,' Mrs Jeffries said thoughtfully. 'But why couldn't you leave with him when he asked you to?' she asked Lottie.

''Cause of me sister. She were gettin' ready to 'ave

her baby and I didn't want to leave the country while she were expectin'. America's a long way off and I knew it'd be years before I could see her and the baby. I wanted to stay until it was born. Her time was close, so Jake said it would be all right. Said he could stay out of their way.' Lottie sighed deeply. 'Jake didn't want to 'ang about, but 'e knew how much I wanted to be here for the baby's birth, so 'e stayed. He stayed because of me and he got murdered . . .'

'There, there,' Betsy murmured softly. 'You mustn't blame yourself. You didn't know he'd be murdered. 'Ere now, what did your sister have? A boy or a girl?'

'She had a baby boy. She named him Jake.'

Inspector Witherspoon's ears were still ringing when he arrived home that evening. Gracious, what a day! Handing his bowler hat and coat to Mrs Jeffries, he sighed in relief at the blessed peace and quiet of his home.

'I've had a dreadful day,' he told her as they walked into the drawing room. 'Positively dreadful.'

'Oh dear,' Mrs Jeffries murmured. 'I'm so sorry to hear that. I thought you were making progress on this case.'

'We are,' he replied, settling himself in his favourite chair. 'I'll probably be making an arrest in a day or two.'

Mrs Jeffries's hand stilled as she reached for the sherry bottle. 'Really?'

'Yes, indeed. As soon as I get confirmation of one or two details, I'll be arresting John Cubberly for Randall's murder.'

Mrs Jeffries forced her fingers to close around the sherry bottle. Her first thought was that her carefully laid plan to bring Lottie Grainger here tomorrow morning might not be a wise idea, after all. 'Cubberly? So he's the murderer.'

'Oh yes, yes indeed . . .' His voice trailed off. 'Actually, I'm not absolutely certain that it's him. But honestly, there doesn't seem to be anyone else who could have done it.'

'You found mud stains on his overcoat, then?' she asked. If that were all the evidence the inspector had, his case was as weak as rainwater.

'Indeed we did. You were absolutely right about Mrs Brown. She hadn't bothered to clean the coat. Mrs Cubberly had taken it upstairs, but she hadn't gotten round to giving it a brush-up either. But that's not the only evidence we have.' He told Mrs Jeffries about finding the note in Cubberly's pocket and the gun in Cubberly's boot.

'So you see,' he continued, 'the evidence is mounting against the fellow. He, of course, protests that he's innocent.'

'Do you believe him, sir?' she asked. She was thinking frantically, trying to fit all the details the inspector had just revealed into the overall pattern. Lottie had claimed that there was no money with Jake's possessions at the lodging house. Therefore, one could assume that Jake had the money with him when he was killed. But did he? And could Cubberly possibly have known that?

'Not really.' The inspector sighed. 'But then again, he seems so sincere. I tell you, Mrs Jeffries, if the man is lying, then he missed his true calling. He should have been an actor. Cubberly seemed genuinely stunned when we found both the note and the gun.'

'May I see the note, sir?' She smiled uncertainly. 'I know it's probably against police regulations, but really, you know how terribly interested I am.'

'Of course you may see it,' he replied. 'Mind you, I should have given it to Barnes to take back to the station, but I'm afraid I forgot and put it in my pocket instead.' He rummaged around in his waistcoat and drew out a folded piece of paper. 'Ah, here it is.' He handed it to Mrs Jeffries.

She scanned it quickly. 'I take it you're now certain that Cubberly met Randall at eight o'clock and killed him. Presumably, he stole the money as well.'

'That's our theory.'

'Then why, sir,' she asked, handing the note back to him, 'did you say you'd had such a dreadful day? It sounds to me like you're making excellent strides towards solving this murder.'

'Oh, Cubberly was blubbering like a baby, Mrs Cubberly was screeching at the top of her lungs, and Constable Barnes was pressing me to arrest Cubberly on the spot.' He shuddered. 'It was terrible, I tell you. Absolutely terrible.'

'Why didn't you arrest Cubberly?' she asked curiously.

He toyed with his sherry glass. 'I'm not sure. But somehow I couldn't bring myself to do it. I've left two police constables at the Cubberly house. We don't want Mr Cubberly makin' a run for it, so to speak. But there's something about the whole situation I don't really like.' He paused and gave her a sheepish smile. 'Perhaps it's that "guiding force" you mentioned yesterday. Perhaps it's telling me to dig a bit deeper in this case. In any event, I didn't think it would do any harm to sleep on the decision. I'll arrest Cubberly tomorrow. Though, mind you, the way Hilda Cubberly was ranting and raving, it will be a wonder if we get the man out of the house without losing our hearing. That woman has a very strong voice.'

'I expect it's normal for a woman to want to protect her husband,' Mrs Jeffries said. 'Though it certainly doesn't help Mr Cubberly's position to have his wife screeching at the police like an enraged fishwife.'

'Oh, she wasn't screeching at us,' Witherspoon said.

'She was angry at her husband?' Mrs Jeffries thought that most odd. According to what the inspector had told her earlier about Mrs Cubberly, she would have expected the woman to be protecting her husband. Not screaming at him.

'That's putting it mildly. She was furious at him. Honestly, Mrs Jeffries, if I hadn't seen her obvious devotion to her husband when we were questioning him yesterday, I'd have thought she hated the fellow.'

While the inspector ate his meal Mrs Jeffries told the others about John Cubberly's impending arrest.

'Well, that's it, then,' Smythe said sullenly. 'Looks like 'e solved this one without much 'elp from us.'

'Don't be too sure about that,' Mrs Jeffries said. 'The inspector isn't certain that Cubberly is guilty. For that matter, neither am I.'

'Who else coulda done it, then?' Wiggins mumbled. 'Even Lottie said there weren't no money at Jake's lodgin' 'ouse. That means 'e 'ad it with 'im. Cubberly's known to be a greedy miser – 'e killed the bloke and stole the money.'

'But how did Cubberly know where to meet Randall?' Mrs Jeffries persisted.

'From the note,' Mrs Goodge said firmly. 'It's quite clear what happened. John Cubberly was in cahoots with Jake. You said the note was addressed to "J" – and Cubberly's the only one at the house with that initial.'

'Perhaps,' Mrs Jeffries mused. She turned to Wiggins. 'I want you to get over to Davies Street early tomorrow morning.'

'Tomorrow mornin'? What 'ave I got to go all the way over there for? I wanted to be here when Miss Lottie come to see the inspector.'

Luty had taken Lottie home with her. Everyone had agreed the girl needed some hot food and a good night's rest before she told the inspector her story.

'That's the point, Wiggins,' Mrs Jeffries told him patiently. 'We need you to find out exactly who Harry gave that note to – assuming, of course, the note isn't a forgery.'

'Lottie should be able to say whether it's a forgery or not,' Mrs Goodge put in. 'She ought to be familiar with Jake Randall's handwriting. But I can't believe that note from Randall was meant for her. Why would he put the wrong initial on it? Besides, if Lottie had gotten the note, she woulda met him at eight o'clock that night. Instead, she spent the evenin' waitin' for him at his lodgin' house.'

'We only have her word that she did wait for him,'

Mrs Jeffries said tartly. 'That's why talking to Harry is important.'

'Do you think Lottie's lyin', then?' Betsy asked.

Mrs Jeffries stared at her sharply. The girl's voice was flat, her expression downcast, and her shoulders were sagging. She'd been this way ever since she'd come back from the East End. 'I think it's possible she could have done the murder.'

'Oh, Mrs Jeffries, that couldn't be true,' Wiggins cried. He looked horrified by the idea. 'Lottie's innocent, I tell ya. She couldn'a shot Jake. She loved 'im. Why, just talkin' about Randall made 'er cry 'er eyes out.'

Mrs Jeffries slept poorly that night. At half past twelve, she got up, wrapped herself in her warm, woolly shawl and stared out the window into the darkness.

There was something about this case that bothered her. Something someone had said. A clue of some kind. A piece of the puzzle that made everything else fall into place. But for the life of her, she couldn't put her finger on it.

She took a long, calming breath to clear her mind. Then she made herself start at the beginning. Jake Randall was shot on the evening of March 7, possibly around eight o'clock.

The only suspects who had alibis for that time were Lester Hinkle and Hilda Cubberly . . . She paused. Perhaps she'd better eliminate Rushton Benfield as well. According to the inspector, the porter at the block of flats where Benfield had been hiding was adamant that the man hadn't gone out that evening.

That left John Cubberly, Edward Dillingham, or Lottie Grainger. Mrs Jeffries smiled slightly. Unlike Wiggins, she had no illusions about what the female of the species was capable of doing. Lottie Grainger had to be considered a possibility for the role of murderess. Luty might well have been right the other day when she was speculating that Lottie could have had the most common motive of all for killing her fiancé. She was going to be abandoned. Seduced and abandoned. It had happened often enough before.

Furthermore, Mrs Jeffries thought, Lottie was the only one who knew where Jake lived. Despite the ready tears and the face like an angel, Lottie could well have been lying through her teeth today. She'd admitted she knew that Jake had stolen the investment money before she ran out of the Cubberly house. Lottie could just as easily have found out Jake was planning on leaving the country without her. The girl also knew the Cubberly household. By her own admission, she'd seen John Cubberly's gun. She could have pretended to leave that day, knowing that she could slip back inside, grab the gun, and meet Jake.

But was that what happened? Mrs Jeffries wondered. And if Jake Randall was planning on abandoning Lottie, why would he send a note to the Cubberly house? Surely, there would have been other, less risky ways for him to meet John Cubberly.

And what motive did Cubberly really have for murdering Randall? True, Cubberly was a miser. But there was no evidence he was having financial difficulties. On the contrary, he was the only one of the investors who genuinely could have weathered the loss. So why would he stoop to stealing and murder? Why risk losing everything he had? Miserliness wasn't a particularly noble character trait, yet it didn't necessarily follow that because one was a miser one was also a murderer.

She closed her eyes and tried to let her mind wander. After a few moments she sighed. This was doing no good whatsoever. Perhaps tomorrow it would come to her. Perhaps a good night's rest would jog her memory.

'Has Wiggins returned yet?' Mrs Jeffries asked Mrs Goodge.

'Not yet, but it may take him a bit o' time to find Harry,' the cook replied. 'How'd the inspector like his breakfast?'

'He enjoyed it very much,' Mrs Jeffries said. 'He'll be in the right frame of mind to listen to Lottie when she arrives. I only hope that Wiggins is able to find the boy. We need to know who Harry gave that note to.'

They'd made their plan most carefully. Mrs Goodge had relented and fixed the inspector a superbly filling breakfast of bacon and eggs. Wiggins had nipped off at the crack of dawn to find the street boy, and Lottie Grainger was due to arrive any moment.

Betsy, who was standing at the kitchen sink, rose on her tiptoes and peeked out the window to the street. 'A hansom's just pulled up in front,' she announced. 'It's probably Lottie, so I best get upstairs.'

Smythe watched her as she left the room. He waited until he heard her footsteps on the stairs before saying, 'What's wrong with the lass, Mrs Jeffries? She ain't acted 'appy since she come back from the East End yesterday.'

'I don't know, Smythe,' Mrs Jeffries replied. She was worried about Betsy, too. 'Perhaps it was going back to her old haunts. Perhaps it brought back unhappy memories. I don't think she was very happy when she lived in that district.' She shook her head and pushed the matter to another part of her mind. She'd have a quiet word with Betsy later. Right now, she had to keep her wits about her. 'I'd better get upstairs. You know what to do?'

'Don't worry,' Smythe said. 'We know exactly what to do.'

'Oh, Mrs Jeffries,' the inspector called. 'Could you come in here a moment?'

She walked calmly into the room, not giving a hint that she'd been hanging about the hall waiting for his summons. 'Yes, sir,' she said politely. 'Is there something I can do for you or your guest?' She smiled at Lottie, who was sitting demurely on the settee.

Witherspoon cleared his throat. 'I'd appreciate it if you'd sit down. Miss Grainger would like to make a statement.' He paused and shot a fast, wary glance at Lottie. 'She'd prefer to have another . . . woman present, if you don't mind.'

The inspector was most perplexed and just a bit offended. Really, he thought, did this young woman think he wasn't to be trusted? But being a gentleman, he did as she requested.

'I don't mind in the least, Inspector.' Mrs Jeffries sat down next to Lottie.

She was delighted that her plan was working. She'd told Lottie to insist on having a woman in the room while she spoke to the inspector. Lottie, of course, believed Mrs Jeffries was there to give her moral support, and to some extent that was true. But Mrs Jeffries was also there for another reason. She wanted to make sure Lottie told the inspector the same story she'd told them.

'Now,' Witherspoon said briskly. 'Could you please tell me where you've been since leaving the Cubberly residence?'

Lottie smiled shyly. 'I've been at me aunt's house over at Wentworth Street. My sister lives with 'er, you see, and she's just had a baby.'

Witherspoon's cheeks turned pink. 'Er, uh, congratulations to your sister, then.'

'Thank you, sir. She had a lovely little baby boy. If you don't mind, sir, I'd like to make me statement in me own words. Is that all right?'

Taken aback, Witherspoon blinked. This was a most odd development. For a moment he seriously considered asking the young lady to wait until Constable Barnes arrived before she began her statement, but that would be so rude. Furthermore, the girl had come here of her own accord. But really, this was most unusual. 'Er, if that's what you would prefer,' he said cautiously, 'then I suppose it's all right.' He knew he could always ask her additional questions later.

'Thank you, sir.' She gave him a dazzling smile. The inspector blushed again.

'I'll begin with a few days before I left the Cubberly house,' Lottie began. She told the inspector everything she'd told Mrs Jeffries and the others the day before.

Mrs Jeffries watched Lottie carefully while she talked.

Today, she had her emotions well under control. Her words were strong and confident. They were also non-incriminating. They'd spent some time last night coaching Lottie on how to phrase her statements. It wouldn't do if the inspector thought she'd had anything to do with swindling the money out of the stockholders of the Randall and Watson Mine.

'Now, let me see,' Witherspoon queried when she'd finished. 'You're saying you left the Cubberly house because you were afraid there was going to be trouble and you wanted to warn Jake. Is that correct?'

'Yes, sir.'

'Hmmm. And Randall was in the habit of sending you notes. Is that right?'

'Yes,' Lottie replied. ''E used to send Harry round with one every afternoon. Jake liked to make sure I was all right. And sometimes he'd tell me where and what time to meet 'im.'

'Excellent,' Witherspoon said. 'In that case, you should be able to help.' He reached into his waistcoat and pulled out the folded note. 'Can you look at this, please, and confirm that it's Jake Randall's handwriting.'

Perplexed, Lottie took the note and opened it. She studied it for several moments. 'This is Jake's writin', but I've never seen this one before in my life.'

'But of course you haven't,' the inspector replied with a smile. 'There's a "J" at the top. We think it was meant for John Cubberly.'

Lottie stared at him for a moment. 'Oh no, sir. You're mistaken. This was meant for me.'

Mrs Jeffries sat bolt upright.

'But Miss Grainger,' Witherspoon said patiently. 'Your name starts with an "L", not a "J".'

'I know that Inspector.' She laughed. 'But Jake always called me by my middle name – Jane. You know, 'e thought it was sweet that way. Jane and Jake. 'E was quite a romantic, my Jake was.'

Witherspoon's eyes widened. 'So this note was meant for you,' he exclaimed. 'Then how did it end up in Mr Cubberly's overcoat? That's what I want to know?'

Mrs Jeffries quietly got up and went to the mahogany table by the window. She pulled open the drawer and took out the heavy oak-rimmed magnifying glass her husband had given her.

'Excuse me, Inspector,' she said politely. 'But if you'll allow me to make a suggestion. Perhaps you might learn something more about the note if you examine it with this.'

Mrs Jeffries was beginning to put the puzzle together. One or two of the pieces were starting to fall into place.

'Er, a magnifying glass?' he murmured.

'Of course, sir.' She smiled. 'You are the one who always said one should never take anything at face value.'

He looked confused for a brief instant. 'Indeed I do, Mrs Jeffries,' he said, reaching for the glass. Holding the glass over the note, he examined it carefully.

After a few moments he said, 'Mrs Jeffries, would you have a look at this for me? I'm not sure, but it does look as though someone has added a top stroke to the number eight. There's a slight difference in the colour of the ink as well.'

Mrs Jeffries stared at the magnified figure. The inspector was right: not only was there a difference in ink colour between the top and the bottom of the '8,' but if you looked carefully, you could see the side stroke of the figure had originally been one long, continuous motion. Someone had added the top 'O' to the number. 'You're right, sir. I believe this eight was originally a six.'

'Then that would mean' – the inspector paused, his forehead wrinkling as he concentrated – 'that the note originally said, "Meet me at six", not eight. Gracious, Mrs Jeffries.'

'There's somethin' else you should know,' Lottie said. She pointed to the top of the paper. 'This 'ere's got a date on it. See, seven/three. But Jake never dated 'is notes to me. Why should 'e? He sent one every day.'

There was a pounding on the front door. Mrs Jeffries, who was thinking furiously, glanced up and saw Wiggins rushing down the hall towards the front door. A moment later she heard voices and then a pounding of feet.

Constable Barnes burst into the room. 'Sorry for interruptin' like this, sir,' he cried, 'but somethin' awful's happened.'

'Egads, Barnes,' the inspector replied. He stared at him in alarm. 'You're in a frightful state. What on earth is the matter?'

'It's that bloomin' Inspector Nivens,' the constable yelled. 'The silly fool's just gone and arrested John Cubberly.'

'Mr Cubberly's been arrested,' Lottie repeated. She seemed most confused.

Witherspoon rose to his feet. 'Nivens has arrested Cubberly? But that's unheard of. Why would Nivens do such a thing? Surely you're mistaken. This is my case.'

'I'm not mistaken, sir,' Barnes cried. 'I seen it with my own eyes. He did it because the smarmy bastard wants the collar for himself. I tried to stop him, but he claimed he'd got the go-ahead from the chief. Said you was takin' too long and that they was afraid Cubberly would make a run for it. Nivens arrested him and took him down to the station.'

'Gracious, Barnes.' Witherspoon was shocked by Nivens's behaviour. 'I'm afraid I really will have to protest. This is an outrage.'

Mrs Jeffries saw Wiggins waving to her from the hall. She backed out of the room.

'What did you find out?' she whispered.

Wiggins checked to make sure the inspector and Barnes hadn't noticed him. 'Sorry it took me so long to get back,' he hissed, 'but I saw Nivens and his boys goin' into the Cubberly 'ouse and I wanted to 'ang about a bit and see what was goin' on.'

'Good work, Wiggins,' she replied quickly. The inspector was starting to pace up and down the room. He was truly angry. 'Now, what did Harry tell you?'

Wiggins smiled. 'You'll never believe this, Mrs J. He took the note there that day, all right. But 'e didn't give it to Lottie nor to Mr Cubberly. I told ya Lottie couldn't 'ave done it, I told ya she were too in love with Randall to kill 'im.'

The pieces were falling rapidly into place now. Mrs Jeffries knew that whoever had gotten their hands on that note was the person who'd killed Jake Randall. She was fairly certain she knew who the person was, too.

'Yes, Wiggins, I know you did,' she hissed impatiently. 'And you were absolutely right. Who did Harry give the note to?'

'Hilda Cubberly.'

CHAPTER ELEVEN

THE LAST PIECE fell into place. 'Excellent, Wiggins, You've done a superb job.'

'You shoulda been there, Mrs J,' Wiggins continued excitedly. 'Nivens hustled Cubberly out of the house fast as you please.'

'Yes, I'm sure it was very interesting.' Mrs Jeffries was trying to think of the best way to approach the inspector. She gazed at him through the doorway. He was still pacing angrily up and down the room. She'd have to handle this most carefully, she thought. She'd never seen the inspector in such a state.

'It were better than just interestin',' he countered. 'It was like watchin' one of them puppet shows at the fair. Five minutes after Mr Cubberly got taken off, Mrs Cubberly comes 'urryin' out with the housekeeper 'ot on 'er 'eels.'

Mrs Jeffries turned to stare at him. 'What?'

Wiggins laughed. 'You shoulda seen it; Zita Brown was 'angin' onto Mrs Cubberly's skirts and askin' for her wages. Mrs Cubberly was strugglin' with her carpetbag and tryin' to push the housekeeper off at the same time that she were tryin' to get into a hansom. Constable Barnes was shoutin' at her that she shouldn't be leavin' and she were shoutin' right back that she couldn't be compelled to give evidence against her husband and that she'd go anywhere she damned well pleased. It were a right old dust-up, I tell you.'

'Oh my goodness. Do you know where Mrs Cubberly was going? Think, Wiggins. Think. It's vitally important.'

'Course I know where she were goin'. She had to shout to the driver over Mrs Brown and Barnes. She told 'im to take her to Waterloo Station.'

'Quick! We've no time to lose. Run down to the kitchen and tell Smythe to bring the carriage here.'

'You mean now?'

'Yes, now. Run. Tell Smythe to hurry as well.'

Wiggins ran down the hall. Mrs Jeffries took a deep breath and calmly walked back into the drawing room.

'Mrs Jeffries.' The inspector stopped his pacing and turned to look at her. 'I'm going right to the chief superintendent. I've never been so offended in my life. This is an outrage. Have you ever heard of such a thing! Inspector Nivens arresting John Cubberly right out from under my nose.'

She smiled serenely. 'I can see that you're upset, sir. But really, you are planning to have a good laugh at Inspector Nivens's expense when you walk into the station with the real murderer.'

Witherspoon's jaw gaped open.

'I beg your pardon, ma'am,' Barnes said. 'But what are you talkin' about? John Cubberly is the killer.'

'Of course he isn't. That's why the inspector didn't

arrest him,' Mrs Jeffries said confidently. She sent up a silent prayer that she was completely correct in her deduction. 'Come now, Inspector, it isn't fair to keep the good constable in suspense. You know very well you've deduced the identity of the real murderer.'

'I have?'

'Naturally you have.' She smiled at Lottie. 'Miss Grainger has just told you that she never received the note that day. Tell me, Miss Grainger,' she asked the confused-looking young woman, 'would your friend Harry have given the note to Mr Cubberly or the housekeeper, Zita Brown.'

'Oh no,' Lottie replied quickly. ''E was scared of both of them. Mind you, he might've given it to Mrs Cubberly. She'd once paid 'im for runnin' an errand for 'er.'

'Mrs Cubberly?' the inspector repeated. He looked confused, too.

'Why yes, sir,' Mrs Jeffries said hastily. 'Why, you've even been giving me little hints about the real identity of the killer. Hilda Cubberly is the only one who could have done it. She was the one who brought you her husband's overcoat that had the note in it. She wanted you to believe that the murder took place at eight o'clock. A time when she had an alibi. Furthermore, she'd made sure the overcoat was still mud stained by taking it upstairs so the housekeeper wouldn't brush it off. Who else but Mrs Cubberly could have slipped the note in Cubberly's pocket? Who else but she knew where Jake Randall was going to be that night? And who else but she had the best motive of all for murder? Money.' She wagged her finger at the inspector. 'Oh, sir, admit it, you've been dropping little clues all along to see if I could figure it out Jake Randall knew that the investors were after him. Why on earth would he have allowed one of them to walk up and shoot him in the chest? If Randall had been killed by any of the other suspects, I'll wager that he'd have been shot in the back. He'd have turned and tried to run if he'd seen a man approaching him on a dark footpath by the river. But he was expecting to meet a woman. He'd think it was Lottie coming towards him. Until, of course, it was too late.'

'Er . . . yes, yes, of course,' the inspector cried. 'Gracious, I'd better get over to the Cubberly house right away.'

'That won't do us any good, sir,' Barnes cried. 'Mrs Cubberly's gone. Packed a carpetbag and left for the train station. I heard her telling Nivens she wasn't going to stay in London and be humiliated by her husband's arrest.'

'Oh dear,' the inspector mumbled. 'I suppose if we miss her at the train station, we can wire the police somewhere further down the line.'

'But, sir,' Mrs Jeffries interjected, 'do you really think that is wise? You don't want to give her an opportunity to hide that carpetbag full of money, do you?'

Witherspoon's brows drew together. 'Er . . . why do you think the money is in the carpetbag?' he asked.

'Well, of course it is, sir. Hilda Cubberly's a lady. If she were really leaving her husband because she couldn't face being humiliated, she'd have spent the day packing her trunks. She wouldn't have run off carrying a carpetbag. Ladies do not carry their own luggage.' It was weak, but it was the best she could come up with on the spur of the moment. And it was imperative that the inspector arrest Mrs Cubberly with the money in her possession.

'But she's got such a head start on us,' Witherspoon said anxiously.

'Not to worry, sir,' Mrs Jeffries assured him. 'As it happens, Smythe is bringing the carriage round this morning. He was going to take me to Elstree to buy some fruit. He should be here any minute.'

'Do hurry, Smythe,' the inspector shouted through the carriage window. 'We mustn't let her get away.'

''Ang on, sir,' the coachman yelled back, 'I know a shortcut.' He whistled sharply and the horses broke into a gallop. They took the corner on two wheels.

'Gracious,' the inspector said as he was bounced back onto his seat, 'I do hope Smythe knows what he's doing.'

The ride got faster and wilder. They careened through tiny streets at breakneck speed and cut through mews with barely inches to spare on each side of the carriage.

Finally, they pulled up in front of Waterloo Station. Barnes leapt out of the carriage and Smythe tossed the reins to a porter. The inspector jumped out and frantically tried to think of which platform to search.

'Why don't we try the boat train,' Barnes suggested eagerly. He took off at a run through the doors with Smythe and Witherspoon right behind him.

Oblivious to the stares of the passengers milling around the entrance hall, they ran toward the gates leading to the trains. They stopped on the other side of the barrier and searched the platforms.

The platforms were crowded with passengers, porters, freight, and handcarts filled with luggage. On the far side of the station, a train was pulling in, while on the platform nearest them, one was pulling out.

'Oh no,' Witherspoon moaned. 'I think we're too late. She was probably on that one that's just leaving.'

'There she is, sir,' Barnes cried. He pointed to the far side of the station. Halfway down the platform, Hilda Cubberly stood waiting to board the train, the carpet-bag dangling in her right hand.

They ran across the cavernous room, dodging passengers and getting shouted at by porters and ticket takers. Reaching the end of the platform, they charged towards Hilda Cubberly.

Smythe ran ahead of the inspector. Witherspoon and Barnes were almost upon her as the last of the disembarking passengers got off and Hilda stepped toward the open door. A conductor shouted, 'All aboard.'

'Halt,' the inspector yelled.

Startled, she looked towards them. She recognized him instantly and turned to flee, the carpetbag clutched to her chest. As she spun around she ran smack into Smythe's massive chest.

'I believe, ma'am,' he said politely, 'the two gentlemen behind you would like to have a word with you.'

'Get out of my way, you great fool,' she hissed.

'Mrs Cubberly.' The inspector skidded to a halt and tried to catch his breath. 'We'd like to have a few words with you,' he panted.

'I've nothing to say to the police,' she snapped. 'Now get out of my way, I'm going to catch this train.'

'Are you in a hurry to go somewhere?' Constable Barnes asked.

'That's none of your business.'

'Mrs Cubberly,' Witherspoon said politely, 'could you please open your carpetbag? I assure you, I'm well within the law by requesting that you do so.'

'And if I don't?' she challenged. 'What are you going to do? Arrest me?'

Witherspoon stood his ground. He looked her directly in the eyes. 'If I have to.' He held out his hand for the bag.

She stared at him for a moment as though she didn't believe him. Then she handed him the carpetbag.

Witherspoon was surprised at how very heavy it was. He gave it to Constable Barnes, who knelt down, flipped the clasp and yanked it open. 'It's filled with pound notes, sir,' the constable said quietly. 'Hundreds of them.'

Witherspoon nodded. He turned to face her. 'Mrs Cubberly, I'm arresting you for the murder of Jake Randall.'

In disbelief, she gazed at him. Then she laughed. 'Do you think they'll hang me, then?' she asked merrily. Her eyes were wild, her laugh hysterical and frightening. 'It doesn't matter if they do, you see,' she continued conversationally, 'I'd rather hang than live one more minute with that bastard I'm married to.'

'Please, Mrs Cubberly.' The inspector was aware of a growing crowd gathering. 'I really don't think you ought to say anything more till we're at the police station. Perhaps you'd best be quiet until we notify your husband—'

'Husband!' She threw back her head and laughed louder. 'He's not a husband. He's a demon. A miserly devil from the pits of hell. Nothing you could do to me would be worse than what he's done . . .'

She kept on laughing all the way to the police station.

'You shoulda seen her,' Smythe said. 'She were even worse once we got her down to the station.'

'Sounds like she were bad enough at Waterloo,' Mrs Goodge said. 'Poor Inspector Witherspoon. Imagine havin' to arrest a woman makin' a right old spectacle of herself.'

Wiggins reached for a piece of seedcake. 'Go on,' he urged the coachman, 'tell us everythin'. What did Mrs Cubberly do?'

'Well, once we got her down there, she confessed to killin' Randall. She couldn't get it out fast enough.' Smythe shook his head. 'She admitted that she was the one that got the note that day. After hearin' her husband and the other investors talkin' at the meetin', she was fairly certain Randall would have the money on him. So she waited till they left, grabbed 'er 'usband's gun and took off for Waterloo Bridge.' He paused and his face grew serious. ''Earin' Mrs Cubberly talk so calmly about 'ow she just walked right up to Jake Randall and shot 'im made me half-sick. Poor blighter didn't stand a chance.'

'Of course not,' Mrs Jeffries said. 'He was expecting Lottie Grainger. In the darkness of the footpath, he wouldn't be the least suspicious of a woman coming towards him.'

'You know what I don't understand,' Luty said. 'Where'd she hide the money? The police searched the Cubberly house and they didn't find hide nor hair of it.'

'Mrs Cubberly was clever,' Smythe said. 'She didn't hide the money in the house, least not when she knew it was goin' to be searched. When she first come back that night, she hid it under her bed. But as soon as the police found the note in Cubberly's pocket, she knew it wouldn't be long before they searched the house. So she grabbed the money and hid it next door in the neighbours' garden shed. She put it under some old tarps.'

'That's a bit risky,' Betsy said. 'What if the neighbours had found it?'

'They was gone,' Smythe explained. 'Mrs Cubberly wasn't takin' any risk at all.'

'So that explains why she was so adamant about the inspector not searching the house when he found the note in her husband's pocket. The inspector mentioned she told them they would have to get a warrant.' Mrs Jeffries mused. 'Now we know why. She needed time to hide the money.'

'Why didn't she just leave then?' Betsy asked. 'I mean, she had the money. Why hang about waitin' to get caught?'

'I don't think her goal was simply to murder and steal,' Mrs Jeffries replied. 'I think she wanted her husband to hang for Jake Randall's murder. It was a way to get rid of him and eventually gain control of her own money.'

'All right now,' Mrs Goodge said to the housekeeper. 'Tell us how you figured out it was her?'

225

'I didn't figure it out until it was almost too late,' Mrs Jeffries replied with a modest shrug. 'But what really made it all come together in my mind was Wiggins getting confirmation that Harry had given the note to Mrs Cubberly. According to Zita Brown, Hilda Cubberly ordered her to have her dinner ready at seven o'clock that evening. Now, that was odd. The household was extremely lax. Being ordered to serve dinner promptly at seven o'clock was unusual enough that Mrs Brown remembered the occasion. As she was meant to remember it. Mrs Cubberly insisted on having dinner served at that specific time to give herself an alibi. She had the note. She knew that she'd meet Randall at six, shoot him and then be back to her home by a quarter to seven. And she knew all of this before she left the house that day. She was the only one of the suspects to make sure she had an alibi for eight o'clock. That was simply a bit too convenient.'

'Is that the only clue you had?' Hatchet asked as he gazed at her in admiration.

'No, there were several others. But I didn't understand them at the time,' Mrs Jeffries admitted. 'Looking back, though, you can see what should have been obvious. First of all, there was the overcoat. Hilda knew her husband was a suspect in a murder that had been committed by the river. Yet instead of cleaning the mud off that coat, she took it upstairs. Why? Because she wanted to make sure that Mrs Brown wouldn't accidentally clean it herself. Also, when the inspector asked to see the coat, it was Hilda who went and got it. I think she slipped the altered note in the pocket at that time, putting it there so the inspector would be sure to find it.'

'Two clues,' Luty murmured. 'That's still pretty danged good thinkin' on your part.'

'Now, now, it wasn't all my doing,' Mrs Jeffries replied. 'I couldn't have done it without all of you. You and Hatchet found out about the gun, Luty. Smythe alerted us to the fact that the investors had gone looking for Randall in the first place, Wiggins located young Harry, Betsy found Lottie Grainger, and Mrs Goodge gave us the information that clearly explained Hilda Cubberly's motive.'

'I did?' Mrs Goodge looked puzzled and pleased at the same time.

'Of course you did,' Mrs Jeffries said warmly. 'If it hadn't been for you finding out that Hilda had been forced to marry John Cubberly, none of this would have made sense. Hilda hated her husband. Yet, like many women, she was trapped. Jake Randall stealing that fifty thousand pounds must have seemed a godsend to her. Not only would she have enough money to live on while her husband was tried and convicted, but she had enough to get completely out of the country.'

'Right,' Smythe agreed. 'That train was headin' for Southampton. We found a ticket for a steam packet in the carpetbag, too. She were headin' for South America.'

'Do you think she deliberately tried to fix it so Mr Cubberly would be arrested?' Betsy asked.

'No, I think originally she just wanted the money.' Mrs Jeffries reached for her teacup. 'She was probably just going to disappear. But then when Randall's body was discovered, I think she cleverly found she could manipulate the police and implicate John Cubberly. She did hide the gun in her husband's boot. And she did it only after she'd made such a fuss about a warrant that the police were sure to be suspicious and search the house.'

Mrs Jeffries was glad to see Betsy taking an active interest in the discussion. The maid had brightened somewhat, but Mrs Jeffries could tell she was still a bit melancholy about something.

'It's kinda sad, isn't it?' Betsy sighed. 'Poor Lottie's lost her fiancé, Mr Cubberly's ruined and grieved, and Mrs Cubberly's goin' to 'ang.'

'Don't be too sure o' that, lass,' Smythe said gently. 'The way she were rantin' and ravin', they may lock her up in a madhouse.'

'Whether she hangs or they lock her up don't seem to make much difference,' Betsy said sadly. 'Nothin'll bring Jake back. What's Lottie goin' to do? Where's she gonna go?'

'Please don't worry about Miss Grainger.' Hatchet reached over and patted Betsy's arm. 'Madam has kindly invited her to stay with us for a while.' He glanced at Luty. 'Haven't you, madam?'

Luty snorted. 'Didn't have much choice, did I? Couldn't toss the girl out on the streets. Her sister and her aunt don't have a hill a' beans. Wouldn't be fair to expect 'em to take in another mouth to feed.'

Mrs Jeffries noticed that Hatchet had been watching Betsy anxiously since he'd arrived. For that matter, they'd all been concerned about the girl. Smythe would barely let her out of his sight, Wiggins had hovered over her like a mother hen, and Mrs Goodge was continually offering her tea. She made up her mind to get to the bottom of what was bothering the maid.

They were all going to worry themselves to death if she didn't.

Luty shoved her chair back. 'Come on, Hatchet,' she commanded. 'It's gettin' late. We'd best be goin'. I've got to go to that danged theatre tonight.'

'But you've been looking forward to going, madam,' Hatchet told her as he got to his feet.

'Yeah, but tonight I'm tired. I'd much rather stay here until after the inspector comes home so we can get the rest of the details.'

'Don't worry about the details, Luty,' Mrs Jeffries said as she got up and followed them down the hall. 'We'll have another gathering soon. A proper tea party. We'll go over the whole case then.'

'Good, I'd hate to miss anythin'.'

'Good night, Mrs Jeffries,' Hatchet said. He reached for the door handle.

'Hatchet,' she said. He stopped and looked at her. 'I'd like to have a word with you. It's about Betsy.'

'Girl's been mopin' about with a long face ever since she come back with Lottie Grainger,' Luty said to her butler. 'Do you know anything about it?'

Hatchet didn't say anything for a moment. Then he sighed softly. 'I'm afraid I do. But it's a rather private . . . oh heavens. You see, I saw something and I'm not sure it's right to tell anyone.'

'Land's sakes, man,' Luty sputtered. 'We're only concerned for the girl's welfare. You kin trust us not to go blabbing to everyone else about Betsy.'

Hatchet hesitated. 'All right, but please, don't say anything to her. This is the sort of thing that Miss Betsy must work out for herself.'

229

'What in tarnation is it?' Luty hissed.

'Grief,' Hatchet said quietly, 'Miss Betsy is grieving. On the way back here with Lottie, she asked me to stop the carriage. We were by a small church. I did as she requested. But after she got out, I became rather concerned. The church was in a dreadful part of the city. So I bade Miss Grainger to stay put and, well, I followed her. She'd gone into the churchyard. She was kneeling in front of a grave. I believe she was crying.' He looked down at the floor. 'It was a pauper's grave. There was no headstone marking the spot, just a large rock. I didn't want to intrude. But Betsy happened to look up and she saw me. She told me the grave belonged to her mother.'

The inspector was utterly exhausted when he came home. Mrs Jeffries hustled him into the drawing room and into his favourite chair.

'I thought tonight you might like a brandy, sir,' she said.

His face was drawn and pale, his eyes sad. 'Thank you, Mrs Jeffries,' he said, taking the glass and putting it on the table beside him. 'That's most thoughtful of you. I suppose I should be happy, but I'm not.'

'I know, sir,' she said gently. 'How did it go?'

'We arrested Mrs Cubberly,' he said, 'but it was rather monstrous. The woman's consumed with hatred. Quite mad, in my opinion. You should have heard the awful things she said to her husband. She actually looked that man in the face and told him she'd rather swing from a gallows than spend one more minute living with him.'

'She confessed, then.'

'Oh yes.' Witherspoon took a sip of his drink. 'Nivens looked a right fool. Yet still, it was a rather depressing day.'

'You're a very kind-hearted man, sir,' she told him truthfully. 'It's no wonder the day's events have saddened you. Yet you must take comfort in the fact that justice was done. Jake Randall may have been a thief and a swindler, but he didn't deserve to be shot and shoved in the river. It was your brilliant investigating that solved this heinous crime.'

'You do make me feel better, Mrs Jeffries,' he said. 'But as for me being a brilliant investigator . . .' He paused and shrugged modestly. 'I'm still not certain exactly how I did it. I think perhaps it was my "guiding force", as you call it. I couldn't quite bring myself to arrest John Cubberly. I expect I wouldn't have determined that the killer was Mrs Cubberly if Miss Grainger hadn't come forward when she did.'

Mrs Jeffries relaxed. The inspector had now convinced himself he'd solved the murder. 'What about Miss Grainger?'

'Oh, we're not pressing any charges against her,' Witherspoon replied. 'She may have been planning on marrying Jake Randall, but she had nothing to do with the theft of the investment money.'

Mrs Jeffries nodded. Poor man, he was still a bit down in the dumps. She decided he needed to talk it all out. Once he got it off his chest, he'd feel much better. 'Are the investors going to get their money back?' she asked.

'Oh yes. With Mrs Cubberly's confession, there won't be a full trial of course, only a sentencing. So the

231

money needn't be held for evidence.' He smiled faintly. 'Dillingham and Hinkle's solicitors were already at the station when I left. I think they were bending the chief's ear to get the process speeded up a bit. Not that it'll do them much good – it's the judicial system which has authority now.'

He continued to talk about the case for the next half hour. Mrs Jeffries listened carefully, occasionally asking a question or shaking her head sympathetically.

'I say,' Witherspoon finally said, 'I'm famished. Er, what's Mrs Goodge cooked for us tonight?'

'A nice roast beef and Yorkshire pudding.' Mrs Jeffries pulled a sheet of paper out of her pocket. 'I know it's not within keeping of the household management scheme,' she said apologetically, 'but we decided that you'd been working so hard, you needed a good meal.' She handed him the paper. 'However, after you eat, sir, we do need to go over the scheme. Mrs Goodge has come up with some wonderful ideas to save money.'

The inspector took the paper, got to his feet, and walked to the fire. He tossed the paper into the flames.

'Why, sir,' Mrs Jeffries exclaimed. 'Whatever are you doing? That's our household management scheme.'

'I know, Mrs Jeffries.' He gave her a wide smile. 'But I've decided we don't need the wretched thing anymore. Life is short. For many, life is short and cruel. We are very lucky here at Upper Edmonton Gardens. My investments may not be doing as well as I'd like, but that's no reason to turn into a miser. Gracious, look at poor John Cubberly. No more penny-pinching. In the future, we shall eat, drink, and be merry.'

★ ★ ★

They had their gathering a week later. To celebrate the event, Mrs Goodge had outdone herself. There were sausage rolls, cock-a-leekie soup, mutton ham, Dundee cake, jellies, currant buns, and plenty of good, strong tea.

'Now, that's what I call a proper feed.' Wiggins patted his stomach and looked down at the floor. 'Even Fred's too full to move.' The dog was sound asleep on his side, his stomach bulging with all the treats he'd been slipped.

'Mrs Goodge,' Mrs Jeffries said, 'this tea was superb.'

'Excellent repast, madam.' Hatchet bowed formally at the cook.

'Danged good grub,' Luty agreed.

Betsy laughed. 'We've all made pigs of ourselves,' she said gaily.

Smythe grinned. 'That's all right lass, we've earned it.'

Mrs Jeffries was delighted that everything was back to normal. Betsy had gotten over her grief, Smythe and Wiggins were out and about and up to their usual activities, and Mrs Goodge had been cooking up a storm.

'Well, I've got an announcement to make,' Luty said. She grinned. 'Lottie's goin' to Colorado.'

'Colorado?' Mrs Goodge repeated.

'In America?' Wiggins said incredulously.

'Whatever for?' Mrs Jeffries asked.

Luty laughed. 'She's goin' to Colorado as the new owner of half of the Randall and Watson Silver Mine. She was Jake's heir. He left her everythin' he owned. He'd done a will.'

'But the mine's worthless,' Smythe said.

Luty shook her head. She reached for her muff and pulled out a piece of paper. 'No, it ain't. It's loaded with silver. I got this telegram from my people today.' She turned to Mrs Jeffries. 'Remember when I asked you to find out exactly where the mine was located?'

Mrs Jeffries nodded. 'Yes, but—'

'No buts about it,' Luty snorted. 'Soon as you mentioned the word "Leadville", I sent off a cable. I knew there might be silver in that mine. There's tons of silver in that part of Colorado. And I was right.'

'Do you think Jake knew there was silver there?' Wiggins asked.

'Probably not. But it don't matter now.' Luty cackled. 'The investors was so happy to get their money back, they give all the shares they bought back to Randall's solicitor. None of them made a profit! Now it all belongs to Lottie. Just goes to show you, don't it?'

'Exactly what does it show us?' Mrs Jeffries asked cautiously.

'That takin' stock would have been a lot smarter than takin' the money,' Luty replied tartly. 'But that's all right. I reckon Lottie'll do a lot more good with a mine full of silver than any of the investors. They were a pretty sorry lot, if you ask me.'

'I think, Luty,' Mrs Jeffries replied with a smile, 'you're absolutely right about that.'